DREAM

of the

WHITE
STALLION

JULIA OLIVER

PAGE PUBLISHING, INC.
New York, NY

First originally published by Page Publishing, Inc. 2019

ISBN 978-1-64544-526-5 (Paperback)
ISBN 978-1-64544-527-2 (Digital)

Printed in the United States of America

Contents

Acknowledgment

The author would like to thank her loving husband for his understanding and patience during the lifetime of hours it took to write this book and to also thank her sister, Sherry, for her support and suggestions during the second lifetime of editing.

Foreword

D *ream of the White Stallion* is a fictional love story set in the early 1700s. It is also an account of the spiritual journey of a shy young Englishwoman born of aristocracy but raised as a commoner. Even though the book purports to be her journal, it's written in modern English for the ease of the reader and author. And finally, this is a tale for those who love horses and everything associated with them.

The villages, historic buildings, towns, and shires mentioned in this manuscript are all authentic locations, as is the famous White Horse landmark. However, the nobility named and represented are purely fictional. In addition, the specific horses and races described are imagined, but the novel's era is the historical period in Britain when horse racing became the rage. Further, by the end of the eighteenth century, the Thoroughbred registry had been formalized, all horses of the breed tracing back to imported Arabian, Barb, or Turkish stallions bred to native English mares, just as portrayed here.[1]

The herbal medicine folklore described in this novel was derived from two medical handbooks, each written over a century ago,[2], [3] and from various other sources, including the author's husband, who is a veterinarian.

Finally, the religious sect named the Way, as used in this novel, is also purely fictional. However, according to *English Society in the 18th Century*, "fringe religious communities gathered and dissolved like clouds" during this period in English history,[4] and the Way is an attempt to describe one such Protestant group.

[1.] https://en.wikipedia.org/wiki/Thoroughbred (accessed November 24, 2018).

[2.] Hon. Jonathan Periam, *The American Farmer's Pictorial Exclopedia of Live Stock and Complete Stock Doctor* (N. D. Thompson Publishing Co., 1889).

[3.] John Nocholson Navin, *Navin's Veterinary Practice or Explanatory Horse Doctor*, (Indianapolis, Indiana: Roach and Thistlethwaite, circa 1860s).

[4.] Roy Porter, *English Society in the 18th Century* (Penguin Books, 1990), 157.

Prologue

The massive stallion, silvery in the moonlight, is rending the
air with his screams. From my vantage lying helpless on the
ground beneath him, it appears as if he is trying to claw a
hole in the sky, his front legs thrashing above me. Any moment now,
he is going to return those hooves to the earth, most likely crushing
my skull. I shriek and try to roll out from under the giant white
beast. I can feel the ground shake below as his feet pound back to
earth—has he missed me by inches? I keep rolling as I hear another
blast from his nostrils, and then he is rearing again. I have the sensation of several men struggling and shuffling around me, hauling
on ropes, shouting, and trying in vain to control the colossal energy
of the maddened animal. I can smell their rank sweat and my own
fear. But none of their faces or voices seems clear. My only focus can
be the piercing scream of the stallion and avoiding those stomping,
flailing hooves.

PART I

Atlantic Ocean, 1737

Chapter 1

BEGINNINGS

I awoke this morning at first light soaked by cold sweat in my creaking ship's bunk. After months of peace, the old nightmare of the white horse has returned. I'd hoped never to relive that dream again, but here it's found me once more. Perhaps it is a premonition? I have no way of knowing if I'm going to survive this long voyage to America. I've had the most awful nausea; others try to reassure me that this misery isn't unusual for first-time sailors. I wish I'd made time to pack some ginger root in my trunk, but our hasty departure precluded that. I also now suspect that I'm with child, a prospect that both thrills and terrifies me despite knowing that I'm in God's hands. I've always wished for more courage.

My "illness" has pressed me to pen this story into my journal. Many mothers die in childbirth—I want to leave a record of all that has happened in the last three years. Some of it is shameful and difficult to write, but I'm hoping my reader will understand and forgive me.

How shall I begin? I suspect I need to go further back in my story, back before the nightmares began. Perhaps my account really starts with my parents. My father, Patrick Alexander, immigrated to England from Belfast, Ireland, in 1712. His Catholic parents were struggling to feed their children, barely able to make ends meet. While he never spoke much of the family he left at an early age or of County Ulster, his homeland always became "my lovely Erin" whenever he was crooning ballads (usually when he was in his cups). I suspect, though, that his life had been hard, and given his seven younger siblings at home, Da had felt pressured to make his own way in the world.

At the age of eight, my father had been apprenticed to a local harness-maker in Belfast, where he worked long, grueling hours at the cutting table and slept in the cold, stable loft. The money he earned, what there was of it beyond his board, went to his family. By the age of sixteen, as a journeyman, he decided that the southeast counties of England offered more promise. There, farmers tilled vast acres of rye, wheat, and corn in the rich river bottomlands and had great need for harness-makers.

As I understand it, after arduously working his passage across the sea, he landed at Bristol, hungry and penniless, and somehow made his way inland to the villages around River Avon. There, he found employment among the farming tenants on the estate of Lord Richard Howard, Earl of Avon. My father was a decent harness-maker, but he excelled at horsemanship, breaking and training young horses and caring for their medicinal needs. These were crafts that he'd picked up during his apprenticeship and for which he had a natural gift. After he had worked several years in the local village repairing and making new harness for the gentle Suffolk Sorrels who pulled the plows in the fields around the great house, word got to the earl of Da's special talents, and he found himself employed as one of the grooms in Lord Howard's stables. Father was hired especially to train and prepare gentle, solid mounts for the earl's three daughters. Lady Anne Marie Howard, the youngest daughter of the three, would become my mother.

I've been told that Lady Anne took as much to her handsome and patient Irish horse master as she did to riding her gentle Galloway cob. Da was four years her senior and equally smitten with the earl's lovely daughter, as impossible as that situation was. It was in my mother's sixteenth year that she was betrothed to an older widower, a marquis with three living children, two under the age of twelve. He was heavy and dour in appearance and a well-known womanizer. It was said he had often unmercifully beaten his servants and tenants alike. At some point, before the wedding could take place, Anne and her Irish groom absconded and were secretly married as they fled the county. Lady Anne Marie Howard became Mrs. Anne Alexander. I don't know how they came to be tenants in the village of Uffington, where I was born, but there, my father scraped a living as a harness-maker for Squire Baker, who owned the manor and farmlands and most of the village where we lived. And my mother never again claimed any family or title save that of wife and mother.

My earliest memories are happy ones. The little cottage we rented was small, just two rooms, but we had a stone floor, which my mother swept clean every day, and our oversize, flagged fireplace kept both rooms warm. Mother's father, the Earl of Avon, had immediately disowned her upon her elopement. It was not only her disgraceful broken betrothal, but as loyal Anglicans, her parents could not accept her Catholic husband, and one so far beneath her station, at that. I never met my grandparents. We had no discourse with them, and as far as I know, my mother never heard from them again. That is, with one exception: several months after I was born, a hired oxen-wagon arrived at our cottage bearing a trunk containing some of my mother's personal articles and her beloved piano forte. We believed Grandmother Howard had dispatched mother's belongings—whether out of affection or pique, who could say? And if the gift had the earl's approval, we never knew. But the music that the blessed instrument provided at my mother's hands, and later mine, would fill our lives and make our little cottage ring with happiness for the next fifteen years—at least until the nightmares and darkness began.

Chapter 2

WITCH'S EYES

I was born Kathryn Anne Alexander in 1717. Although my father had the ruddy hair and emerald green eyes of the Irish and my mother, the fair hair and grey eyes of the Saxon, I was endowed with neither gift. My hair was not auburn, not flaxen, something in between and more ordinary and unremarkable. My eyes were of such a clear, light blue that they sometimes appeared almost colorless. I believed these plain features, along with my mortifyingly thin frame, helped account for much of the name-calling I experienced while growing up.

Still, I know I was a fairly happy child, especially compared to others in our small village. While I would have loved having a brother or sister to play with, it was not to be. Twice, my mother conceived after my own birth and twice the midwife delivered a still-born child. From my earliest memories, my mother had experienced recurring fevers, sweats, and weaknesses. At those times, my father would prepare her a tea of lemon oil and willow bark. And usually the fevers would subside after a bit. Whatever I lacked in sibling companionship, Mama and Da made up for in attention and love. I know I was a lucky child, for I saw no others, either then or since, who possessed such caring parents.

Our village was relatively small. We were situated in the long Ock River Valley, having just a central cobbled street lined with squat, close-built structures of white blocks and thatched roofs, outbuildings and privies in the rear. There were also a few side roads of dirt with more cottages outside the main thoroughfare. But the main claim of Uffington was our imposing St. Mary's Church, constructed centuries before. The chief glory of this building was its central octagonal tower, which boasted a ring of five bells. On any Sunday morning and for all holidays, weddings, and funerals, the multitonal chimes could be heard tolling for miles. I remember thinking that the harmonies of the bells must sound to God like the angels singing in heaven. Besides the church, along the main street were also an apothecary's shop, the Fox and Hound Pub, a tanner's, smithy, shoe-maker, and cooperage among the other tradesmen and homes.

Our little cottage was on the outskirts of town, one of the few rental properties to boast a massive oak tree in the front yard. We also had a small ramshackle stable, pump, and shed in the back, where my da plied his harness trade. We never had a permanent horse residing in our little barn, only our milk cow, Molly, but sometimes my da had a gelding or mare in for training. By the time I was five years old, it was my duty each morning and evening to milk the gentle cow. I didn't mind this so much. Molly was fairly compliant, coming down from the grazing commons, her bell ringing, morning and evening, right at six on the hour. On cold mornings, her warm, sweet breath would cloud the air in the stanchion as she ate her breakfast of corn and chewed her cud complacently while I pulled the steaming milk from her teats. Sitting on my rickety, three-legged stool, I would sing little Irish ditties that my da had taught me. My favorite mornings in the barn were when my father would have a horse in for training. Almost without fail, the beast would hear me coming and add his whinny of greeting to the lowing of the cow. I've loved horses for as long as I can remember. Da always let me feed the horse when we had one in and allowed me to help with training as I got older. Yearning for a pony of my own was the only wish I could have had as a child— that and to be beautiful like my mother.

There was an Anglican Charity School at St. Mary's Church for the children of our parish. It was overseen by our rector, Reverend Michael Davies, who taught reading, arithmetic, handwriting, and geography along with the Anglican doctrine. Many of the village children, if they were not laboring in their fathers' shops or apprenticed to a tradesman, attended this school. Even girls were welcomed, although most were expected to stay home and perform household duties while their mothers sewed, tatted, brewed, worked in shops or did whatever they could to bolster the family income. My own mother excelled at embroidery, having been taught this gentlewomanly art as part of her own upbringing, and she usually had a shirt, kerchief, or skirt ready for the needle. In the lean times, the extra money her sewing brought in would stand between us and destitution.

I did not get my education at St. Mary's for several reasons, one being that we were not accepted as part of the congregation. My father remained staunchly Catholic, but since there was no Holy Roman priest or service in all of the Salisbury Plain, he was left to say his rosaries and do his penance on his own. I later learned that larger towns often had a Methodist, Quaker, Catholic, or Protestant church, but for our village, this was not so. Whether it was due to her being the wife of a papist or because it was obvious by her speech and carriage that she was "apart" from the common village folk, my mother was not encouraged to join the church and had few friends.

Neither was I welcomed by church, school, or playmates. I will never know if this had more to do with my parentage, my appearance, or my own behavior. I was always quite shy and was probably considered backwards. If they thought Mother's speech to be haughty, then my own tongue must have seemed stranger still, being a unique mixture of aristocratic accent and Irish burr. I usually tried to keep silent while around the other children. When they would laugh and call me a papist, I would drop my head and not know what to say. Or sometimes I would just run away, their calls of "bean pole" or "witch eyes" echoing after me. As I was such a coward, it was no wonder they delighted in tormenting me.

I remember wondering why I didn't seem to fit in, wondered what was wrong with me. But then I would remind myself that most of these children had hard lives at home—not just scarce food and hard work, for we all experienced that. But other parents didn't seem to care about their offspring; curses and beatings were common, and affection rare. So I could feel compassion for the other children, even the bullies, and this gave me comfort.

I had one tormentor in particular, Tom Burlington, who seemed to take more pleasure in harassing me than most. Tom was larger than other boys his age; he had a sprinkling of freckles over his nose which would have made him seem charming and boyish if they hadn't been on such a menacing countenance. When Tom would yell, as he often did, "Ye think ye're better than us, don't ye?" and begin to throw stones, I would run away, back to my mother, his "Ye skinny little witch" echoing behind me. Surrounding me in her arms, Mother would tell me not to worry. "Children will be children. It will all work out." I wanted so much to believe her. I wish she had been right in the end!

I do remember one time when I found the courage to stand up for myself, or, rather, for something else. I was on an errand to the tanner's for my da and ready to cross the stone bridge over the stream that ran down through our valley. Before reaching the span, I noticed a number of children in a group at the top of the archway, Tom at their center. He was dangling something over the stone side on a long string, and the children were laughing. As I got closer, I could see that there was a wriggling animal—it looked like a kitten—tied by the neck at the end of the string. And then Tom began dunking the poor little creature into the river.

I started to run, and when I reached the group, I tried to grab the string. "What are you doing, Tom Burlington?" I shouted as I fought him for control of the rope. The other children had moved back.

"My Marm told me to drown these puny cats, and that's what I'm doin'. I just thought it were be more fun this way than the sack she given me." He was shoving me back, but I was having none of it.

"Stop it!" I shouted again, but this time he pushed me hard, forcefully enough that I landed on my backside. Rising quickly, I gathered my strength and slammed into him as hard as my slim frame could manage, since he was nearly twice my size. Catching him off guard, I saw that he had dropped the string, and the kitten plopped back into the water. Ignoring his curses and the other children, I raced off the bridge and down the slope to the stream's edge. Now I could see four little shapes in the water. Three were downstream, not moving, but the fourth, the one with the rope still tied around its neck, was mewing and spitting and paddling desperately against the current, doing its best to reach the shore.

Hiking my skirts, I waded into the blackwater. The cold took my breath away, and I knew I was soiling my stockings, but I kept going deeper, forgetting that I didn't know how to swim. Fortunately, the little animal kept paddling toward me until I was able to grab it by the scruff and haul it dripping out of the water. It was a miserable little thing, gasping and gagging and looking half-drowned, which I guess it was. But after I removed the rope, dried it off, and carried it home, the kitten turned out to be a beautiful calico. I named her Cally, and she became my best friend and playmate. The little cat would accompany me to the barn for milking, wrapping her lithe torso around and around my ankles. I would feed her some cream right from the pail each morning, and she never left our homestead again. Mother tolerated her because Cally was an excellent mouser. She was even allowed in the house, where she slept with me on my pallet in the loft above our sitting room. I could spend hours dragging a little piece of string for her to chase or watching her pounce on a ball of cotton lint. I could also wile away time brushing my hand over her soft brown-black-and-white fur and listening to her purr—that is, I could do all these things when I wasn't expected to be working on my lessons or at some chore, which was most of the time. Still, at night she would snuggle her little body close to mine and her soft purr would lull me to sleep, even when it was cold, or my stomach was empty. I had saved her from one merciless fate. But I could not save her from another in the end.

Tom Burlington was not one to let an insult go unpunished. I had to be very careful from then on when it was necessary for me to venture away from home. Unfortunately, this was most days of the week. My main household duty was not simply to milk the cow twice a day but also to make and deliver the butter each morning. This involved separating the cream from the milk and then churning it in a wooden container with a plunger. The process became less difficult as I grew older and stronger, but it was no mean feat while I was still young and slight of weight. For nearly three quarters of an hour, I would sweat over that churn. Cool water would also need to be carried in from our pump in back several times to wash the butter once I had poured off the buttermilk. After scraping the yellow globs from the barrel, I would then wring it in a cream cloth, salt it, and pack the oily substance into a tin. This had to be delivered down to the pub in middle Uffington, not too far from where we lived, but just past St. Mary's. I believe my mother traded the butter for other foodstuffs, particularly sugar, rye flour, tea, and bacon—anything we couldn't grow in our own garden—and I would sometimes carry a note with me to the pub and a bundle back home again.

Each morning, if it was possible, I dallied inside until I knew most of the children would be in school, and then I could safely make my delivery. But when the weather was too warm to risk the butter melting, or on days when school was out, I was forced to venture into Tom's territory. I believe he watched for me. I became very adept at slinking behind buildings and traveling different routes, coward that I was. Tom delighted in jumping out from behind a bush to frighten me. He especially enjoyed making me drop my bundle, once in a while even spoiling the butter. He was often accompanied by other village children, and they usually chanted, "Skinny witch, skinny witch!"

One time I found myself sitting on the ground after being tripped, and winded, with Tom leering above me. As usual, I stared at the feet of my tormentor, unable to look up. But somehow I found the courage to ask, "Why do you all call me a witch? I'm no witch!"

"We see the way ye look at us with them eyes—ye look right through us. Ye think ye're better'n us," he sneered. "And to boot, ye'r never in church." I had no answer to that.

Although we did not go to St. Mary's as a family, or worship together, for that matter, Mother always said grace over our porridge or lentil stew, and Da would make the cross and whisper "Amen." Mama taught me about God and his Son, Jesus, and that I had to be *very* good in order to go to heaven. She also taught me to play the old psalms on the piano forte and Bach's *St. Matthew Passion*. I had started at the keyboard at the age of four with finger exercises and could play most any music by sight at the age of twelve. Sundays we had our own worship service, Mother and I, while Da lit candles and said "Aves" out in his shop. With my parents, my Cally, and Molly, I didn't miss the other children so much. Life was good enough in those early years.

When it came to lessons, I expect I worked harder than those attending the church school. Besides the subjects the village children learned, Mama also taught me piano, French, needlework, and drawing, as well as exposing me to such literature as she could find. She herself had been taught by an excellent governess, and later a tutor, her father assuming that such education would suit her well as the wife of a nobleman. I never was very talented at drawing and only gained a rudimentary understanding of French. But Mama said I had a lovely singing voice and I was quite proficient at the piano keys. I loved books, and Mother and I were both equally excited whenever we secured a new text or novel, taking turns reading to each other in the evenings. During those days when the fevers would come upon her, I would sit and read to her for hours or play her favorite songs on the piano forte—that is, when I could spare the time from housework, gardening, or milking in the barn. There were always chores to do.

Along with the musical instrument that Grandmother Howard had shipped to us was a trunk of Mother's things. And when I was six years old, Mama called me into her bedroom and invited me to look through her "treasures." While there was nothing of any great value, no gold or jewels, there were several lovely gowns of silk and lace (which she never wore), a velvet cape, an ivory comb and brush set, a brass looking glass, and a small pewter locket on a silver chain. The pretty ornament was engraved with a family seal, that being of the Howards. My mother took the inscribed locket and opened it so that I could see the tiny portrait inside. She told me it was a rendering of my grandmother. I peered at the tiny picture; the woman had fair hair like my mother's and, I thought, a rather long face. Not much more than that could be discerned from such a small portrait. But Mother said that she wanted me to have the locket, and she fastened it about my neck. Every now and again, I would open the piece and stare at the grandmother I had never known and wonder what she would think of me. Even as I daily wore this memento of the past, I had no idea of the part it would play in my future.

Chapter 3

GOLIATH

By the time I was ten years old, I was helping with the training of the few horses that were consigned to my father. Da worked all day in his shop, making, repairing, and selling harness. But once in a while, someone would bring him a young colt to train or a mount with a bad habit of throwing its rider. I believe my father had a gift with horses, but his methods were unconventional, so much so that he was ridiculed behind his back, and sometimes to his face. I always thought this surprising, since the horses he had trained were known to be well-behaved and valued in the county. But people will believe what has been passed down to them, and it was "understood" that a person had to crush a horse's spirit to truly "break" the horse. If this took hobbles, whips, and spurs, then so be it. Conversely, my father believed in "gentling" the animal, especially a young one, and he refused to use the harsher methods. Because of this, we didn't often have a horse stabled in our barn for training.

But when we did, my excitement knew no bounds. I could barely work at my studies, practice my sewing, or help Mama with the garden, knowing that after supper, I would be invited to come and watch my father as he worked with a two-year-old gelding or mare in to have their first experience with saddle or harness and cart. (If the animal was a stallion, my father would not let me help, claiming they could be more dangerous and "bockity, to be sure.") I remember the summer of my tenth year, when I was first allowed to really take part in the training. The horse Da had in was a coming three-year-old gelding, fairly old for his first experience with saddle or collar. His owner, Squire Baker, who was also our landlord, had paid a lot of money for the animal, and I could see why.

"This gent," my da was saying, patting the neck of the giant black steed, "be an immigrant, just like meself. Imported from Holland he was last fall and just now growin' into those long legs." He continued his explanation, giving the horse another affectionate caress. "He'll be seventeen hands and more when he's finished, says I." We had brought the gelding out from his stall into the field behind our barn. My father had been working with him every night for a week on the long longe, and the horse was now blowing gently into my father's hand and standing quietly. "These Friesians be so gentle for such high steppers—I've never seen t' like for lookin' like a spirited beast when really just a gentle lamb," Da said warmly.

The horse was named Goliath. I thought that a pretty apt name, as he seemed to tower over me. The gelding had already been broken to head-collar before he came to us, that being a necessity for his shipment into our country. Now Da had him leading so well that even I could bring him from his stall to the lot with no help whatsoever. Today, Da told me, we were going to introduce him to the saddle. "Now, bring t' wool pad over, Katie darlin'…but gently, gently," he corrected. "Now, let Goliath get a good whiff on." The big Dutch horse flared his nostrils and lowered his muzzle to sniff at the blanket. Then he snorted loudly and threw that massive head back up in the air, which startled me, and I stumbled back.

"Always watch 'is ears, daughter," Da instructed me. "He'll be tellin' ye everything ye need to know with them ears, for sure. If 'is ears are pricked forward, e's interested. If 'is ears are a-swivelin' back and forth, 'e's nervous like. And if they're pinned flat on 'is head, then 'e's scared or angry, 'e is, and ye'd best wait a moment. Just now when ye approached, he'd laid those ears flat. For sure, if 'e does that again, just wait 'n be patient."

"Now be brave and approach 'im again wi' the pad. But don't be nervous, darlin', or 'e'll be pickin' up on that for sure!" To the horse, he murmured, "Whisht, quiet now."

I came up slowly, holding the woolen article out to the horse, who lowered his beautiful head once again and sniffed the blanket all over. This time, his ears were forward, and neither of us startled. Next, Da proceeded to rub the pad all over the horse. When Goliath tensed or tried to move away, Da just patiently followed, continuing to hold the lead, talking low and reassuring the beast that there was nothing to be afraid of. When the animal stopped moving away, Da would retreat the blanket and give the horse a reprieve. Then Da would repeat the whole process again until Goliath was allowing the blanket to be rubbed all over his body. Only once did the big horse kick out with one hind foot. But Da was standing off to the side and kept approaching and retreating patiently until the gelding stopped his fidgeting and stood completely still for the process.

Da also taught me how to watch for signs of submission. He said that even though Goliath probably weighed half a ton, the big animal was still looking for leadership from his handlers—the best horses always did. "Now, Katie, you see 'im lickin' those lips and chewin' like 'e's got some grass in his gob? That's 'im sayin' that 'e gives up. Another horse would recognize that, and we can read it, too." I had seen Goliath licking when he had finally stood still and allowed himself to be rubbed with the blanket, but I hadn't understood what the horse was saying. I loved the idea that the horse could "talk" to us.

Next, Da placed the blanket on the horse's back. Since this had already been done before, the gelding did not tense. But my father left the pad where it was this time and stepped back. Immediately Goliath shook the blanket off. Da chuckled. "This horse be brah for being a Dutchman!" Again, the blanket was placed on the horse's back, and again it was dumped on the ground. But the third time, the horse allowed the pad to stay, and Da scratched the shiny black neck and crooned, "Good lad, good lad, now sure." It was an easy job after that to lead Goliath around with the pad perched securely on his withers.

"Now, Katie darlin', do ye think ye can manage the tack?" The light hunting saddle was resting on a keg by the barn, and I dutifully hefted it and brought it over. "Now let 'im sniff it just like before."

This time, I watched Goliath's ears carefully, but there was no issue. This accomplished, my father removed the girth from the leathers and then lifted the saddle toward the horse. Evidently, the gelding, having experienced the blanket already and knowing that if he moved, my father was just going to follow him, stood still and allowed the tack to be placed on his back. When the animal had remained still for a few moments, Da removed the saddle and again told the horse how good and smart he was. Then the tack was replaced and again removed. When Goliath was showing no tension at all and would walk with the apparatus in place, Da picked up the girth and buckled it loosely to the leathers.

"Now, Katie Anne, you need to step back. Sure, when I tighten this girth around 'is belly, 'e may take issue. If 'e does, I'll let 'im circle on the longe and buck, if 'e must. I want you clear and out of the way."

"Yes, Da," I replied dutifully and went to stand by the barn. As my father reached under the horse's taut belly and slowly tightened the girth, he spoke reassuring words in a quiet voice. Goliath's eyes became round, and he pinned his ears, but he stood stock-still. As before, Da praised him and then loosened the girth straps. When the horse was calm again, my father repeated the process. After the third time, Da asked Goliath to move forward. The animal did not move. Da pulled on the head-collar, but Goliath would not budge. Man and beast were at a standstill. When Da finally pulled the giant black head to the side and pushed on the hindquarters, the horse, off balance, finally relented and took a step.

"Stay where ye are, daughter, 'e's still got a hump in 'is back and may decide to be an eejit yet." But Goliath continued to walk forward in little starts and shuffles, and soon he was walking calmly, and it was decided that we had done enough for the evening. I could tell Da was very pleased with the horse, and it appeared the gelding was very attached to the man. Goliath was walking close to Da with his head almost on his shoulder, licking and chewing as he went. I remember thinking, *When I get my pony, this is how I will do it.*

Over the next few days, Da proceeded to exercise Goliath in the saddle every night, working on the longe at the walk, trot, and canter. He introduced the bridle and reins with snaffle bit, which the big gelding took like a gentleman. Finally, the evening came when Da told me it was time to familiarize Goliath with a rider. "What do ye say, Katie-girl? Are ye ready to mount up?" I noticed that he did not inquire about this until we were out of the house. We both knew what my mother would have said. Normally, I was rather timid in new situations, but I had waited so long to ride a horse. And Goliath seemed very gentle in my father's hands. I nodded my assent.

Da again worked the horse around and around in the tack, changing direction and paces, all at the sound of his voice. When the command was given to "Whoa," the horse stopped and stood dead still. Da nodded at me; it was time. He had me tuck my long skirts up into my waistband, and then I approached. By this time, Goliath knew me well; I was the one who fed him in the mornings and sometimes led him out to graze on the lush grass of the meadow. I reached out my hand and stroked his soft black muzzle. "Don't hurt me, big boy," I pleaded.

Next, Da hoisted me up to the saddle but told me to just lean over the top. The horse snorted a little and reached his big head around to see what we were doing. Da took me down and then back up again. When the gelding seemed comfortable with that, Da said he was going to lead him with me just hanging over. "Like a sack o' potatoes," he said. This wasn't exactly what I had had in mind, but I trusted my da. When the giant horse began to walk with my father leading him, I felt like I was being slung to and fro like...well, like a sack of potatoes! Da spoke to me over his shoulder. "This lad shows a big gait. Sure, ye'll feel like ye're on a ship!" I hadn't ever been on a ship, but I *was* feeling quite uncomfortable. I felt relieved when Da finally gave the "Whoa" signal and pulled me off. There were more "Good lads" and even a "Good girl."

Ultimately, it was time, time for Goliath's first ride. Time for my first ride. Da swung me up on the wide back and told me to sit still. Whenever I feel overwhelmed by my own timidity, I have a habit of narrowing my point of vision. If I can focus on just one detail, I can forget that I am frightened almost senseless. Up on the horse, my vision tapered until all I could see were Goliath's ears. They were flicking back and forth nervously, first toward Da and then back toward me. Da was stroking the big horse's neck, and he told me to do the same, but my arms wouldn't work. Next thing I knew, we were walking. That big, swinging gait was moving my body forward and back, almost like riding a rocking chair. It was wonderful! Still, I continued to stare at those ears to keep my composure. In no time, my father was reaching around my waist and pulling me to the ground. We had done it, my father, Goliath, and me. I was in heaven!

Chapter 4

STRANGLES

T hings weren't always so easy with my father. While he and my mother usually got along well and were commonly affectionate with each other, there were times when they argued. This was almost always after my father had been paid for a set of harness or some other job. I noticed Mama often arranged to be out at the shop when a customer was due to collect an order. It was Mother who settled our rents and purchased our foodstuffs. She even kept the accounts for Da's business, having learned bookkeeping from her tutor. She was the one who paid the tanner for the leather supplies, the brass-maker for buckles, etc. But on those occasions when Da received the coinage himself, he was often off to the Fox and Hound before my mother even realized he was gone.

It wasn't just that he would come home more drunk than sober. Da was a happy drunk, unlike so many who turned mean when they were intoxicated. He would return to the house singing, maybe staggering a little as he came in the door. Mother learned there was no point discussing anything while he was in this condition, and she would merely usher him off to bed. The trouble would come the next morning.

At daybreak or even earlier, our household would arise and set to the day's work. Knowing my da had been in his cups the night before, I always made sure to be up and out before both my parents were awake. Even in the barn, I could still hear the arguing over the *hiss hiss* of steaming milk hitting the pail. I would bury my head in Molly's flank and try to ignore the row.

"Pat, how much did you bring home from the pub last night? I know you got paid for the Darbys' harness yesterday afternoon."

"Now, Annie, give a man a break. Me head's a-poundin'."

"I'm sure it is. How many pints was it this time?"

"Only enough for a good time, to be sure. A man deserves to spend 'is own hard-earned pence."

"It's not the ale I mind. You know you're always welcome to the price of a tankard. But it's the whiskey that goes to your head and blinds your good sense. Did you bring home the rest of what you were paid, or were you gambling again?"

"Whisht now, Anne. I've another harness nearly ready for Mr. Flynn and a horse a-comin' for training next week, to be sure."

"Pat, you know our rent is overdue. I can't make another excuse to the squire. Please tell me you stayed away from the drink and cards last night." My father must have started out the door at this point, with my mother right behind him, because the voices grew louder.

"Anna Marie, I'm done and sure discussing this! You'll not be tellin' an Irishman 'e can't have 'is whiskey!" Knowing the argument was coming toward the barn, my mother always persistent, I would abandon the cow to her breakfast and run out the back, out to the commons and away from the bickering, run as far as my legs would carry me up the green hill, until I had no more breath. Cally would always follow me, and I would eventually slow and find a sheltered spot to sit and pant. Burying my face in her soft fur, I would cry. I had heard this same quarrel or a version like it so many times. It would end with my mother in tears and my father stalking away. Mother would take in even more needlepoint and work until late in the evenings to try to help make ends meet.

The worst part was that her fevers were coming upon her more often now and she was beginning to cough. Her hacking would go on so long and so hard that she found it difficult to breathe, difficult to place her needle correctly, and her sewing suffered. I was desperately worried about her, and I knew my father was, too. One day he came home from town bringing the village physician, Dr. Thomas, with him. I knew Da must be getting anxious about Mother's illness, because he and the physician did not see eye to eye. Da was an herbalist, at least in the treatment of animal illnesses, and did not believe in bloodletting. Mother protested that they couldn't afford the services of the physician, but Da was adamant. I know he loved Mama, but I also think he felt some guilt over all the extra work she had been taking in because of his gambling.

Dr. Thomas took Mother into her tiny bedroom and then called for Da about ten minutes later. I had anxiously climbed up to my loft retreat and was focusing all my attention on Cally, listening to her soft purr. But I could make out just enough of what the physician was saying to understand the dreaded diagnosis: consumption.

I was then eleven years old and realized that my mother would probably not live to see me become a woman. However, Father was not one to give up. Refusing to allow the physician to lance her, he made a trip to the apothecary and returned home to mingle powdered bloodroot, ginger, camphor, and laudanum, dissolving them in warm water. Each morning and evening thereafter, he gave Mama several spoonfuls of this concoction, and by the next week, Mother had rallied. The cough mostly went away, and we could pretend that everything was going to be all right. I thought maybe my father would slow down his drinking and gambling, and for a while, he did. But like my mother's illness, it only went dormant for a time. Meanwhile, I began to pick up some of the embroidery, and between the three of us, somehow the rent must have been paid, for we continued in our little cottage.

Besides occasionally training horses, my father was also sometimes asked to come and doctor one of the animals. Like his training methods, his "medicine" was considered unorthodox. Most physicians, whether treating a person or beast, considered bloodletting as their foremost therapy. Because my father stubbornly refused this course, believing it harmed more than helped, most farmers avoided his services altogether. However, Squire Baker, our landlord and sponsor, had been so taken with Goliath's training—the horse became an excellent hunting mount and carriage horse—that he occasionally procured Da's help with an ill beast, especially if the local physician had not found success with it. Unfortunately, this meant that my father was only called in after the animal had worsened (and had already been bled.)

Often, Da let me accompany him on these appointments, if Mother could do without my help for a time. I always enjoyed going with my da to visit the farmers, but especially when it was the manor property. Walking with my father up the landscaped drive lined with elms whose foliage created a tunnellike canopy and whose branches were full of songbirds, I could imagine I had entered a fairyland. The large manor house itself stood at the center of a manicured lawn and was surrounded by flowering shrubs. On this particular visit, the squire led us behind the cobbled stables to a paddock with several yearlings milling about. They appeared to be hackney or Irish hobby types, lighter than draft horses, high headed and beautiful to my eyes. But in the corner stood one colt with obviously labored breathing. His head was lowered, and he was standing dejectedly, ropy snot hanging from his nostrils.

"How long has the illness had 'im?" my father asked.

"About a week," Squire John answered. "The physician has been out to bleed him three times, and we've been drenching him, but he's only gotten worse."

"Judging from that big knot under 'is throat, 'e's got the strangles. Have these other ones shown any illness?"

"No, not yet."

"Well, ye need to get 'em separated, though it's probably too late and they'll all be sick soon. But let's take a look at this 'un. Can ye get ahold o' 'is head-collar?" Squire Baker sent over his groom, who had no problem in grabbing the poor beast's head. The young horse didn't even seem to notice the men approaching—so dull was his eye and so difficult his breathing. My father gently palpated the throat of the colt, who looked anxious but did not move, and then Da stated, "Ta', 'tis definitely strangles. Ye can see the thick discharge comin' from 'is nose and the swollen gland under 'is throat. 'Tis that swelling that's makin' it so hard for him t' draw breath, it is." We all stood back and gazed at the poor creature.

My father continued, "We're gonna need to lance that tumor, but it's too solid right now." He went on to explain that he planned to draw a blister over the swelling that afternoon. Then, if the colt survived the night, they would hope to do the surgery in the morning. "Do you have a fleam, Squire?" John nodded.

My father opened the case he'd been carrying and drew out a flask containing a mixture of cantharides and turpentine spirits, which he then smoothed over the colt's neck using a rag. "Keep using t' drench t' physician gave you, but by King George, don't let 'im draw more blood, and I'll see ye t' mornin'!" The squire nodded, looking apologetic. "And for t' sake of yer herd, remove t' rest of t' beasts but don't put 'em with any others until ye know they're right."

Father and I got home in time that night for a good meal of pulses and greens with a little salt fish for flavor, and Mother had made an apple tart, an unusual treat. But the main pleasure of the day for me had been attending to my father and observing his work with the colts—anything to do with horses was always special to me, even when it involved one so sick as the yearling we had seen that day. I knew well from experience that the poor creature could be dead by daybreak—strangles was often lethal. And even though I was not allowed to go with my father the next morning—I had my butter and studies to attend to—I could envision what he would do, driving the lance deep into the swollen gland, putrid pus ejecting in a stream, the colt rearing back in pain but then taking a deep breath in relief as his air passageway cleared. I said a prayer to God that the animal would live and that his paddock-mates would not sicken. And God answered this prayer. Although two more colts did come down with strangles later that week, they all survived with Da's assistance. It was too bad, though, that Father's doctoring and God's intervention were not going to work to save my mother.

Chapter 5

THE WHITE HORSE

I t was that same summer that Billy Simpson apprenticed to my da. The thirteen-year-old was from nearby Fernham and was about two years older than me. He was stocky-built with dark curly hair and a wide smile. No one in our village had been willing to sign one of their sons to a papist, but Billy's father didn't seem to have the same compunction. For me, it was a treat to have another person of similar age in "our family." Billy took his meals with us, although he slept in the shop. I didn't really see all that much of him outside of meals unless I had an errand to run for Da. Father kept him working sunup to sundown. But once in a while, when Mama was feeling poorly and needed to lie down, she would give me a little free time, and I was then unerringly drawn to the shop to see what "the boys" were up to.

They were usually hunched over the worktable. Da had shown Billy how to draw a pattern on the stretched tanned hides and then make sweeping, smooth cuts with a leather knife to create the various straps necessary for each harness. Soon the apprentice would learn how to sew in the buckles, turrets, and other metal fittings using waxed thread, but for now, that task was left for the master. It would be quite a while before the novice could attempt the more-difficult sewing of the ornamented blinders, crupper, or saddle or, especially, the all-important work collar stuffed with straw. One small blemish or stiff stitch where the harness lay around the neck of the horse against the shoulder, and the animal could be sored or even ruined. Once a harness was completed, it was Billy's job to rub and clean the finished tack with neat's-foot oil to soften and waterproof the leather.

One afternoon, when I was working in the garden, hoeing the potatoes and peas, I noticed a farmer leading the biggest horse I had ever seen up to our shed. He was a shiny black, like the Dutch horse, but much larger. He also had heavy feathers, nearly from his knees all the way to the ground, and was marked with four white stockings. I had never been up close to such an awesome animal! I left the garden quickly and came up behind Da. The farmer was saying, "This here's a Shire horse from Dishley Grange. I was lucky enough to pick 'im up at an auction last week. Ain't 'e grand!"

"He is indeed," said my da, walking slowly around the great beast admiringly. "I've not seen one so large in these parts, for sure!"

"I figure he can do the work of two Suffolks," the farmer stated proudly, "but none of my harness will fit 'im. Can ye get me one made up quick?" Da went into his shop and came out with his two biggest collar patterns.

"My largest housing is a twenty-five-incher," Da explained, "but I'll be blessed by King George if this guy don't take a thirty-inch." My father and Billy proceeded to take measurements for the collar, from withers to the shoulder insertion, from side to side, every which way, it looked to me. "It's important to have the collar fit snugly, but you want at least four fingers' leeway at the bottom, ye do," he was explaining to Billy, holding up his fist. They also took measurements for the girth, backstrap, breeching, crown, and cheek pieces.

"I've never seen a drafter measure even close to this," Da pronounced to the farmer, shaking his head. "Week from now, come back and we'll 'ave this lad plowing the deepest furrows in the county."

Billy and I were becoming fairly good friends. He told me about his family (there were six siblings) and about his village (it was smaller than ours) and about his plans (he hoped to become a harness-maker in a big city like London). I hadn't had much opportunity to talk to other children, let alone boys, and I was engrossed by his stories. On Sundays, when Father took the Lord's Day as Sabbath and our shop was closed, Billy would sometimes walk to town with me in the morning when I was delivering butter. On these mornings, I had no fear of Tom or the other children! I noticed that, like us, Billy didn't attend St. Mary's and was inclined to spend Sunday afternoons resting or fishing. Neither did he seem interested in joining Mother and me in our devotions. Once in a great while he would catch a ride in a farm wagon to go to visit his family but was always back bright and early on Monday morning.

I liked Billy for the most part, but once in a while, he made me feel a little uneasy. I couldn't say exactly why; it was just something about the way I would catch him looking at me. Usually, I enjoyed being around him and I was grateful for his company, especially when I had to go into the village. Whenever he was around my mother or me, he was always polite, and the truth was that sometimes, when he didn't know it, I stared at him, too.

One Sunday morning, Mama was feeling poorly, and I knew we would be skipping our usual worship together. After milking and churning, I was ready to head off for the village when Billy appeared and said he was coming with me. I was always glad for the "defense" of his company, and we set off. He seemed to know that I didn't need to hurry home that morning, and he asked if we might go up and see the famous White Horse. The great chalk animal had been carved into the side of White Horse Hill at some ancient time by some unknown people and was famous far and wide in its shrouded history. I had grown up knowing of its presence (it was only about one and a half miles south of our village) but had never climbed high enough on any of the surrounding hills to see it clearly.

It was a beautiful day, blue skies with a light breeze. Billy seemed excited to go, and I figured neither Mama nor Da would have any need of me for a while. So we headed up the hill in the direction of Coxwell, where I thought the view might be a good one. Billy was not his normal, talkative self, and I stayed quiet, too, watching carefully where I laid my feet as we picked our way up the stony embankment. At last we reached the crest and turned around to look across the valley. The view took my breath away. Even from this distance, the three-foot-deep trenches filled with white limestone against the backdrop of the green hillside made the carved outline of the graceful, galloping steed stand out and appear almost to be floating. "That thing must be at least four hundred feet long!" Billy exclaimed as he gazed, astonished at the sight. We stood, staring at the ancient landmark for several minutes.

I was still lost in my imaginations when I realized that Billy had taken my hand and was looking at me, not at the historical site across the valley. I felt that strange prickling again and quickly stepped back from him. "What's wrong, Kate?" he queried, but I was already turning to retreat down the hillside.

"I'll be needing to get back to Mama," I quickly answered, but Billy had grabbed my shoulder and turned me to face him. His face, normally so pleasant, now appeared almost angry, and it frightened me.

"I thought you wanted to come up here…with me," he asserted. "I thought you favored me."

I didn't know how to answer; I couldn't really say how I was feeling. I just knew I needed to get away. I turned again to head down the hill, and this time he let me go. We walked all the way back home in silence, Billy following behind me. He didn't mention the incident again. Nor did he act like anything had changed between us. And I wasn't sure that anything particularly had. It was just that I didn't understand my feelings, especially toward the apprentice. My body and emotions were changing, and I couldn't explain why it made me feel so unsettled and awkward. I was not as thin as I used to be, although I certainly didn't have the figure of most girls my age. But I noticed that the other village children didn't make fun of me much anymore, and that left me wondering too.

I got up the nerve to ask Mama one day if she thought something was wrong with me, and she answered with a small smile. "Why, Kate, you're simply growing into a young woman. You know you're becoming more beautiful every day, don't you?" But sometimes I would go into her bedroom and look at myself in the little brass mirror. To me, nothing had changed. My wide, pale eyes still looked strange, and I longed for the fairer hair and fuller figure of my mother. If this was growing up, I didn't much care for it.

That night, I had my first vision of the white horse. While I slept, it began as more of a pleasant dream than a nightmare. The beautiful white stallion was cantering, not so much upon the plain as *over* the plain. He was coming nearer, now galloping, or perhaps flying, through the air. And when he was directly over me, I began to sense the danger of those thrashing hooves. Now he was no longer lovely, but threatening. I felt the scream catch in my throat as I started up from my sleep—wide awake, on my pallet! This dream wouldn't come often in the next year, but I realize now that it might have been a portent of things to come.

One other incident involving Tom Burlington occurred that same summer. On my way home from the pub, having delivered my butter bucket on a Sunday morning, I heard what sounded like a youngster crying and other children laughing. My first impulse was to run the other way, but the child's sobs arrested me. Peering around a corner, I saw a small girl I didn't recognize crumpled against a stone wall, with Tom and his younger siblings standing menacingly in front of her. The Burlingtons looked like they were dressed for church. Finding courage I didn't know I had, I approached the group. "What's going on? Why is she weeping?" I asked, while keeping my eye on the little girl. "What happened?"

"This uns a big crybaby," Tom said for the group. "We gave her a little scare, just trying to say 'Howdy,' and she peed herself. Lookit, her skirt's all wet," he continued as the others laughed and pointed.

"Leave her alone, Tom," I ordered as I approached the child.

"Who's going to make me?" Tom demanded right back. My legs began to shake, but I fastened my eyes on the little girl's tear-streaked face to keep my composure and tried to think how to reply.

Just at that moment, St. Mary's bells began to toll, and one of Tom's brothers warned, "Come on, Tom, Ma will be mad if we're late for church, and we'll catch a switchin' for sure." With that the other children left, Tom departing reluctantly after them, leering at me over his shoulder.

"What's your name?" I asked quietly, slowly approaching the little heap on the ground. "I won't hurt you. My name is Kate." Slowly the small girl turned her face up toward mine, and I could see her tears were slowing. "What's your name?" I asked again.

"Ruby," she whispered, and then added, "I wasn't doing nothing, but those others started chasing me, and then…and then…" And she began to cry harder again.

"Don't worry. They've scared the pee out of me before, too. Come on, let's get you home to dry clothes. Where do you live?" I kept talking, attempting to calm her sobbing. "I don't think I've ever seen you before." I tried gently taking her arm and lifting her to her feet, but she was having none of it. "Come on, let's go find your mother."

Through her tears she stammered, "This is the only skirt I have. Ma's going to be upset." Now she had started to cough, and once the hacking started, she couldn't seem to catch her breath. I watched as the fit finally lessened and her color came back. I had seen this same thing at home, too often!

I had to think for a moment. "Well, why don't you come to my cottage, then, just around there?" I pointed. "My mama can help get you cleaned up." I could see she was considering this, as her tears slowed again. I asked, "Will your ma wonder where you've gotten to?"

"Na, she worked last night and won't be awake before noon." She paused. "Do you think your ma would really help me?"

"I'm sure she can get you fixed up. Come on, let's go see." And with that, she finally rose, and we set off up the dirt lane. But I had to go slowly for Ruby to keep up, stopping every few yards to ease her breathing. No wonder the Burlingtons had caught her so easily.

As I knew she would, Mama was anxious to help. We took Ruby into the bedroom, managed to get her soiled clothing off, and draped her in one of my old shifts. I say "draped" because the dress would have fallen right off her shoulders if we hadn't used a sash and sewing pins. I couldn't help but notice (the child wore no underclothes) how painfully thin she was, much thinner than I had ever been. Every rib showed—she looked like a skeleton! Several times we had to wait for a paroxysm of coughing to subside. I could tell that Mother was as taken aback by the child's condition as I was.

"Have you had anything to eat this morning?" Mama asked once we had gotten Ruby decently clothed. Ruby shook her head. "Well, I had breakfast ready for Kate. Would you like to join us? Sorry it's only warm milk with bread sop, but I have some apple jam we can dab on top for flavor," Mama added.

We all three sat down at the table, and Ruby proceeded to slurp her breakfast down in just a few seconds and then, with wide eyes, watched Mama refill her cup. When Ruby had finally slowed her eating, Mother began gently asking a few questions. How old was she? Ten. (She was the size of a six-year-old.) How long had she lived here? She and her ma had just come from London to live with her aunt last week. How did she like Uffington? Well, the children here seemed just about as mean as those in London. But then she added, "Except for Kate, that is," and she gave me a heart-warming smile.

"Well," Mama finally said, "we'd better get your skirt washed." Mother pulled me aside and whispered, "I'm going to use lye soap on her things, but I want you to help give her a sponge bath. Her hair needs a good dousing of vinegar for the vermin. Can you do that but keep your own hair pulled well back?" Luckily, it was a warm day with a good breeze, and Ruby's clothes were mostly dry by the time we needed to walk her home.

Mama decided to come along with us as it was only to be a short walk. I think Mother was surprised and concerned at how weak the child seemed as we made our way, each of us holding one of her hands. The house Ruby and her mother were living in was a small cottage, very similar to our own. But when we started to walk up to the door, the child pulled my mother's hand and led us around to the back instead. There was an entryway in the rear going down to the cellar, and Ruby's mother met us at the top of the stairs. Ethel, who seemed relieved to see her daughter, went on to explain that Ruby had been sick for a long time. Her husband had died, and on the advice of a physician, the two of them had come here to live with Ethel's sister.

"The air in London is really bad," she continued, "and I wanted to get my girl out into the fresh air of the countryside." I had heard that the big city was choked with smoke and soot from the multitudes of coal fires, and also that reeking, human sewage ran in rivers down the streets. But I had to wonder if the foul, dank air that I could smell coming up from the dirt cellar would be any healthier for the child. No wonder Ruby had taken the opportunity to explore outside by herself.

"Is there no room for you in the upper house?" my mother asked, but Ethel shook her head. "I was lucky that my sister was even willing to let us sleep down here. She has a houseful of her own to feed and care for. I've found a job down at the brewers tending to the fires all night, and I hope to be able to find a better place for Ruby and me to stay soon."

"Hmmm," my mother replied. "Well, we've brought you a jug of milk. We are blessed to have a cow and often have extra. I'll send my daughter over now and again with our spare, if you'd like? It may help put some weight on Ruby's frame."

We headed home, and I could tell from Mama's silence that she was worried about our new friend. But her concern was short-lived. It was less than a week later that I arrived at that cellar door bearing another jug of milk. Getting no response in the back, I rapped at the front door and was informed by the aunt that her sister was gone. Ruby had died in her sleep two nights prior. I wondered if the fright from Tom and his siblings had advanced her illness. I worried that the bathing or delousing or even the milk might have harmed her and hastened her death. But mostly I agonized over the question, Did Ruby and Mama have the same condition? And would they both come to the same kind of tragic end?

Chapter 6

SNOWFLAKE

The summer I turned twelve, my life changed. I was sewing in the house with Mama, who had been feeling poorly. I was worried about her; she was losing weight and coughing more often. Da and Billy were out in the workshop that morning when we all heard the clop of horse hooves and then someone hailing us from the yard. It was a liveried servant who was speaking to Da when Mother and I stepped outside. Father came excitedly back to the house and was retrieving his medicine case as he explained, "I've been called up t' the Earl of Faringdon's estate, I 'ave. He's got a stallion with the colic." The earl had never called on Father before, although everyone knew who Lord Charles Stanley and his late wife, Lady Janet, were, being the only English nobility in our neighborhood.

"Please, Da, please, can I come?" I begged. Da looked over at Mother, who paused and looked at me. "Please, Mama. I want to see the stallion."

She slowly smiled and nodded. "Well, be sure and look at the grand house and grounds, while you're at it." She laughed, shaking her head. Da and I quickly headed off with the servant to the trap, which was hitched to a flashy bay hackney-type. Da left Billy in charge of the shop.

On the road, the driver explained that the earl's best horse had been ill off and on for two days. Lord Stanley's own physician had already bled the horse, but with little improvement. We drove at a sharp clip, the servant urging the horse to a fast trot for the hilly four miles. I'd never had the pleasure of riding in a carriage, and the experience exhilarated me. I could barely enjoy the changing scenery for gazing at the beautiful bay haunches laboring in front of us. In less than thirty minutes, we were pulling through pillared gates and rushing up the long stone drive toward the stable area. Our cart horse, by this time, was in a lather and breathing heavily.

We dismounted quickly, and Da headed toward the small knot of men who were watching a sweating grey horse being led around and around. I was glad to see that our driver immediately began tending to his hot carriage horse, and I jogged to catch up to my father. I couldn't take my eyes off the stallion—he was shockingly silver in color. I had never seen a grey horse before. I had seen older black horses turned white with age or roan animals, but this horse was the same color as the shiny silver of my neck chain with dappling over his rump and barrel.

A stocky, older gentleman in a fine linen coat and breeches was saying, "And I've had him since spring last. Comes from the finest Arabian stock in the peninsula. My mares have already dropped several fine foals this spring, and I was hoping to race him next year. The Arab breed's stamina is legendary. But now…this!" He paused, glancing at the stallion, who was being led in circles by a groom, a dark stain of sweat marring his dappled coat. "Squire Baker tells me you're good with equine ailments. I hope he's right. I can't afford to lose this horse! My entire breeding program is based on Cloud—that's his name, Cloud of the Desert."

"Yer man says 'e's 'ad the colic for a couple o' days now?" my father stated.

"Yes, off and on. He's been bled, and I thought he'd improved, but then he started pawing again."

"Has 'e been t' eatin' and drinkin'?" Da questioned.

"He took a little water last night but won't touch his oats. We've been keeping him walking so he won't roll and kick."

"Has he passed stool?"

"No, not for two days."

"How long 'ave ye been moving 'im?"

"Since midnight last night."

"He's bound t' be tired. Sure, let's let 'im stop and see what happens. If 'e don't pitch, let's let 'im rest." The groom at the head of the horse looked even more relieved than the animal by the command to stop walking.

At this, a younger man in equally fine dress whom I hadn't yet noticed stepped forward. "I'll take another turn handling him now, Father," he said. For a while, the stallion just stood, his head hanging dejectedly, his sides heaving. I couldn't help appreciating how splendid the Arabian must have looked when not covered in sweat and exhaustion. His delicately chiseled head with its wide, finely dished face, tapered muzzle, and small expressive ears was set on a long, handsomely arched neck. His back was short coupled, but with a long flat croup. I could imagine, when the horse was in health, that his tail would be held high, regally above his back. Now it hung stiffly behind his rump. My father had approached the horse and was bending by his side, his ear pressed to the horse's barrel. Da stepped back and scratched his head, watching the horse.

Suddenly, the animal let out a loud groan, his tail swished, his body quivered, and his head swiveled to bite at his belly. Then he began to drop to his knees, continuing to moan. "Get 'im up and walking again before 'e rolls," my father commanded, and the younger man urged the stallion forward to keep him on his feet. Da returned to the trap quickly to retrieve his medicines. To one of the grooms, he said, "I'll need a bucket o' warm water and some distilled spirits." The groom looked surprised but, after glancing toward the earl for approval, went off in the direction of the stables.

Now Da explained to Lord Stanley, "There's no gut sounds. To be sure, if the horse has twisted entrails, there's not much I can do. We can try to relieve some of 'is pain, we can, but 'e'll probably die and t'would be kindest t' shoot 'im." At this, the earl looked shocked and then almost apoplectic. "But," my father continued, ignoring the man's reaction, "if 'tis something packed up and stuck in his gut, then we might have a chance, if we can get 'im to pass stool. Then we might save 'im."

"Do whatever you must," the earl pressed. "I can't lose this stallion!" he repeated, again. I had gathered that the tall, handsome, young man leading the ailing animal was the earl's son. He was speaking quietly to the horse, patting his neck and trying to comfort him. Meanwhile, Da was mixing a drench of prickly ash berries, distilled spirits, laudanum, and warm water. He had poured the liquid from the pail into the drenching bottle. Asking the younger gentleman to grasp the horse's muzzle and hold his head in the air, he forced a cow horn into the side of the steed's mouth and proceeded to pour the drench into the funnel. The horse struggled, but the younger man stubbornly held on. "Grab 'is tongue and pull it out the side," Da ordered. This accomplished, it was obvious that the horse had no choice but to swallow the distasteful liquid.

"Now we need oil. What kind might ye have on hand, in quantity?"

"I have a gallon of linseed oil," Lord Stanley answered.

"Get that quickly and see t' more warm water," Da commanded, and grooms were dispatched. Soon they had the drenching apparatus in place again, and Father, after adding oil of peppermint to the bottle, soon administered it, followed by more warm water. The horse sputtered and shook his head and spewed some of the liquid out of his nose in a loud snort, but most had obviously been swallowed. The young man at his head, though he had been sprayed by the oily mess, did not complain, only continued to talk softly to the animal. I noticed two other younger gentlemen pointing at him and laughing. "Now we wait t' see what happens, we do," Da finished. "It may take well and over an hour afore we know if this will work."

"Well, come up to my study for a drink, then. I'm tired of standing out here, and my lumbago is acting up," the earl complained. "Sorry, is this your daughter?" he said, finally glancing my way.

"Ta, this is my Kathryn," Da answered rather proudly, and we followed the earl toward the house. "Kathryn, say g' day to the earl." I did a clumsy curtsy and stared at the ground.

"My eldest son, Viscount William, is the one at Cloud's head." The tall, young man was still leading the horse in circles. "He's quite good with horses," the earl said with pride. Then he nodded toward the two other younger, obviously well-dressed men standing off to the side among several grooms. "Those are my younger sons, Anthony and Clarence...not worth so much," he added cryptically. As we watched, the two younger men headed off toward the back of the house, laughing, knowing the entertainment was now probably at an end. I noticed they did not offer to help their brother. But neither did any of the grooms, who had perhaps been up all night.

As we walked toward the mansion, I felt my nerves begin to set in. I knew we were passing through manicured gardens and along a bricked walkway, but all I could concentrate on was my father's heels and trying not to trip. It was the same as we entered the hall and turned into some sort of large room. I was barely conscious of the bookshelves, large stuffed chairs, fireplace, or desk that occupied the space. I know the earl offered my father and me something to drink, which I declined. Perched on the edge of one of the cushioned chairs, I barely was conscious of their conversation. I believe it concerned breeding and racing and the future of Arabian horses in the country, but I was too nervous to really listen. All I could think about was the suffering grey horse and the handsome, young gentleman handling him.

Finally, we were interrupted by a knock on the door summoning us back out to the paddocks. There was good news. The stallion had passed stool—evidently a great quantity of hard balls followed by looser, watery manure. The viscount was still at the horse's head, patting him, telling him what a good boy he was. The animal himself seemed much relieved and was picking at some grass at his feet. Now that he was calm, I could confirm that he was the most magnificent horse I had ever seen. His coat had dried and was now a steely, dappled grey, his legs, mane, and tail a darker charcoal color. He had a white stripe down the middle of his wide forehead between large, expressive eyes and a white snip on his pinkish nose. He was absolutely breathtaking.

"Do you think he'll be set right now, sir?" the younger man was asking my father in a deferential tone that impressed me.

"Sure, there's a chance the trouble is over. But if not, I be thinkin' drench 'im just like you saw me do. And by King George, don't let that quack come and bleed 'im. Does no good, only weakens the animal." The earl looked at him askance but didn't argue.

"Would you like to see some of Cloud's offspring?" Lord Stanley suddenly invited, and we walked up toward the large, bricked stable. I was in awe of the wide, cobbled aisleways, the oak-fronted, large stalls bedded in bright straw, and the striking animals inhabiting them. At every cell, the earl stopped and described the bloodlines of each beautiful mare and her colt or filly.

"See those small white spots on the rump of this colt?" the earl said, pointing. "Did you notice that Cloud has the same markings? They aren't very noticeable because of his dappling, but I've never seen them on a horse before. Now some of his colts carry the same pattern on their coats. I'm hoping it's a sign of speed!"

I was interested in all the mares and the earl's discourse, but I couldn't help noticing that we had skipped past one stall, and I peered in as Lord Stanley and my father went on down the aisle. Inside, a chestnut mare was nuzzling a small, grey filly lying in the straw. The mare would nicker, push her nose against the little horse, even nip the baby's back. Each time she did this, the foal would struggle to rise, but her legs would not seem to unfold properly, and it appeared she was unable to stand. The mare seemed quite anxious about this.

"Wait," I called to the men. "What about this filly? Something seems to be wrong."

"Come away from there, miss. That's nothing you need to see," said the earl.

"No, please. Da, come and look at this foal."

Despite what Lord Stanley had said, my father came to stand beside me and peered in at the two horses.

"This filly was born last night," the earl resignedly came back to explain. "She can't stand. There's something wrong with her legs, and she still hasn't nursed. I've been meaning to have her shot all morning, but I've been too preoccupied with Cloud."

"Do ye' mind if a look I have?" Da asked.

"Help yourself, but I've seen this before. She's not salvageable, I'm sure of it."

My father entered the stall and spoke quietly to the mare, who became agitated. "Davey, come get a head-collar on Belle," the earl directed, and the mare was soon confined. Da bent down next to the little animal in the straw and gently began to draw out her long spindly legs. Her two front limbs would only uncurl so far.

Da spoke to the groom who was holding the mare. "Davey, drop the lead and come help me get this foal on 'er feet," he directed. Between the two of them, they picked up the wobbly baby. She seemed to be able to shuffle her hind legs underneath herself, but her front legs were curled at the fetlock, the hooves unable to reach the ground. "Let's hold 'er up t' the mare so she can get a drink o' colostrum," Da said. I knew that colostrum was the "first milk"—a watery substance that all mothers produced for the first few hours after birth.

The little filly didn't seem to know what to do when her muzzle was placed against the mare's udder. But instinctively she began to root and shove on the teats. The mare grunted and turned to look but seemed to know and even desire that her baby would relieve the pressure she felt in that area. Suddenly, with a loud sucking sound, the foal attached and began to nurse. She would suckle for a few moments, then struggle backward against the arms holding her, and then find the nipple again. After about five minutes of her suckling, my da and the groom lowered her back into the straw, her little muzzle dripping milk. She lay back, seemingly exhausted but satiated.

Now Da rejoined us outside the stall. "I've not seen a foal with this condition," he began, "but I've heard o' it. The cords in 'er front legs are contracted and stand she can't. But now that she's gotten 'er first feed, she's goin' t' get stronger, and I think she'll get up on 'er legs, even though she'll be standin' on 'er front pasterns. Sure, she'll be able t' shuffle around in the straw, but once she's out on firmer ground, she'll rub the flesh right off t' the bone, she will."

The earl nodded and replied, "Exactly. That's why I'm going to put her down."

"But," my father continued, "I believe you can bring 'er right. She'd need t' wear splints on 'er front legs for a while and have 'er fetlocks and pasterns massaged and stretched twicet day. Surely, ye've got grooms t' see to such?"

"That's not the issue," Lord Stanley interposed. "Once grown, the mare would most likely never be sound enough to race, and I wouldn't want to breed her for fear of producing another foal like herself. No," he pronounced with finality, "she's not worth the trouble."

The two men turned and headed back down the aisle, but I desperately grabbed at my father's shirt. "Da," I whispered frantically, "please don't let them kill her." With tears in my eyes, I was making my case. "We could take her. We could fix her."

Father stepped off to the side and spoke quietly to me. "I know ye've a tender spot for creatures, Katie, but we couldn't keep 'er. Sure, we could probably help 'er legs, but she needs her momma. What would she eat?" He looked at me with sympathy. "Just best to let 'er go."

"No, please, please," I begged. "We could give her Molly's milk. I'd take care of her!"

"Cow's milk be too rich for a foal. And besides, she'd be needin' to nurse every two to three hours right at first."

"We could dilute Molly's milk. And I would do the feedings—I know Mama would give me the time. I'd do whatever it took, Da. Please," I finished with a whine.

"Well, diluted milk might serve, but it's a huge lot o' work. Ye know yer ma needs ye in the house. And besides, I don't want ye in the stable at night."

"I'll work extra hard for Mother when I'm not in the barn," I promised earnestly, "and Billy might take some of the night feedings, if I ask him. He sleeps out there, anyway." I could see my da was seriously contemplating. I jumped on the advantage. "You know I've always, always wanted my own horse."

"What if she ain't thrifty? What if she sickens from cow's milk? What if she develops scours 'n dies?" Da asked gravely. "T'would be easier to let 'er go now than t' lose her later when yer gra had grown, never mind the time 'n work wasted." But I could see he was relenting.

I threw my arms around him. "I promise that I won't complain if we lose her later. But please, please, we have to try." With a sigh, Da nodded.

I heard him talking to the earl, asking if he might take the foal as payment for his services with the stallion. Lord Stanley looked at him like he was crazy. "She's of no use to me, but why would you want her?" he asked.

"'Cause me daughter has a soft spot for animals and believes she can nurse yon foal back to health. We'll have t' try raisin' her on cow's milk, but I can't say nil t' 'er," Da finished.

"Then I can't say no to her either," the earl said, looking at me quizzically. "Take the filly with my blessing, but I doubt this is going to have a happy ending." And with that, the deal was struck. Little did I know, with this agreement, that my future was also settled, for better or worse.

After giving instructions for the stallion to be fed a bran mash, blanketed, and fed lightly that evening, we set off for home with Snowflake—so named because she also had her sire's little white spots on her rump. I never caught a last glimpse of the handsome, young viscount, but I was too excited about my new horse to care. We made sure to give Snowflake a final feeding before we carried her from the stall, the mare's desperate calls ringing after us. This time the earl had his servant hitch the farm wagon to a large drafter, and we piled straw in the back, where we held the filly during the trip. It took much longer to get home than our previous journey had been, and by the time we arrived, the three of us—Da, me, and Snow—were all exhausted.

Da and Billy carried the foal into her new stall, which we bedded deep in sawdust. She had continued to whinny for her mother the entire trip. Now she was so exhausted that her cries were just feeble whimpers. She looked so forlorn that I almost regretted my decision. But I got right to work milking Molly, and Da retrieved some clean rags from his shop. Billy was there to help, too.

"Difficult this may be, Katie Anne," Da warned. "She may not take it. She may never take the milk." We had diluted a pail of the warm liquid with water, and he dipped a rag and brought out the dripping mass. "Billy, get ahold of 'er head, and let's get this into 'er gob."

Over and over Da pried Snow's lips open and dripped the diluted milk into her mouth. Again and again the little filly shook her head, shaking out the liquid, stubbornly refusing the nourishment. Finally, after several minutes, we were all covered in milk and discouraged. "Let's leave 'er for a bit, and then try again later," Da suggested. Mama had come out to watch, and she put her arms around my shoulders. She knew how important this was to me.

"Go on in the house now, daughter, and we'll all try t' get some work done. For sure I'll call you when we're ready to give it another go." I wasn't much use at my embroidery, so Mama set me to breaking beans, something I could do without paying much attention. I leaped up when I heard Da's footsteps approaching the door.

This time as we opened the stall, Snowflake gave a little whinny of greeting. I suppose she was glad to see any creature, even if it wasn't her mother. Cally came in following me, and the little cat approached to sniff the filly's face. Snow snorted and pulled back, but the cat didn't take fright. Then the two animals sniffed noses for several seconds and seemed to relax. This was the beginning of a long friendship.

We tried the milky rag again, but without success. Snow was obviously getting weaker, as she didn't shake and fight us as strongly as before. But she continued to refuse to swallow her milk. It had gotten late. Mama had brought us each a dish of beans and bacon with a crust of rye bread for our dinner, which we ate right there in the barn. I couldn't take my eyes off the sad little foal curled on the floor of the stable. I noticed that Cally had remained in the stall and was curled up beside the filly. Snow had her eyes closed; Cally was licking herself and purring.

"Da, I can't go in to bed knowing that Snow is out here all alone and hungry. Please, just for tonight, can't we stay out here with her, only until she starts eating?" I begged.

"All right, daughter, I'll get some blankets for a pallet." I knew Da had gotten attached to the little filly, too. Billy went to his own bed in the shop, but Da and I lay across the opening to the stall, where Snow could see us. There was no worry of her treading on us trying to escape—she was too weak to even attempt to rise from her bed in the sawdust.

Sometime toward midnight, Da woke me and I picked up the bucket of diluted milk. I knew it wouldn't be as palatable cold, but Molly was out on the commons and wouldn't be back until dawn. Da and I sat down by Snow's head. She woke and sat up but didn't struggle as Da circled her neck. She was getting so weak! I brought a rag full of the cold fluid to her lips. She didn't back away like before but just remained unmoving, as if she was too tired to care. I put the rag down and rubbed her soft neck. "Da, maybe you were right. Maybe it would just be kinder to put her down," I said with my voice choking.

Cally sensed my emotion, as she always did, and came over to curl against me. I felt her rough tongue licking my finger where there was still some wet milk. Suddenly, I had an idea. I dipped my finger into the pail and then pried my finger into the filly's toothless gums. I felt her tongue wrap around my finger, and then she began sucking. I removed the digit, dipped again, and replaced the finger. "Da, look, she's sucking on my finger," I whispered carefully, but excitedly.

"Try wrappin' some o' the rag around your finger so t'will hold more milk," Da suggested. When I did this, the slurping, sucking noise increased. Suddenly, the filly came wide-awake, interest finally showing in her eyes. It took a long time to get maybe a cup of milk into the little animal, but she eventually stopped suckling and appeared ready to sleep.

"It's time for us t' sleep, too, daughter. Go up t' yer pallet. I'll feed 'er again later tonight and then see you 't milkin' time in the morning." I knew there was no point in arguing. Besides, my eyes were drooping. As I headed into the house, I noticed that Cally had stayed behind with Snow. I knew I would miss the little cat in my bed, but I also knew she was where she was needed most.

Snowflake began to thrive as she began to eat better. She was soon sucking on just the rag. And a day after that, she took to the bucket, drinking right alongside the lapping cat, who she seemed to be copying. Once she was adept at slurping directly from the pail, the filly was able to drink her fill at each meal. It also meant fewer feedings at night. Billy had not been happy with the idea of rising every three hours to feed the little horse, but now Da agreed to his feeding just once in the middle of the night, leaving the pail with its remains in the corner, where Snow could find it.

It was amazing how quickly her little gaunt frame filled out and her fur smoothed. She also learned to stand, especially after we had splinted her legs, and could move around her stall at will. She did develop the scours, as Da had warned, but he gave her a draught of powdered rhubarb, ginger, and opium mixed with milk and a little gruel three times a day, and after two days, the scours improved. He also experimented with the strength of the milk dilution until it seemed to agree with her.

Once we had overcome her nutritional needs, we began concentrating in earnest on her forelegs. Da made splint supports out of willow shoots, six for each leg. He notched these and tied them all together using his saddler's thread. The knots between each slender branch kept them apart and straight once they were tied around the leg. We used heavy muslin wraps under the wood to prevent chafing.

The splint supports helped keep her legs from curling and collapsing. But Da stressed to me how important it was to stretch and massage her ankles every morning and evening. With first Da's, and later, Billy's, help, I would do this starting with the filly lying, and then with her standing. It was important to get her sustaining her weight on her hooves, not her pasterns. Da also applied a salve to her ankles each morning.

Obviously, Snow did not take kindly to all this well-meaning attention, but she had a gentle nature and never did kick or bite but submitted willingly enough, even if not eagerly. It helped that she looked forward to seeing us and the milk bucket, greeting us with a loud whinny as we approached her stall. Once she had finished her meal, we would work on the massage, and it was a victorious day when she finally placed her heel on the ground and was not just walking on her tiptoes. From then on, her own weight was all the physical therapy she needed. I wish I could say that I had kept my promise and maintained all my housework duties during this time.

But the truth was that I just couldn't stay out of the stable. Often, when I should have been working, Mama would find me just sitting in the stall with Snow and Cally or standing outside, watching the filly cavort in circles and jumps around her cell. But Mama was patient with me, knowing how important this gift had been. And Da never complained about it either.

By the end of the summer, I was able to take Snow out for long walks up to the commons. She was allowed to graze on grass while on the lead and also in the paddock. She loved to kick up her heels and race around in the sunshine. She played games, rearing and fighting imaginary foes, and then tearing off, bucking in feigned fright. You would never guess that she had ever been unable to walk. By three months, she was weaned onto grass, hay, and a few oats. These provisions were a terrible expense for my family, I realized. But Mama somehow found the means, and I never asked how. If it weren't for Mother's continuing weakness and our financial concerns, my happiness would have been complete.

Chapter 7

TRAINING SNOW

A ll that next year, I continued to milk twice a day and churn in the mornings, help with the housework, and sew in the evenings. Mama seemed weaker some days, at times not even rising out of bed, her coughing severe. Other days she would almost seem her old self. We had pretty much finished with my studies. Mama still expected me to practice on the piano forte, and we continued to read as many books as we could borrow or procure. But on days when the sickness would come on her, the cooking, cleaning, gardening, washing—whatever needed doing—would take most of my time. On those days, the only moments I had to spend with Snow were on the trip up and back to the commons, where she was tethered.

Other days, after the morning work was done, Mama would release me to the stable. She knew that was where my heart longed to be. I had watched Da train many horses by now, and I needed no help with my own filly. I started her on the longe when she was one year old. I knew I couldn't work her too fast or hard on the big circle because of her weakened legs, but I could see they were strengthening each month.

Snow learned voice commands and to read my body language. She would walk, trot, canter, and "Whoa" on signal, whether on the circle or on the lead. She would turn or back up just with a nod of my body or a flick of my wrist, licking and chewing the whole time.

When we went for walks, she matched my pace, step for step, so much so I imagined we looked like some sort of tandem, six-legged creature.

Billy would sometimes step out of the shop to watch us. I couldn't help but notice that he was maturing into a broad-shouldered, handsome young man, but I continued to feel awkward around him. It didn't help that I had witnessed him lose his temper with Snow one day. I usually cleaned her stall, but that morning, Mama had been more ill than usual, and I hadn't even gone to take the butter to the village. I heard Da ask Billy to clean her stall after breakfast, and I felt badly about this, knowing how much work our apprentice already had waiting for him in the shop. My father was depending on him more and more, and sometimes Billy complained about it to me.

This particular morning, feeling Mama could be left for a few moments, I stepped out to the stable just to say hello and see if I could help. Billy was in the stall with Snow. He was using a pitchfork to pick up her waste and throw it in a barrow that was parked in the doorway. He seemed to be muttering under his breath, and as he moved into the corner, the filly, curious and following him, misread his direction and stepped on his foot. Slinging a curse—something I had never heard him do before—he hit Snow on the nose with the handle of the fork. She backed up in panic and confusion, ears laid flat, not knowing why he had hit her.

I rushed to the stall door. "Billy, you hit her," I blurted, not knowing what else to say as I entered the cell and approached the filly, my hand outstretched. "Easy, girl. He didn't mean it."

"She's spoiled and needs to learn respect, Kate. She shouldn't have been walking on top of me. You need to teach this horse some discipline, or she's going to hurt you one day." I couldn't believe what he was saying and just shook my head. "Besides, you give her all your attention. I don't even get to walk to the village with you anymore, you're always so busy with *her*." He waved the fork at Snow again, and she backed as far into the opposite corner as she could get.

"I think you need to leave the barn now, Billy," I said as calmly as I could. "I'll finish cleaning the stall." He glared at me for a moment and then threw down the fork and left. I was beginning to shake. I wondered why he had said what he did. It was true that we hadn't spent any time together alone for a long time, but we saw each other every day at the meal table, and we talked there. And why was he taking this out on my horse? I determined to keep a closer eye on his dealings with Snow in the future and wondered if I should tell Da about it. But I didn't. Billy apologized to me later that day, and I put it out of my mind.

When Snowflake turned two, I got more serious about her training. I introduced her to the tack much as I had seen Da do with Goliath years before. Snow acted like she had been carrying a saddle for years. She also accepted the bridle with little complaint, although she did mouth the bit for a while until Da suggested I tighten the cheek pieces so that the snaffle rode higher in her mouth. That seemed to solve the problem.

The next step was to work her in long lines, extended reins that ran from her bit on both sides, through the stirrups of the saddle, and back to me walking behind her. This confused Snow at first. She kept trying to circle and come back to me, ignoring the pull of the rein on the corner of her mouth. I finally asked Da to come and lead her for a time while she learned to understand that a pull from the rein meant turn and both reins meant "Whoa." Before long, I could guide her anywhere using the long lines.

Snow had never been a spooky horse. When she was younger, I practiced leading her all through the village and up into the meadows. The first time she saw something new, she would prick her ears and want to stop and look at it—a chimney sweep carrying brushes and brooms, a matron pushing a coal cart, an ornamental flag. But rarely did she step sideways or try to turn and run, and after she had looked for a moment, she would usually walk on calmly. The one time she did spook and nearly got away from me was her first time seeing a large wagonette pulled by a pair of leggy Norfolk Trotters. I wasn't sure if it was the strange horses (she had mostly been isolated from other horses since the day she was born) or if it was the sight of the "monster" wagon that was chasing them. This time she bolted away from me and I nearly lost the reins. Only my calm voice and command to "Whoa" and a strong pull on her mouth kept her from running all the way back home.

When the moment came for me to mount Snow for the first time, it was straightforward. Da came to help me by holding her lead and giving me a leg up. But it was almost as if Snow said, "What took you so long?" We were riding through the countryside within a week. Mother and Da did have one argument over this. Mama felt it was unbecoming for a woman to ride astride. But the only saddle we owned was the hunting saddle Da used when training young horses, and it would have cost more than we could afford for Da to buy the tree and forms to build a sidesaddle. Besides, I told both of them that I preferred just riding bareback, with no saddle at all. Mama finally gave in and fashioned for me a full skirt that was split and sewn in the middle to preserve "my modesty." She wasn't happy about me riding without a chaperone either, but in the end, she gave up. She didn't have the energy anymore to fight both of us.

That winter, when Snow was a long two-year-old and I was still fourteen, we had another incident with Tom Burlington. I was riding down by the stream in our village. There was no ice on the ground, but the weather was cold. I could hear voices up on the stone bridge, and I recognized my old tormentor and his siblings. They were roughhousing, and there was yelling going on. Suddenly, there was a splash as something significant hit the water. I was downstream a little ways but heard Tom frantically calling as he exited the bridge and headed down the slope to the water's edge.

"My little sister's fallin' in the water!" he screamed. "And I can't swim! Please, someone, help!" He and several other children were running up and down the bank, and I could see a mass of skirts and what might have been a head bobbing out in the current. The sad truth was that none of us village children had been taught to swim. As far as I knew, no adult in the village ever swam either. Besides, there seemed to be no one else nearby.

I made a decision almost unconsciously and began guiding Snow toward the bank. I could see that the current was carrying the child, who was still struggling, downstream toward me. I had never asked Snow to step into the river. We had practiced walking through puddles, but I had no idea if she would enter the stream. She hesitated and pawed at the water. I kicked her sides harder than I had ever done, and suddenly, she plunged in. As the splashing waves reached my legs, I gasped with the cold. Suddenly, I was very afraid. I knew that most horses could swim, but I could not. What if I got swept off her back?

But there was no turning back now. The little girl had stopped struggling. She was only a few yards ahead of me, but the water had reached Snow's back and I could feel that my horse had begun to swim. My own body was lifted off her back by the buoyancy of the water, and I had to grasp the filly's mane to keep from falling off entirely. Thank goodness for my strong, milking-trained hands! We were now almost to the child, who was submerged just under the water. I reached out and grabbed ahold of her hair, pulling her up to the surface even as I kept a death grip on Snow's mane with the other hand.

The child's head was above the water now, and I used my legs to turn the horse toward the bank. Snow needed no further urging as she surged toward dry land. When her feet found purchase and she began to struggle through the mud, I lost my grip on her mane and only just managed to grab the filly's tail as she scrambled up the bank in front of us. Somehow, Snow dragged both me and the child I was gripping up to dry land and the frantic Tom. I let go of Snow's tail and sank, shivering, to the ground. Tom had picked up his sister and was wailing over her body. Suddenly, we all heard her gasp and begin to cry. I was too cold to do much more than crawl to my horse, who had thankfully stopped and returned to my side, her head reaching down to sniff my cold form. Now others had come to surround me, and I managed to ask through chattering teeth if they would help me remount. Lying on Snow rather than properly riding, I turned her toward home and a warm fire. But as we left the scene, I heard Tom call out through his tears, "Miss Kathryn...thankee." I didn't look back.

Chapter 8

LAMBOURNE

That next summer, I turned fifteen and Snow was a three-year-old. I guess we were each about the same age mentally and physically, but Snow had a better sense of herself. She was a beautiful filly-mare now, not so tall, maybe only about 14.2 hands, but finely featured, a lighter grey than her sire. I thought she was the most beautiful horse on earth. I sometimes secretly worried that Lord Stanley would see her one day and want her back. I was coming into my own woman's figure, too, already taller than my father, but about the same height as my mother. Da said I looked more like Mama every day, but I couldn't see it.

I hadn't had a lot of time to ride Snow that spring. Mama and I were just too busy planting garden along with all the other work we had to do, and I tried to be sure that I did all the heavy digging and lifting. Mama had come through the winter poorly. But sometimes, if the day was warm, I would take a few minutes and go up to the commons with my gorgeous horse on a lead, sit in the sun, and just enjoy watching her graze among the grasses and lilies. She seemed to always keep one of her large expressive eyes on me while she searched all around for the most tender shoots. It amazed me how her lips could sort through the grasses and find exactly which ones she wanted to tear from the earth, avoiding those less tender or tasteful. Horses really could be quite picky in what they ate. I felt so blessed to be able to just sit and observe such a magnificent creature. Life was good on those days!

Da and I received an exciting invitation that summer. Squire Baker had purchased a new stallion that had been imported all the way from Northern Africa. Diamond was a Berber horse, another grey like Cloud of the Desert, but lighter, closer to white in color. Diamond didn't resemble any of our English countryside animals. He had very high withers and a sloping back to a short croup. He needed a breast collar fastened to the saddle leathers in order to keep the seat from slipping rearward toward his tail. But the squire was very excited about his horse's amazing speed and stamina.

Ever since the outbreak of strangles on the squire's property, he had relied on Da to keep his stock of horses healthy. And now he was planning to take Diamond to the big regional horse race at Lambourne the next month, and he wanted Da to accompany him just in case Diamond experienced any problems along the way. The plan was to take several wagons carrying grooms, servants, supplies, tents, etc. and make the twelve-mile trip two days before the race was scheduled, returning the day after the event.

When I heard about the proposal, I became excited. Mother had been having mostly good days lately. The light, early-summer weather had seemed to help her feel better. I wanted to approach Da about allowing me to come with him, but I knew I needed to have my arguments in order first. I would remind him of the help I provided when he was working with a horse. I would reason that Mother was feeling much improved right now and could do without me for three days. And finally, I would plead that I had never been far from home, had never experienced such an exciting adventure, and that I would promise to stay close to him the whole time, but out of his way.

The morning I made my appeal, I was so nervous my legs were shaking. Da let me list off all my reasons without interrupting and then smiled. "Your mama and I 'ad already decided to let you come," he announced. It took me a moment to realize what this meant, and then I let out a whoop of joy. Billy, on the other hand, was not happy when he learned that he was to stay home and tend to things at the shop and cottage. When my da wasn't looking, I saw him lift our small ax from the woodpile and throw it as hard as he could out toward the privy. But Billy's reaction could not temper my own excitement. It grew even greater when I learned I was to be allowed to ride Snow on the excursion, *with* a saddle was the stipulation, since there might not be room for me in the wagons. But the squire had already agreed to my attendance. John Baker evidently had great admiration for my da.

The day for our travel dawned bright and clear. I had groomed Snowflake until she was gleaming. Da and I had packed a change of clothes and also bread and cheese, apples, dried oatcakes, and a bottle of cider for sustenance along the way, and these were stashed in a saddlebag behind my seat on Snow. We were invited to eat from the squire's provisions, as was my horse, but Mama wanted to be sure we would not be hungry on the road.

The lengthy trip was a blur to me. There were villages, hills, woods, and streams all very similar to ours at home, but exciting, nonetheless, just because they were new. The land eventually broadened out into a rolling green landscape that looked ideal for grazing animals. Even though we stopped several times along the way to water the horses and relieve ourselves, it was still a long time for me to be in the saddle, and I confess I was quite stiff at journey's end. Everyone else, including Da, rode in the wagons. Several men, under head groom Milty's oversight, took turns leading Diamond on foot to spare him for the race.

As we came down the last slope toward our destination right at twilight, I could see that Lambourne was a much larger village than our own. It occupied most of the upper valley of the River Lambourne, which could be seen wending through the vale. We made camp in a fairly level field right outside of the town next to many other caravans who had evidently also made the trip for the race. Our grooms unhitched and saw to the horses, who were then tethered and fed for the night. The servants bustled around, setting up tents and cook-fires, and we soon had a little village of our own. Even though I was exhausted from the ride, I took my time brushing out the saddle sweat from my equally tired little mount and checked her feet for stones. She had performed perfectly the whole day, never making a misstep. Da brought us a bucket of water and several flakes of hay from the squire's stores, and then he and I finally made our way to one of the tables that had been set up to feed our party.

There was already gossip going around about what other horses were here, who had the fast ones, and what festival events were going to take place in the village in the next days besides the race itself. We were told that Lord Stanley and his three sons had come down from Faringdon two days prior and were planning to race Cloud and also one of his three-year-old sons, a horse named Baron. The talk was that these were expected to be two of the fastest animals, but Squire Baker was adamant that his Diamond could beat them. There was also another grandee present, Lord Brian Herbert of Bath. His son, Viscount George Herbert, was expected to ride their stallion, but no one knew much about the horse. And of course, there were several other entries to the race from the local gentry around.

My head was swimming with information by the time I finally began to nod and Da led me off to my pallet. We were supposed to sleep in one of the tents with the grooms, but I convinced Da to let us put our blankets out close to Snow, where we could keep an eye on her and where she could take comfort in our presence. By the time I woke the next day, Da had already taken care of the morning chores and was smiling and calling me sleepyhead. He reported that both Diamond and Snowflake had eaten their morning rations, had drunk water, passed stool, and appeared to be sound and recovering from the travel well.

"What would ye like t' do today, daughter, since this be your big holiday?" he queried with a smile. "I thought ye might like to walk down and see the town o' Lambourne. I hear there'll be a small carnival with jugglers and puppet shows, food booths, 'n even bull baiting." He went on more somberly, "I wish yer mama could have come…she would have loved the carnival, she would." He paused thoughtfully. "But the trip would've been too hard on 'er." Then he asked more cheerily, "So what's it t' be?"

I thought for a moment and answered, "I'm sure the carnival and village would be interesting, but what I would really like to see are the other horses that are here."

"Now, why don't that surprise me, Katie dear?" Da asked in mock seriousness. "All right, go 'n look at horses we will." And so we began walking around the large field full of tents and camps, wagons and drafters, and of course, those animals that had come to race. Most of the competition horses were being walked around by grooms this morning to let them stretch their legs. A couple were being ridden, even given a few quick sprints to blow out their lungs and ease some of their nerves as they waited for the race tomorrow.

Most of the horses looked like the common hacks I might see in our village on occasion. There was one long-legged bay stallion that caught Da's eye, and we talked to his owner, Squire Baxter, for a while. He told us his horse was a Cleveland Bay from the Yorkshire area. The animal was usually part of a four-in-hand put to his coach, but he thought this particular beast might have some speed. Another flashy animal being ridden by a groom turned out to be of Andalusian descent, but Da figured the horse had too big of a gait up front to last the four miles of the race.

At the far end of the field, set apart by the largest tents, we saw the flags sporting the crest of the Earl of Faringdon. Lord Stanley was easy to spot in his hunting jacket, standing among some others, watching his two stallions as they trotted together a little way down the field. Da and I approached the group, but I could not take my eyes off Cloud. His silver coat gleamed in the bright sunshine, the muscles of his arched neck taut with excitement, his tail raised proudly in the air. Snow looked a lot like him, I thought, but in a more feminine, refined way. Cloud gave a little buck of excitement, and we could see that his rider was having trouble controlling him. It was obvious that the horse wanted to run.

The other stallion, the three-year-old that I understood was Cloud's progeny, was a gleaming chestnut with a flaxen mane and tail. He, too, was beautiful and prancing proudly, sporting the dished face and high tail set of his Arabian sire, even though his dam had been of local breeding. Baron, as he was named, was obediently minding the requests of his rider despite dancing in anticipation.

Suddenly, the two stallions lunged forward, their riders obviously giving them the cue to run. The horses were at full speed almost instantly and ran neck and neck for about a furlong before their jockeys, as I learned the riders were called, were able to pull them back to a more gentle canter. Lord Stanley seemed quite excited, speaking loudly to those around him about the attributes of, first, Cloud of the Desert, and then Baron. It was obvious that he thought one of his stallions was going to win tomorrow.

The two horses and riders had ridden back to Lord Stanley's group, and I could see that the older son, the one I had been so taken with three years ago, was riding the chestnut, while one of his brothers was on Cloud. Anthony, I thought he was called, was speaking to his father while trying to get Cloud to stand still. But Viscount William had spotted my father and was riding toward us, stopping in front of Da. I ducked behind my father, self-conscious for some reason I couldn't name.

"Alexander, wasn't it?" the young viscount asked. I peeked around Da's shoulder. This was the same handsome face, the same gentle voice I remembered from the day when he had comforted his colicky stallion. But had he grown even taller, even more attractive?

Da gave a nod of acknowledgment.

"I want to thank you again for your help with Cloud three years ago. Look at him now, sir," he said, pointing back toward his brother. A pause, while Da exclaimed over how fine the older stallion looked. "And what do you think of his son here?"

"I think Cloud throws fine progeny, he does," Da answered truthfully. "I'm surprised, though, that yer not riding the pureblood yerself?"

"Well, my brother Anthony is set on winning this race, and I didn't mind giving up the ride to handle this boy," he said, giving Baron a pat. "Besides, I'm the one who broke and trained Baron. If anyone is going to give him his first race, I want it to be me so that I can pull up if I think it's getting too much for him."

"Well, good luck to ye both," my father concluded with another nod, and William reined back toward his brother and father.

Da and I continued full circle of the field, but we never found the location of the Earl of Bath or his horse. When we returned to our own camp around noon, the talk was that Lord Brian Herbert had disdained making camp with the rest of us "locals" and had, instead, stabled his horse in town and was staying at the Lambourne Inn. Still, no one seemed to know much about his entry save that his son, the viscount, would be the jockey.

That afternoon, Da and I did walk into the town, which was not far. Besides it being larger than any village I had yet seen, there were also many attractive, two-story buildings along High Street, with their bay windows and flower boxes peering out above our heads. I was particularly taken by the old Norman church, which was an edifice at least twice as large as St. Mary's and more ancient. St. Michael and All Angels had a notched parapet along its roof in front of its large square bell tower, which gave the building a castle-like appearance.

Da and I had stepped back into an alcove across the street from the church in order to study its wide arched stained glass windows. As we quietly observed the structure, we became aware of heavy-booted footsteps approaching and low conversation. A rather-pompous voice in an angry tone was saying, albeit quietly, "You'd bloody well better win this race, I tell you!"

His companion answered in a more nasal, wheedling tone, "I will, I promise, Father."

"I've got two hundred pounds riding on this farce, not to mention the cost of importing that blasted horse. He should be made of gold for what I paid for him!"

"I know, I know, but we'll make a fortune with him when he proves to be the fastest stallion in the country and mare owners line up to purchase breeding rights."

Their voices were fading as they passed by, still whispering, "I don't care how you do it, fast or not, you'd better win this race, I tell you." I peeked around the corner at their departing forms—both were dressed in fine clothes, with flowing capes about their shoulders.

But what really arrested me were the dressed white wigs underneath their top hats. I had heard this was becoming the fashion among grandees in London, but I had never seen a gentleman wearing one. It almost made me laugh.

Da and I looked at each other and nodded. "The Lords of Bath," we said at the same time.

That evening, Da told me he was heading back to the town pub with some of Squire Baker's men, but he introduced me to Milty, the squire's head groom and also Diamond's jockey for the race. "Now, daughter, Milty is staying t' keep an eye on Diamond, and sure I asked 'im to keep an eye on ye, too. Will ye be all right with that?" So, it was arranged, both Da and I doing what we each loved best. I had Snow on a long lead heading out to where there was meadow grass that had not been trampled following Milty, who had Diamond in tow.

Milty had warned me to keep quite a distance between the two horses. Even though Snow was not in season, a mare could still be a distraction to any stallion, but, he said, especially with Diamond. The groom explained that the Berber could be fractious to the point of being dangerous in the breeding shed, and Milty was very glad that there were to be no mares in the race tomorrow. So I was keeping Snowflake well off from Diamond's quarter. It was a beautiful early evening, and there were others walking about, other horses being allowed to graze. Snow seemed grateful to be pulling at the green grass rather than picking through hay, and I was happy just to sit on the turf with my arms around my legs and watch her. The evening air was lovely, and there was a sense of excitement and anticipation all around.

I saw by their legs that two men had approached and were talking to Milty, but I didn't take much notice. There had been a lot of interest in the Berber stallion. I was surprised when a hand appeared above Snow's back, and I heard a quiet voice say, "Hi, there, girl. You've become a beauty."

It was the viscount, William Stanley, himself. He was running his hand over my filly's croup, obviously studying the little white spots that she carried. He spoke again as I scrambled to my feet. "You're Alexander's daughter, right?" I nodded. "And this is the new-born filly you took home with you the day your father helped us with

Cloud." It wasn't a question. "She's turned out splendidly. I can't tell you how happy I was to learn that you were going to try and save her. I knew Father planned to put her down, but all my attention had been on Cloud that day."

Now he turned his notice from gazing at Snow to looking at me. I hadn't taken my eyes off him. He was at least a head taller than me, with fair wavy hair and an open countenance that was friendly and inviting. His blue eyes sparkled, and I thought I had never seen a man so handsome. But I couldn't seem to find my tongue.

He went on, "Is she broken to saddle yet?"

I finally gained my voice. "I trained her myself," I said, not so modestly, "and she's just the gentlest horse ever."

"Her mother, Belle, was a great saddler. I learned to ride on that mare. I was really sad when Father sold her after she dropped…what is her name?"

"Snowflake," I stammered.

"You say Snowflake is a good ride?"

"She wants to please. I've never had a moment's trouble out of her."

"Well, your father is certainly good with animals. And she surely looks like Cloud, doesn't she?" he said earnestly, returning his eyes to the filly. He was scratching her neck now, just under her mane, where she liked it, I couldn't help but notice. And Snow had stopped grazing and was sniffing his coat. "Would you mind if I hopped on?" he suddenly asked.

"All I have is her head-collar," I stammered, not really knowing how to answer.

"That will do, if she's as gentle as you say," he finished. He had taken her lead from me and was tying it so that it was made into two reins. Before I could blink, he had swung right up on her from the ground, and my traitorous girl was moving away with him, apparently being guided by his long legs. He put her through a few maneuvers and paces and then brought her back to me. Sliding to the ground, he handed me her lead and said, "Great job. Your father should be proud." And with that, he went to join the other two men.

Chapter 9

THE RACE

The next morning, there was much bustle and excitement. The race was due to start in front of the church at the noon bells. Milty, the thin, wiry groom who was the squire's appointed jockey, had Diamond saddled a full hour before lunch, and Da pronounced him sound and ready to go. There was a lot of discussion about where best to view the four-mile race. It would begin in front of St. Michael's and travel down High Street, through the village, and then two miles up to the top of Windmill Hill. There was an ancient barrow and ruins at the top, where the racers were to circle and return to the church. There was no set path for the race; just get up to the barrow and back.

Squire Baker had opted to watch the race from a hill just on the outskirts of the village that posed such a good vantage that most of the other owners were found there too. Once the horses would be seen coming down the hill, closing to the finish, it would be possible to dash down a side street and catch the ending in front of the church. Many of the more well-to-do gentry had brought seats, and there was even a raised platform for those willing to pay a fee. Da and I stood just to the side of the platform, John Baker near enough above to call down to us among the crowd as he watched the race. He had a pair of Galilean binoculars, a set of two telescopes joined together, that he would use to watch the competition. Many others sported spyglasses around their necks.

We were able to watch the parade of horses as they came from the camp and down into the village to the start. Each jockey had been assigned an apron of colored silk to wear. These pinafores were of varying bright hues so that the jockeys and horses could be identified from afar. Diamond had been allotted an emerald green. I noticed the prancing Cloud in light blue and Baron in red. The Cleveland Bay was in yellow and the Andalusian in orange, but his rider was having difficulty controlling his stallion and finally dismounted and withdrew from the race. There were three other entries that passed by us, horses of more common breeding and appearance. There was a sorrel, a black, and a roan in dark blue, grey, and white silk respectively. Finally, a rider in royal purple joined the procession, Lord George Herbert, the man with the nasal voice, the man who was "to win at all costs." His mount, it turned out, was a Turkomene, imported all the way from Central Asia. The bay was slender and tough-looking, with a long back and long neck. He reminded me of the greyhounds that Squire Baker used to hunt rabbits. There was much murmuring as each entry and rider had passed by, but especially as this last horse, strangely named Ahkil, drew near.

Then they were all around the corner and visible no more. It seemed like an eternity before the noon bells rang, and consequently only an instant before the horses and jockeys appeared exiting the town and charging up the hill in front of us. I could hear the squire saying to himself, "Steady, steady, Milty. You've a long way to go. Save him."

The hill itself appeared to take a terrible toll on the horses. Of the original nine, eight horses had started the race. By the time they had galloped midway up the long incline, the sorrel, black, and roan had been left far behind the others. The Cleveland Bay in yellow was doing his best to keep up, but it was obvious he was struggling. The other four horses all seemed to be running efficiently, first one and then another taking the lead. It was apparent that all four riders were spelling their mounts; none was in a flat gallop. The hillside was too rough; there were rocks, ditches, and hedges besides the slope itself.

Sometimes the riders would disappear entirely as they rode down into a gully or behind an outcropping. So far, they were taking, more or less, the same course, if not exactly the same path. Now and again, one of the horses would stumble and fall behind, but then there would be another lead change after the next hillock. When they approached the barrow at the top, we lost sight of all of them. There were several anxious moments among the crowd, and then with a cheer, we saw them all appear again, galloping down the hill. Squire Baker was shouting, "We're ahead. Diamond's ahead!"

There were parts of the mountain where it would have been foolhardy to hit a full run; horse and rider would have found themselves cartwheeling down the hillside. There were other places where the animals were more sliding than running down the steep slope. But as they approached the flatter bottom and the last half-mile of the race, it was obvious that the jockeys were asking for an all-out effort. And their game mounts were giving it to them. The Cleveland Bay had now been left behind, but the Arabian, his son, the Turk, and the Barb were all giving chase and coming down the hill nearly in a row.

As the riders rounded a little outcropping about a quarter mile from us, it looked like Ahkil had rammed solidly into Diamond and the Berber had lost his footing and gone down hard, causing a gasp from the crowd. Squire Baker was immediately on his feet, but it was still too far away for us to see clearly what had happened or what the outcome might be. Diamond, it appeared, had soon regained his feet and begun running again, but Milty was not visible. We all saw William pull up Baron and ride back to the place where apparently the fallen jockey still lay.

Meanwhile, Cloud and Ahkil thundered on. We could hear their hoofbeats plainly now, and Diamond was running close behind them, riderless. The two jockeys were driving hard, asking for more speed. Then it seemed that the bay swerved again, this time toward the grey, just as they passed our last vantage point, but Cloud scrambled catlike and remained upright. The crowd were all running now down the little side street to try to catch the end of the race, but Da and I stayed back with the squire. Some of his grooms had followed the racers, aiming to catch Diamond, but the rest of us were all staring at the hillside. Lord William was leading Baron slowly down the gentle slope, with the lifeless body of Milty slung over his saddle.

We learned later that Lord Anthony and Cloud had won the race by several lengths. It had looked like Ahkil had come lame and pulled up just after the collision with Cloud. Lord George was claiming foul, insisting that Lord Anthony had intentionally bumped his horse. But everyone who had witnessed the incident agreed that it was quite the opposite. Squire Baker was incensed and also felt his horse had been intentionally rammed, resulting in Milty's death, but there was no way to prove it in such difficult footing as the race had been run on. Diamond had a cut on one flank, which Father stitched up, and a few bruises, but otherwise seemed unscathed.

Our group from Uffington was quite somber that evening as we prepared to leave the next morning. We would bear Milty's body home to his family for burial. The squire, Da, and the grooms all went into town that night to drink away their disappointment and grief. Milty had been well loved. Da left me with the servants who were remaining behind, asking me to stay in the tent until he returned. But when it became late, and the group still had not come back, I began to worry about Snow, tethered out by herself, and decided to go to my pallet and wait for Da there. Unable to sleep, I lay on the ground listening to the horses munch on their hay.

About midnight, or so I judged it to be, I heard what sounded like stealthy footsteps and low voices. "Here he is," I heard someone saying. It sounded like the hushed words came from the area near Diamond. All our grooms were still in town, and I was afraid there was no one on guard. I didn't know what to do.

After a few moments, I gathered what courage I could find, stood, and said in a tremulous voice that betrayed my fear, "Who goes there? What do you want?" In the next moment, I could hear several pairs of footsteps running, although the night was too dark for me to see who it might have been. It wasn't too long after that before Da and the others returned, some obviously drunk, but all still subdued. I related my story about the intruders to the squire, who nervously inspected all the horses and then posted guards.

Da was unhappy with me for not staying in the tent. "What if something had happened t' ye, Katie? How could I live with meself? How could I live with yer ma?" Still, under the influence of the night's drinking, he was soon fast asleep. But it was a long time before I was able to join him in slumber. And when I did, my nightmare of the white stallion visited once again.

The next morning, before we were completely hitched and ready to head home, the Viscount of Bath visited our camp. I was packing my bedroll but could see that he was speaking with Squire Baker, who did not seem happy. After a short conversation, the squire shook his head and turned his back rudely on the nobleman. I learned later that Lord George had tried to buy Diamond but had been refused. The viscount stood there for a moment, whether taken aback, embarrassed, or angry, I couldn't tell. But he and his servant then exited our camp. On their way out, they passed close by my filly, and I saw the viscount gesture to his man as they approached Snow. I shuddered as Lord George ran his hand over her croup in recognition, just as Lord William had done two days before. I felt a shiver of dread run down my spine. I didn't need to be sleeping to experience another nightmare.

Chapter 10

CLOUD

Less than a week later, a liveried servant from Faringdon arrived once more on our doorstep. Could Father please come, because Cloud had a nasty wound that needed stitching? My father shook his head. "Please tell Lord Stanley that I'm truly sorry, I am, but I can't leave the shop right now. Squire Baker's race saddle was ruined in the fall at Lambourne last week, and 'e's waitin' for the one I'm finishin' right now."

The servant looked irritated. "Can't your novice finish the work?" He was nodding toward Billy, who had stepped out of the shop behind Da.

"My apprentice be good," Father went on, "but the squire's me landlord, and I promised 'im me best work." Da stopped and considered a moment. "Me daughter can sew as well as meself, maybe better, 'tis sure," he added with a twinkle in his eye. I knew he was referring to my needlepoint. I had helped stitch up a few animals but had never done all the work myself. "If yer set on gettin' any help from here, she's yer only choice," Da concluded with finality.

"But...but...the wound is in his...private parts," the servant stammered.

"No difference. The girl helps me castrate sometimes. She'll not be discomfited." The servant looked like he didn't know what to say. Da took the initiative. "Katie, go get me case and see that ye have everything ye need." The other man still stood there uncertainly, but when I entered the cart a minute later, he sighed, got in beside me, chucked to his horse, and again, we made the fast trip up to Faringdon.

Neither of us spoke as the horse trotted gamely back toward his stable. For me, I was lost in my thoughts. Normally, I would have been very reluctant to travel away from our village on my own, but riding out on Snow had afforded me more independence lately, and I *had* been to the Faringdon estate before. I was elated that Da seemed to trust so much in my abilities, but I was not so certain of them myself. Had the request been from almost any other quarter, I might have resisted. But the truth was, I would take any opportunity to see William again. William! Of course, he would be Lord Stanley, Viscount Stanley, when his name was spoken out loud. But in my head, he was always William. I wasn't just attracted to his handsome features; it was even more his gentle voice, the way he treated horses and people. I felt a kindred spirit with him and a fascination I couldn't name. I knew he was an impossible fantasy, but just being near him would be enough for me.

As we pulled into the stable yard, a burly, red-headed groom named Smitty was introduced. He didn't seem any happier than my driver to see that Da had sent me, a girl, in his stead. But the situation with their valuable stallion soon took precedence, and I was led into the barn where Cloud was standing, crosstied in the aisleway. Smitty explained that since Cloud had won the regional race, a number of mare owners had sought to book breedings with him. They had gotten a new mare in that morning, but she had taken exception to Cloud's amorous intentions and had kicked him "in the balls." Smitty did not seem embarrassed to tell me this (although I couldn't help blushing a little), but I was glad he could be direct. There was no point mincing words. This could be a serious injury, especially now that the stallion had gained notoriety in the breeding circles.

I walked to the back of the grey stallion and could immediately see the long gash in the scrotum that was dripping blood onto the cobbles. "How long has he been bleeding like this?" I asked. All morning since it happened was the answer. The wound needed closing! We decided to move out into the wide foyer, where they hitched their carriages, in order to have room to maneuver. While I opened my case and threaded the needle I had brought with some of our saddler's silk thread, the grooms set about to wash the injured area, as I had requested. I soon heard Cloud's hooves clattering, and then harsh cursing, as one of the men took a kick to the leg and began hopping about. "Let's get a twitch on him," I suggested, glad to see the injured groom could still walk.

Smitty brought out a wooden bat with a leather loop on the end. He expertly grabbed Cloud's upper lip, looped the leather over it, and began to twist. As the thong tightened on the stallion's sensitive flesh, his eyes focused on the groom and he became very still. The twitch, as my father had taught me years ago, did no harm to the horse but got their attention in a very strong way. And often, they would feel no pain in any other part of their body while they concentrated on their lip. I could completely relate to that, as focus was often my own coping mechanism.

As soon as the stallion was subdued, I began to examine the injured area. I warned the grooms to have a rope ready in case we needed to tie up a front leg to prevent more kicking. But Cloud never again moved a foot off the ground. I was glad to find that the horse's testicles were intact. The wound was only skin-deep, and the loose flesh should be easy to sew, so long as my patient stood still. I hoped the bleeding would then slow and all would be well, providing no festering set in. This was always a possibility, especially since it was summertime, with flies ever present.

One of the men held the stallion's tail off to one side, and I took a deep breath. The first stitch was always the hardest. Stabbing the needle into the flesh, I began to sew. I had about half of the gash closed when I heard voices and felt Cloud tense. I had been standing to the side of those massive hind quarters, leaning down and around the rear haunch as I performed my task. Now I straightened and could see several well-dressed men and women approaching.

"We heard there was some excitement in the barn, and we came to see," a beautiful, dusky-voiced woman was explaining. She had dark hair, a creamy, pale complexion, and deep-blue eyes. Most striking was her curvaceous figure in the lavish red gown she was wearing.

"Yes, someone said a *female* was doctoring our stallion," Lord Clarence contributed in a wheedling voice, "but I only see this slip of a girl!" I knew that Clarence was William's youngest brother. He was as tall as his older brother, but thinner, with a narrow face and shifty eyes.

A similar mocking voice added, "Are you sure it's a girl?" I was certain this was Lord Anthony, the middle son who was shorter and stockier than his two brothers. I could hear the other guests snickering. The women had their hair piled high in curls, faces powdered, jewels at their throats. Suddenly I felt very drab in my bloody brown muslin with my hair pulled into a long braid down my back. The women were tittering, and I felt as if I were eight years old again, waiting for the taunt of "witch's eyes."

William stepped forward, my William. If he was surprised to see me, he didn't let on. "Sorry," he began, noting both Cloud's and my disquiet. "We have a house party going on, a celebration of our victory last week. There was some talk that a 'female' was in our barn, doctoring our 'guest of honor,' and some of our other visitors insisted on coming to see." He looked a little sheepish. Then in a quieter voice he said, "I was told your father couldn't attend." Walking to the rear of the stallion and glancing at the stitches, he went on, "But I see you are competent in his stead. Thank you for coming." Then he nodded and stepped back out of my way, and I could tell I was to resume my surgery.

Now, with so many spectators, I felt twice as nervous as before, as did Cloud, who began to fidget. I leaned back around my patient and forced myself to focus on the task at hand. By pretending that no one existed except Cloud and me, I was able to continue stitching—that is, until I realized that the woman in the red gown had also come around to Cloud's rear. A moment later, she was fanning herself and declaring, "Oh, my…oh, my…I feel I'm going to faint!" William and Clarence were immediately at her side, arms about her, and she and the rest of the crowd moved back toward the house. As much as I had wanted to see William, I was glad to see them go. I stood again and took a moment to quell the tears that had been threatening to spill over. The rest of the stitching went without incident.

I applied some of Da's healing ointment to the wound and then signaled Smitty to release the twitch. The horse snorted and pawed, but the groom rubbed the animal's nose gently, and soon he was quiet again. We watched over Cloud until I was certain that the bleeding had stopped and there was no swelling yet of the scrotum, and then he was turned into his large well-bedded stall. "Obviously, he needs to stay as quiet as possible for a week," I said. "Only hand walking and grazing, and *no* breeding." The groom nodded. "But I *am* concerned about the wound becoming putrid."

"How soon would we know to be worried?" he asked.

"If there's no real swelling or redness by tomorrow, that will be a good start," I answered.

"What if we're seeing swelling later today?"

"Then it might need a poultice. Can you do that?"

Smitty looked doubtful. "On any other horse, I might feel up to it, but this horse is too valuable to the earl," he replied. "Miss, I would ask you to stay, just for tonight, to help us keep an eye out for trouble. If he's fit in the morning, then we can take you back home." I had to think about this. I knew that the first twenty-four hours would tell us most of the tale, and I knew how important Cloud was, but I also had duties at home. Still…

"Could you send word down to my parents that I won't be home until tomorrow?" I asked. "If so, then I'll stay, just in case you need me," I added, and I hoped I was making the decision Da would have expected.

Soon a maid was commissioned from the house and I was shown up to the back of the great mansion. Smitty promised that he would send word up to me if anything changed with the stallion. Whereas Da and I had entered the massive front doors three years prior with the earl as escort, now the maid and I entered the lower kitchen door at the back. I was becoming anxious as I followed her—she said her name was Alice—through the large kitchen, feeling the eyes of most of the scullery staff on me even as they scurried about preparing the large meal I assumed was to be served to the houseguests.

I kept my eyes on Alice's apron strings as we wound our way up through narrow stairways and back halls used by the servants.

At last we were in the attic area, where the maids' rooms were. Alice told me she had been assigned to see to me and was bedding me in her own room, which turned out to be at the very end of the narrow dark hallway. At least there was light when we entered her apartment, since there was a narrow slit of a window, open in the pleasant breeze and sunshine. Alice left me for a minute to retrieve some bedding, and I relaxed a little, looking around. The room was small, about half the size of Cloud's stall, and contained a narrow cot, pegs on the wall for a few clothes, a chest with a basin and pitcher on top, and a stool by the little window. When she returned, I told her I would be fine sleeping on the floor, which I was used to at home.

I couldn't help noticing that she spoke with an Irish accent. This was not uncommon among grooms and servants, as many immigrants came to England and found work in the great houses. Alice asked my name, and I told her I was Kathryn Alexander. She looked a little surprised and said, "Me name's Alexander, too." Then she amended, "Alice O'Grady Alexander."

"My da's from Belfast," I explained, "my mother from Avon."

"Me people are from Belfast, too, sure they are!" she said excitedly. She began asking me about Da's relatives. I didn't know many names, but I did know my grandfather's, and Alice decided that we were possibly second cousins. She was so excited, but not more so than I. It had always been my wish to have extended family! Alice was probably five years older than me, with the ruddy hair and complexion of my father, and I immediately felt a strong kinship. Unfortunately, the rest of her relatives were still in Ireland, but even so, I couldn't wait to get home and tell Da.

Alice said she only had a few minutes to spare; there was so much work to do with all the visitors in the house. She'd been assigned to the guest room of Lady Grace Middleton, the daughter of a baronet, a very wealthy baronet, she informed me. Alice thought Lady Grace was beautiful but too proud and vain to be likable. "'Her Highness' had brought 'er own ladies' maid, who also was very 'uppity,'" Alice informed me.

Then she began sharing gossip. The earl was hoping to make a match between William and Miss High and Mighty, but Alice was desperately hoping this wouldn't happen. She couldn't stand the thought of Lady Grace coming to live permanently at Faringdon. She also shared the rumor that "Her Highness" was simultaneously being courted by Lord George Herbert of Bath. At that name, I caught my breath. I knew that the aristocracy was a tight circle, but I was still unprepared to even hear mention of the despicable man who had caused Milty's death and might yet covet my beloved filly.

Finally, offering the use of the water pitcher and inviting me to come down to the kitchen if I got hungry, she scurried off to her duties. At loose ends, I was considering going back out to the stables when I heard a commotion below. Sitting on the stool, I was able to look down through the window, which was perched high on the house, just below the eaves. Sitting to the side, I felt sure I was invisible from the ground. The guests were exiting the manor below me onto a large paved courtyard surrounded by flowering bushes and trees. I could see this terrace overlooked landscaped gardens sloping down, away from the house, toward a glistening lake in the distance. The servants had set long tables of dishes, and it seemed they were about to have afternoon tea. The setting was lovely.

I immediately noticed the dusky-voiced woman in the red gown. She appeared to be the center of attention, being surrounded by several gentlemen. I couldn't really see faces from this angle, but their voices were somewhat audible. The woman was laughing at something one of the gentlemen had said, and I heard him call her Lady Grace. I was not really surprised that "Her Highness" had turned out to be the beauty from the stable.

I searched through the crowd below until I spotted William. He, too, seemed surrounded, but by ladies, all in beautiful costumes that seemed to sparkle in the afternoon sun. They were gazing up at him with appreciation in their eyes, I imagined. Lady Grace's voice was raised several times, as if vying for attention, and soon I saw William take his leave from his admirers and make his way through the other guests to her side. He escorted her over to one of the tables and was soon carrying a teacup and plate of dainties over to a low stone wall, where they both perched and began conversing. Other guests were now also helping themselves to tea, but I only had eyes for one couple.

So enrapt was I by this idyllic scene that I didn't hear the maid come into my chamber. It wasn't Alice, but a servant reporting that Smitty was asking for me, and I soon found my way back down the stairways and out to the stable. The groom was concerned because the stallion's belly, high on the right side, was also beginning to sport a hot, swollen area. We both agreed that the mare had probably gotten him with both of her hind feet, and this was a bruise from the second hoof. Using buckets of cool water, we bathed both injured areas to ease some of the inflammation. Cloud stood like a champion; I hoped the cold water was soothing to his hot flesh.

I spent most of the evening in the barns with the grooms, taking my dinner meal with them. And when everything appeared stable with the stallion, I finally headed up to my pallet, knowing that one of the grooms would keep watch overnight. Alice got in even later than me, complaining that her charge had lingered long after the dancing party had concluded. She feared that Grace and William had taken a very late, evening stroll and worried that this boded evil. She was unable to leave the bedchamber area until the lady's maid had reported they needed nothing further. Alice complained that even though the guests would probably all sleep late the next day, she would be required to be up at dawn, carrying trays and awaiting their every request. I was up at dawn the next morning, too.

Chapter 11

THE FOXHUNT

When I entered the stables early the next morning, the night groom reported that Cloud had experienced no problems. Smitty arrived at the stall, and together, we examined the wound. There was no bleeding, no unexpected heat or swelling. We were all relieved. The grooms escorted me up to the manor, where we ate breakfast together in the servants' hall near the kitchens. When I asked about an escort for the drive home, I was told that the stable hands were all on alert that morning. There was to be a foxhunt, but it wouldn't take place until the gentlemen had all breakfasted and were ready. There was some speculation that a lady or two might attend the hunt as well, which meant there might be even a further delay.

Smitty explained to me that he couldn't spare any of his staff until after the hunt was concluded. I reconciled myself to staying into the afternoon—there was nothing to be done about it other than to walk home, which I was loath to do. Besides, I had always wanted to witness a traditional English foxhunt. However, Smitty warned me that this hunt was out of season and would not really be in earnest. Apparently, a couple of their prominent guests, the Lady Middleton in particular, had requested the experience, and the earl was complying.

Several of the guests had brought their own mounts with them, but a number would be borrowing the estate's hunting horses. Since one was to carry a sidesaddle, I expected Lady Grace would be riding. I assisted the grooms in readying all the animals—they were expecting at least fifteen riders to follow the hounds along with the earl's own huntsman and whippers-in. I understood that the master of the hunt would be Lord Charles himself. His professional huntsman, Charlie Duncan, kept and trained the pack of specially bred hounds in a kennel at his cottage, which was toward the rear of the estate. The whippers-in were riders that traveled on the outskirts of the pack. They carried long whips, and their main job was to keep the hounds in order. I learned that it was easy for hounds to get distracted by the scent of red deer and coyotes, and they would sometimes leave the main pack to follow a forbidden trail off on their own. The whips were there to try to keep discipline. Ordinarily, Smitty said, the earl's three sons would carry the whips. But today, the sons would ride with the field and act the part of hosts, so two of the grooms would whip-in instead.

The later it got in the morning, the more excited I became. Smitty finally told me I should go up to the manor house to watch; he said the hunt would begin right in front of the mansion. I gathered with some of the other servants before the main hall as the riders began to mount in the stabling area. Others were already astride and milling about in the front yard. They were wearing an assortment of hunt jackets, breeches, tall boots, gloves, and top hats, all with broadcloth stock ties at their throats. When the master and two sons appeared, I couldn't help admiring their red wool jackets with brass buttons shining, the "colors" of the hunt. Last to make it up from the stables were Lord William, astride Baron, and Lady Middleton, on a gentle-looking mare. Her green velvet riding habit accentuated her lovely figure and capped off the picture of aristocracy.

Servants began passing trays with the "stirrup cup" among the field; most imbibed, although some pulled their own flasks from beneath their coats. I noticed that William waved away the cup. Alice, who was watching beside me, whispered that His Lordship never imbibed. Then we all heard the distinct cries of the foxhounds coming over the hill and entering the front grounds. The huntsman's horse was in the lead, the pack swarming all around and behind him

84

with two whips, one to either side. Now the hunt was truly beginning, even if it was only for entertainment.

The huntsman and pack moved off ahead toward the woods, the field of riders remaining well behind, William and Baron at their head. I couldn't help but notice how elegant Lady Grace appeared, balancing easily on her sidesaddle, her green gown flowing down and over the rump of her gentle mount.

The huntsman played several notes on his horn and picked up a trot, as did the field. It was a grand sight; so many beautiful horses and people, all moving with one intent. When they neared the woods, there were more notes from the horn, and Alice explained that the hounds were being "cast." All the riders now held up in anticipation except the whips, who moved into the forest with the hounds.

Suddenly, there was a chorus of cries from the pack and notes from the horn. The huntsman moved into a gallop, following his hounds, the field also cantering behind. Alice, who had seen all this before, told me that if I hiked down toward the lake, I might get lucky and see the pack move into one of the many grazing and crop fields that were interspersed among the forested lands. It all depended upon where the fox decided to travel, that is, if he didn't just go to ground; the hounds, if they could, would follow the fox, with the hunt field following the pack.

Gratefully, I made my way down the slope toward the sparkling water. I passed through a rose garden and then a sunken garden, several landscaped terraces, and then proceeded along a stretch of low flowering hedges lining what I assumed to be a walking path. Down by the lake I could see a dock and what I took for a boathouse, and that was my destination.

Off in the distance, I could still hear the chorus of yelping and an occasional blare of the horn, but I never did see the pack or field in full flight. I sat silently on the edge of the dock, just enjoying the peace and the beauty of the day. While I was sitting there quietly, out of the corner of my eye I caught movement. It was a stag, not a large one, but it came running from the direction of the woods, jumped the hedge that ran down to the water, and then traveled along around the lake. I don't believe the animal ever saw me sitting there, and it made me smile.

About five minutes later, I noticed that the hunt group was returning slowly from the woods, up to the house and stable area. The huntsman was tooting on his horn, the hounds milling in a group around him. Then I also saw that William and Lady Grace had left the others and were riding slowly down and away from the terraced lawns. It looked like they were going to take a leisurely ride by themselves. At that moment, a lone hound broke from the woods nearby and came barreling and bugling up the same path the deer had taken. The hound crossed under the hedge and headed on around the lake on the path of the stag, his nose to the earth.

Next came one of the whippers-in. He was galloping his mount, yelling loudly, "Farley, Farley, heel to!" and snapping his long whip. His horse approached the hedge, gathered himself, and made a graceful jump and a-not-so-elegant landing, stumbling slightly, but regaining his balance. Unfortunately, the rider lost his, momentarily clinging to the side of the saddle as the horse continued in flight, and then sliding off the rear. I saw the horse kick out as the man slid off, catching the rider in the face, snapping his head backward. Then the man landed on the ground, left leg first, before crumpling in a heap. The horse ran off toward the stables, the hound now nowhere to be seen.

I ran to the man, who was about fifty yards away. He was inert on the ground, not even moaning. But I could tell he was breathing, although his left leg was sprawled out behind and under him at an unnatural angle. The cut from the kick on his forehead was bleeding profusely. I gathered the hem of my skirt and pressed it against the wound with firm pressure, but I was not sure what else to do. Then I became aware that William had galloped up and was vaulting off his horse and kneeling beside me.

"Is he alive?" I didn't have to answer, because the man began moaning, and then even tried to sit up. But he immediately fell back in severe pain.

"My leg, my leg!" he screamed.

Without thinking, I spoke to William. "We need to get his leg out from under him and straighten it out. I don't know if it's broken or dislocated, but either way, it must be moved." Together, with the man continuing to scream, we bent to the task. William lifted the man's hips while I grasped the leg and, as gently as I could, adjusted it back into a more natural position. Immediately, the man's screaming diminished to a moan. William was removing his stock tie and had it folded against the fallen rider's head wound.

Now the dusky-voiced woman called, "William, can't you leave him to the girl? We can go call for help."

Ignoring Lady Middleton, William spoke urgently to me. "We'll have to get him up to the house and call the physician and surgeon. I'll need to go up and get a wagon. Can you stay here with Steven until I return? Keep this pressed against his head." William briefly touched his hand to mine as I took the bandage.

As he mounted Baron, he called, "I'll be back in just a few minutes."

He and Grace were riding briskly away, but I could hear her complaining pettily, "Can't you just send the servants back? You promised to give me a tour of the grounds." And then I could hear no more. Steven had lapsed back into quiet moaning, and it indeed was just a few minutes before William, followed by several grooms in a wagon, rumbled up. Lady Grace was no more to be seen. The servants loaded the fallen man as gently as they could onto the wagon.

"I've sent for the surgeon," William informed me. "We have a physician quite nearby, and he may be at the house when we get Steven up there." Then he paused and really looked at me. "How old are you?" he asked.

"Fifteen," I answered, gazing back. "Well done again, Kathryn Alexander," he commended, and then he was gone and I saw him no more that day. Later, when I was waiting for the grooms to finish with the hunt horses so that someone could drive me home, I found Alice, who was helping in the kitchen, and invited her to come to Uffington to meet Da and Mama. She said she would if she ever got the day off and the means to make the journey. Then she proceeded to tell me the day's big news: William and Grace's engagement had been announced that morning. She was miffed that she had only just heard about it, and also by the news itself.

"But good it might be t' have a lady in attendance in the house again after all these years," she conceded. I asked for an explanation. It seemed that the earl's wife had died fifteen years ago, but under some questionable circumstances. After her third son had been born, she had eschewed keeping company with her husband or children at Faringdon, and had lived exclusively at their townhouse in London, where she had flaunted several affairs before becoming pregnant again. There was obviously no way that the earl could have been the father, but she came home for her laying-in. Neither she nor the baby survived childbirth, and rumors had flown ever since. This information was just more evidence to me of how lucky I was. William and his brothers might have wealth and station, but they had never known the love of a mother.

Chapter 12

BILLY

B
ack at Uffington, I was able to put William and his upcoming marriage out of my mind. There was simply too much to do. While Mother had improved as the fair summer weather continued, she was still weak, and most of the housework and gardening fell to me, along with the milking twice a day, mucking Snow's stall, taking her to and from grazing, and sewing in the evenings. Mother told me often how sorry she was that she couldn't be more help, but I didn't really mind. My only regret was that I couldn't spend more time with my filly, who was growing fat and lazy, especially since the earl had sent me home from Faringdon with enough grain sacks to last most of the winter. Well, Snow wasn't the only one gaining weight. It seemed I was finally "blossoming" into that woman's figure I had always wanted, albeit still a slender one.

Billy and I had formed a friendly truce. He was nearly eighteen now and approaching the day when he would be released from his apprenticeship and become a journeyman. Sometimes after dinner he would stay in the house and help me clean up, freeing a little time for us to take a short walk together. Billy was still stocky and broad-shouldered and now sported a man's beard and deeper voice. I was more comfortable with him than before but knew in my heart that I could never love him. I was afraid that he was growing an attachment for me that I couldn't reciprocate. At night, I would talk these feelings over with Cally, who always listened so patiently.

I would ask her for advice about how to keep things on a friend-ly-but-not-serious note with our apprentice, but she would only look at me with those big green eyes and purr.

Billy had also begun accompanying Da on the evenings when he would head for the pub. It wasn't too often these days, but when they did go, both would come home staggering. I had hoped at first that the younger man would help keep my da sensible, but it seemed to be working oppositely. The mornings after these excursions, Da would seem his usual self, but evidently, Billy didn't handle the drink or the morning after quite as well, and he would be sullen and morose at breakfast—that is, if he came to the table at all.

Summer turned into autumn without note. I was busy gathering the last of the garden, storing roots and apples in our cellar, making preserves. Once in a while, I would take time to mount Snow and ride off down the valley. The hardwood trees in our village were turning from green to golds and reds. In my mind, it was the most beautiful time of year! Snow also seemed to appreciate these jaunts. Sometimes she would prance and snort and almost act like an untrained youngster again. But like me, she was growing up now, becoming a mare, not a filly any longer, and sometimes I wondered about having her bred and raising another little Snowflake. Diamond, I thought, would make a perfect mate for her, but then I remembered what Milty had said about the stallion's dangerous behavior during breeding, and it gave me pause. I couldn't stand the thought of my precious girl getting hurt.

In October, there was to be the annual Harvest Fair in our village. There was always music and dancing, followed by a harvest bonfire on the commons outside of the village. I had attended this celebration most years with Mama and Da, at least until Mother became too ill to go. Da had taught me some of the local folk dances, and when I was younger, all three of us would join hands and partic-ipate in the footwork, often culminating in me pirouetting inside of my own happy circle. Last year, Mama had not been able to attend, but this year she deemed herself able to walk down to the village, for just a little while, anyway.

The evening of the fair was cool and clear, perfect for the cele-bration. Billy was walking beside me, Mama and Da behind. They were holding hands, and soon Billy took mine as well. I decided not to make an issue of it as we entered the square, where the booths were located and music was already beginning. We each purchased a pasty for a penny and ate the flaky treat as we walked along the street, greeting a few people here and there. The broadest part of the square had been cordoned off, and lamps had been lit all around for the dancing, even though it was not yet quite dark. There were three musicians playing, sitting on the steps of St. Mary's, and people were already dancing in the twilight. A light jig was being performed, and since this was my father's favorite—he insisting it was a traditional Irish dance—he pulled Mama into the square, she laughing and pro-testing at once.

Billy and I also joined the performers. He was objecting that his dancing was rusty, but I called the steps to him: hop, hop, back; hop, hop, back, two-three-four. We were both miss-stepping and laugh-ing in amusement before long and panting by the end of the round. (Da and Mama had only danced for a minute, but I had delighted in watching them!) As the next reel began and we moved out of the circle, Da came up holding a tankard and handed one to Billy. I was not happy about this but decided that festivals were no time to be critical and resolved again to enjoy myself regardless.

Billy and I danced several more times—a line dance, a circle dance, a rigadoon. And each time when we paused for breath, I noticed he would join Da for a drink. Mama had found a seat and had been watching the dancing with great relish, but now she told Da it was time to go home. I really desired to leave with them, espe-cially worrying about the amount Billy had been drinking, but so far, he didn't seem intoxicated, and he pleaded with me to stay for the bonfire. It did sound like fun, and I hated to miss it. So we left the lighted square and headed out toward the area where we could already see the sparks flying high in the air.

Reaching the open field, I pulled my shawl more tightly around me. It had become chilly, and there was a dew falling. Billy noted my shiver and put an arm around my shoulders. "Feelin' cold?" he asked.

"Don't worry, I'll keep you warm." I could smell the ale on his breath and pulled back a little, but he just held me tighter.

"Come on, let's get closer to the blaze," I suggested, especially since that was where the crowd was gathering. "It will be warmer up near the fire." There was a tall pile of poles that had been lit, and great walls of flame were now reaching toward the sky. People were talking and laughing as they watched the pyre light up.

But Billy was pulling me in the opposite direction. "Cm'on," he instructed, "there'll be more privacy over here. There's somethin' I wanna ask you." I didn't want to leave the area of the bonfire, but I wasn't having much luck pulling us in the opposite direction. At this point, I still didn't want to make a scene. I wasn't really afraid of Billy, but I *was* afraid of his temper.

Finally, Billy stopped when we reached a stone bench that was placed under a large oak tree. We were a distance from the other people now, and it was quite dark. He asked me to sit on the bench, and then he sat beside me and began. "I'm gonna be a tradesman on my own in just a few months, and I plan t' open my own shop in one of them big towns, maybe even London," he said proudly. "I've been savin' my money, and I've got quite a bit," he bragged. "Anyway, I'm gonna need a wife." At this, he seemed to have to stop and think about what he was going to say next. He had begun slurring his words, and I could tell that the ale was finally getting to him.

"I hope ya know how much I'm 'tracted to you, and I think you like me pretty well, too," he gushed. "It only makes sense that we marry. How 'bout it?" At this, he leaned over and attempted to kiss me, but I drew back and put my hands on his chest.

"Wait, Billy." I was scrambling for words that wouldn't offend him too much. I was afraid of his anger now. "You must know that I have no desire to leave Uffington. I could never leave Mama—she needs me."

"But I need you too," he said, rather plaintively. "Besides, everyone knows your mama ain't gonna last another year."

Now I said with more feeling, "You're wrong, Billy Simpson! But long as she *does* live, I'll be here to take care of her."

"Well, in that case, she and your da can come live with us. You know, don't ya, that his gamblin' debts are worse and worse? One day his creditors are gonna come fer him. When that happens, ye'll all need me." He had said this last with some rancor, but now he softened. "Come on, sweets, I need ya, and ye need me." He was beginning to paw at me, brushing my hands away, pressing my breast as he leaned his face toward mine.

Now I was fighting in earnest, trying to stand. "Billy, stop it!" I said loudly, hoping others would hear, hoping he would give up. I was pushing at him, but he had pulled me back down, literally on his lap. He was very strong and had his long arms wrapped tightly about me. One of his hands had ahold of the top of my bodice, and when I pushed off again, I felt it rip. "Billy, stop!" The next thing I knew, I had been shoved to the ground and he was on top of me. His sloppy mouth was assaulting mine, his ale-breath nauseating me. I was frightened beyond being able to scream.

Suddenly, Billy was being lifted off me and there was a scuffle. "Run home, Miss Kathryn," bellowed a familiar voice. The two men were locked in a fierce battle now, punching and grappling with each other. I didn't wait to see what would happen but turned and ran as fast as I could. I would leave Billy at the hands of Tom Burlington.

The next morning, Da was waiting for his apprentice at the shop door. Da had seen my face, seen my torn dress when I ran into the house panting the night before. Only my mother grasping his shoulder had kept Da from going to look for Billy. But this morning, his anger was couched in cold control. Billy, who had not come home the night before, now approached the shop. His clothes were filthy and torn. It looked like he had spent the night in the open, and his face sported several bruises. I think my father took some pleasure in seeing him so.

"Ye'll leave now, Billy Simpson. Take yer belongings and git out. I'll give ye your certificate, but I don't want to see yer face again." Billy looked like he wanted to argue, but after a pause, he entered the shop and came out again a minute later bearing a bundle.

He walked down the path toward the town, then suddenly turned and said, "You'll be sorry. You'll pay for this!" And with that, he left. The night before, my nightmares had returned with a vengeance, and now I knew I would not be rid of them, not for a very long time.

Chapter 13

THE NIGHTMARE

That winter, the year of 1733, I turned sixteen. And as the cold and ice progressed, so did Mama's illness. She began coughing fiercely again, sometimes hacking so hard that she coughed up blood along with phlegm. As she got sicker, Da spent more and more evenings at the pub. It was as if he couldn't bear watching Mother suffer, but his drinking and gambling only added to her distress. She had lost so much weight that she appeared almost skeletal, and I struggled to get her to eat much.

I was paying the bills now, and our rents were falling further and further behind. Da was still working hard, but our business had slowed since Billy had gone. One night, as I lay in my attic, I overheard Mama and Da talking.

"We're going to have to make some decisions," Mama was saying weakly. Da was silent. "The rent to Squire Baker *must* be paid if we're to keep this cottage." Again, Da had nothing to say. I'm sure he was feeling guilty because the income from his last two consignments had been drained away in whiskey and cards.

Now he did speak. "A gentleman came by here yesterday. He offered a good price for Katie's filly," Da suggested.

My heart leaped into my throat, but Mama countered quickly. "No! That would break our daughter's heart. I would rather be destitute than sink to that," she concluded. My heart slowed down a beat, even as I knew how desperate we all were.

"Well, there's always the cow. We didn't have the means t' get 'er with calf this summer," Da said regretfully, "so for sure she's goin' dry this coming spring anyway."

"Do you think you could sell her, Pat? It would mean we'll have nothing to trade for the foodstuffs we don't grow ourselves, but what else can we do?"

"She's always been a good milker, she has, even though she be gettin' old. Still and all, I think we could get a fair price for 'er," Da finished. And so the decision was made. That next week, a local farmer came and led Molly away. I cried as I watched her go and took my solace in the fur of my little cat and a quick ride on Snow. But every morning after that, for a long time, I mourned the loss of our cow, of the precious milk in our diet, and the rich trade that her butter had provided. But at least our rent got paid up that month.

One night, when Mother was well enough to sit up while I worked at embroidery and Da was in town, I got the courage to ask, "Mama, do you ever regret marrying Da? I sometimes think of the wealthy life that you could have had and wonder."

"Don't you ever think that, Kathryn Anne Alexander," Mama reproved. "Money will not keep you warm at night. Once upon a time, I was betrothed to a very rich man, a grandee with money and power. But he was also a cruel man and a womanizer. And yes, I was swept away by Patrick's good looks and charm, but even more so by his patience and sweet nature. He does have his faults, but your da has worked hard and been faithful all our married days. He loves both you and me, and that's all a person can hope for from marriage. And besides, without Pat, I would never have had *you*." Then she added, "Our life here is not so bad, you know, better than very many!"

"Yes," I said thoughtfully. "I understand what you mean. But how do you know when you're in love? How can you say when it's right?"

"I don't know how to answer that, dear," she said. "It's sometimes easier to know when it's wrong. But when you find that you can't imagine your life without a certain person, that you know you'd give up anything to be with him, well then, you know you're in love."

That was the last time Mama felt well enough to sit up with me in the evenings. By March, she was constantly in bed. I was doing my best to keep up with everything, but the work and bills were overwhelming me. I would fall into bed at night, and then the old nightmares would come.

The massive stallion, silvery in the moonlight, was rending the air with his screams. From my vantage lying helpless on the ground beneath him, it appeared as if he were trying to claw a hole in the sky, his front legs thrashing above me. Any moment now he was going to return those hooves to the earth, most likely crushing my skull. I shrieked and tried to roll out from under the giant white beast. I could feel the ground shake below as his feet pounded back to earth—had he missed me by inches? I kept rolling as I heard another blast from his nostrils, and then he was rearing again. I had the sensation of several men struggling and shuffling around me, hauling on ropes, shouting, and trying in vain to control the colossal energy of the maddened animal. I could smell their rank sweat and my own fear. But none of their faces or voices seemed clear. My only focus was on the piercing scream of the stallion and avoiding those stomping, flailing hooves.

I don't know how long it was after the nightmare ended that I woke—hours, days? Mama was leaning over me, a cool cloth on my forehead. "Katie, Katie, are you awake?" she was begging. A fit of coughing took her, and then she was back. My eyes were having trouble focusing.

"What happened? Where am I?" I asked, feeling foggily that I was not on my pallet, but in a bed.

"Easy, daughter, you've had a shock. I'm just so grateful you are back with us," said Mama, and then she began to cry and then cough again. It was a while after that before my mind cleared and before Mama was able to speak to me again—another day? Time was a blur. Eventually, though, I came to understand that a dreadful affair had occurred. Mama had found me in front of our cottage, unconscious, but unmarked, save for a blow to the head. Wretchedly, Da was not so fortunate. He had also been found with a crushed skull, his body lifeless. The grass in front of our home had been trampled, as if many hooves had pounded there. And adding to my grief, as if it could be worse, Snow was gone.

I was saddened to learn that Da's funeral had come and gone while I was unconscious. He had been laid in a simple grave out back of the house, the Anglican Church refusing him internment in the sacred cemetery beside the sanctuary. It would be several days before I was steady enough to visit his grave. I wondered how my grievously ill mother had found the strength to cope with all this. She told me she couldn't have done without knowing that I would need her when I awoke.

Once I was recovered enough from my ordeal, Squire Baker, who was also our local magistrate, came to talk to me. The squire was a large man with a normally jolly face. But that day, his expression was full of concern. He and Mr. Bennet, the local justice of the peace who was with him, asked what I remembered from the night—had it been a week ago now—that my father had been killed. I told them about my "dream," but also that it was similar to the one I had been experiencing ever since I had seen the White Chalk Horse, and I couldn't be sure what was real and what was imagined. This didn't seem to satisfy either man. But I simply couldn't remember anything specific.

The JP told me, although I could see it made Squire Baker uncomfortable, that there were folks who thought my father had been involved in something dishonest the evening of his death. It happened that both the Earl of Faringdon and the squire had lost horses that night—the two stallions, Cloud of the Desert and Diamond, had been taken without a trace. Squire Baker was understandably very upset. It was well-known that my father had large gambling debts, and well, they didn't have to spell it out, although the squire professed that he couldn't think such an evil thing of my father.

"But," I protested, "my horse was stolen, too. My da wouldn't have had any reason to steal my own horse." And I added, "If he were an accomplice, why is he dead now, too?" There weren't any answers. The men left, asking me to get in touch with them if I remembered anything further.

By the time another week had passed, I had recovered my strength while my mother had relapsed to her bed. The JP came by again, asking more questions that I couldn't answer. So one evening, after feeding Mama, I left the rest of my work undone and walked down into the village and then back up the hill toward Coxwell, climbing until I reached the crest where Billy and I had first glimpsed the White Horse. As I climbed, the flesh on the back of my neck began to crawl, and I had the sensation that I was being followed, or at least watched. I turned around several times and scanned my surroundings. While there were boulders and occasional trees where someone might hide, I couldn't spot any movement. Finally reaching the top, I surveyed the distance but saw nothing suspicious.

Sitting on a rock near the crest, I stared at the carved outline on the far hill, the graceful, galloping steed as arresting as ever. I had so many questions running through my head. Was the white beast in my nightmares merely an apparition of the chalk horse? Had I actually seen a white stallion the night of my father's death? Had it been Diamond? Or Cloud? Or some other flesh-and-blood animal?

I strained to remember any of the voices I had heard in my nightmarish state. Could one of them have been the nasal drawl of Lord Herbert? The deep slur of Billy Simpson? One of the men my father gambled with? Who else might want to see harm done to Da...or me? Who else might want to steal the stallions? And why take Snow, my sweet, sweet filly?

I sat there for a long time, but no answers came. Twilight was drawing near, and I began making my way back down the hill. Again, I had the sensation of being watched, but I encountered no bogey-men, no flying stallions. It was nearly dark when I finally approached our cottage and began to feel safer. But a movement caught my eye; there was something shifting underneath the big oak in our yard. I became too frightened to move, but finally, after noting no change other than a slight swaying motion near the base of the tree, I found the courage to creep forward. When I finally reached a spot where I could see through the shadowy darkness, a scream caught in my throat. A calico cat was hanging by its neck, swinging on a rope in the breeze. It was Cally.

Chapter 14

Aftermath

Morning came, but I doubted I had done much but occasionally doze between my bouts of crying. "God," I had sobbed, "if you are there, why has this happened? What have I or my family done to deserve this? Please help us!" But no answers came.

I had lost so much in the last week, and now this. Who would want to hurt my sweet little cat, and why? Years ago, I might have suspected Tom Burlington was exacting some sort of revenge. But after he saved me from Billy's assault, I was certain he now held no grudge. Was someone trying to warn me, caution me not to remember, not to tell?

I stayed under my cover, not having the energy or will to get up. What was the point? But then I realized that the house had gone cold. I heard Mother coughing and knew I needed to lay a fire. Billy had been right; we did need him, needed his help now. But what would that have cost me, I speculated, and would the cost have been worth it?

I finally dragged myself down the stairs and started my morning routine. We still had half a rick of firewood in the pile, but what would happen when that was gone? We had some apples and vegetables stored in our cellar and half a crock of rye flour, but we were going to need more supplies, and soon. There would be rent to pay, and I had no idea if Da's creditors would start knocking on our door.

I had to think! There was still a mound of sewing to see to, but that would not bring in enough even for food.

I decided to walk to town that morning and begin looking for work. I asked at the tannery first, and then at the pub, because I had a working relationship with both owners. But neither had any work. At the tanners', I asked if the owner knew whether Billy might still be in town, but he didn't know what had happened to our apprentice. At the pub, I fancied I felt animosity from the brewer—my da probably owed him money. I tried at the smithy, the cooperage, the spinning shop, and every other business in our small village, but either no one had work or no one was willing to hire me. Was it my imagination, or were people looking at me and wondering if my father had been a thief, or worse? I knew if we lived in a larger town, there might be factory work, but that wasn't available here. Neither did we have an almshouse in our parish.

I decided to try at St. Mary's. I wondered if, indeed, my family's problems were tied to our lack of attendance here for worship. Would I find God here? I had heard others talk about the charity of the church and knew that, on occasion, they would help the poor. I had never been into the structure before. As I entered the nave, my footsteps began to echo off the stone walls, giving me the feeling that I had stepped into another world. I was too nervous to look around but kept my eyes straight ahead as I entered the central chapel. I did not look to the right or left, where I knew the two transepts must veer off.

Suddenly, I heard a sound to my right. "Can I help you?" a pompous voice intoned.

I jumped and had to regain my composure. The voice asked again, more firmly, "Can I help you?"

"Rev'd Davies?" I asked in a small voice, even though I knew very well who the squat, balding man was.

"Yes," he answered, "and you are Kathryn Alexander?"

I nodded. Now that I was here, I didn't know how to begin. We both stood there staring at each other until I lowered my eyes and finally began, "My mother is very ill, sir, and my father is gone—"

"I know all about your father, and how he passed," he interrupted in a not-too-friendly manner.

"Well, there's just Mama and me now, and I'm not sure how we're going to make ends meet," I continued. "I was wondering…I was hoping that the church might have some help for us?" I ended on an optimistic note.

"None of your family has ever set foot inside of God's house and yet you apply here for sustenance?" he asked in a disapproving voice. "There's no help for you here."

"But, sir," I pleaded, "my mother is a good Christian. She prays every morning and has never harmed a living soul. She is so ill, and I don't know how to pay for food or medicine, let alone find our rent to keep a roof over our heads."

"That's not my concern. If your mother were such a good 'Christian,' then she should not have married a papist," he finished. "I know all about her high-and-mighty ways. She was always too good for this 'country parish,' and you are just like her, parading through town on your fancy horse, riding astride like any common trollop would. No, there's no help for you or your mother here." And turning on his heel, he strode away, leaving me standing in the chapel in tears.

For the next week, I did not leave our cottage save to pump water, bring in wood, and use the privy. There were no animals to care for in the stable, no reason to venture outside. I had felt humiliated in the village and could not think where else to turn. Then we were paid a visit by Squire Baker. At least this gentleman still appeared friendly to us. I could tell he did not believe my father had taken any part in stealing his stallion, and I believe he felt pity for Mama and me.

He inquired about my mother's health and then about our state of affairs. I understood that he was asking about our rent, but I didn't know what to say. Then he offered me a solution. He said that Mrs. Baker had always wanted a piano forte so that her daughter could be schooled in the art. (I had never met his wife—she seemed to avoid his stable area and horses.) He offered to bring Mrs. Baker down to our cottage to examine the instrument and said that we might make some sort of deal. I told him to bring her by, but I knew I would need to talk this over with Mama. The piano was our most-highly-prized possession. When I visited her bedside and spoke to her, she rasped, "Do whatever you must do, Katie." I knew we really didn't have a choice, and I had little interest in making music anymore, anyway.

Mistress Leona Baker, a reedy woman with a long nose and a wheedling voice, was on our doorstep with her husband the next morning. I invited them into our small cottage, and Mrs. Baker peered around dolefully and looked like she couldn't believe anything desirable could come out of such surroundings. But she asked me to play a piece on the instrument, and when I did, I saw her begin to smile. She conferred with her husband, and then they told me they would like to make an offer for the piano. As Squire Baker began to speak, his wife interrupted and asked, "By the way, does your mother have any other 'things' she might like to sell?"

I started to answer no, believing we had nothing else of value, but then I remembered the chest that Grandmother had sent. "Wait here a moment," I requested and then entered Mama's bedroom and told her what the squire's wife had said. Again, Mama told me to do whatever was necessary, and so I dragged the old chest out into our sitting room.

Mrs. Baker pawed through the contents, murmuring disparaging comments. Regarding the silk and lace gowns, she muttered, "These costumes are out of date and wrinkled beyond repair." Then she added, "Too bad the moths have gotten to this velvet cape." But she did handle the ivory comb and brush set with more relish and seemed interested in the ornate, brass, looking glass.

She and her husband conferred quietly for a minute, he looking unhappy, but finally the squire turned and offered, "We could give you six months' free rent for the piano forte," and added, "And one pound six for the chest of items." He sounded regretful, but got a hard stare from his wife.

I wasn't sure what Mama's possessions were worth, but I guessed at least four times what he was offering. I gathered my courage. "I will gratefully accept your offer for the piano, sir, but for the price, I believe we would rather keep Mama's things."

Again, the husband and wife conferred and then proposed, "We'll give you two pounds for the chest, but that's our last offer." Again, the squire looked uncomfortable, as if he wished he could be somewhere else, but his wife looked unyielding. I knew there were no others in the village who would have any interest or use for Mother's precious items, and so I agreed to the bargain. We needed so many things: butter, lard, meat, soap, candles, milk, never mind tea, sugar, or new clothes. I wasn't sure just how far two pounds would go, but it would serve for now.

A few days later, servants from the squire's manor house came with a wagon and removed our beloved piano. It was sad to see it go, but I also felt relief that I would not have to worry about rent, at least not for a while, and this consoled me for the loss. I was able to purchase supplies and get more nutritious food into Mama, and like other years, as spring bloomed and the weather warmed, so did Mother's condition seem to improve. I was able to leave her and go into the village, when necessary. And I sometimes took short walks out into the verdant fields behind our house, finding what joy I could in the flowering and reawakening of creation. However, it always felt like there was a heavy weight hanging right over my head or a threat just around the next corner. And I could not escape the nightmares.

When I had used the last of the pound notes, I began to worry in earnest. Although Mama could sit up for spells and even help a little with some of the cooking, she was not able to sew. I was doing my best, but I did not have her fine skills, and though I spent many hours a day bending over my needle, I could see that we were still lacking in sufficient income. So I made the decision to go to Faringdon and ask for help. I was reasonably certain that the earl had respected my father, and I was going to have to depend on his charity. I felt I was out of options.

Leaving a large pot of turnip soup simmering and warning Mother I would be gone all day, I set out on the four-mile trip. It would not have been a hard journey except for the myriad of hills between our two towns. Just half an hour into my walk and I was flagging and wondering how I was going to make it home again by nightfall. Gratefully, though, about two miles from my destination, a farm wagon rolled by carrying chickens destined for the butcher in the village, and the farmer graciously gave me a ride, at least to the outskirts of town.

I had been through Faringdon twice before, but each time, being conveyed in the earl's trap and moving at a fast clip, I had not taken the time to look about me. Now, on foot, I had the leisure to notice that Lord Stanley's village was quite a bit larger than ours at Uffington. There were more shops and more tradesmen. There were at least two pubs and several cobbled streets besides the main. Their All Saints Church looked a lot like St. Mary's, except that the central bell tower was four-sided and not so tall. I had heard that meeting halls called clubs were springing up in populated areas, and I noticed two such buildings here, one with a printed sign stating, "Gentlemen's Card Club," and another, "Ladies' Book Club." How Mother and I would have loved the latter, had our own community boasted such a place!

I finally reached the upper end of the village and neared the gate to Faringdon Manor. Being occupied with the trip, I had not had much opportunity to worry, but now my nerves set in. I was hoping to encounter Smitty or Alice when I arrived, knowing that a friendly face would make things feel easier, but it was not to be.

I faltered in my decision of whether to approach the front entrance or servant's door in the rear. My class rank would send me to the back, but hadn't the earl himself led Da and me in through the massive oak doors at the entrance? Still, I wasn't brave enough to face the butler's inquisition that I knew would await me there, so I instead rapped at the doorway to the kitchen. Telling the maid (or was it cook?) who opened the door that I wished to speak with the earl, I received a piercing look. She took in my worn, common clothing and my nervous disposition and guessed immediately why I was there. Beggars might have been common at that door.

"We've no extra food today," she said firmly. "We've no need for workers in the house, neither. But ye can go see Smitty out in the barn—I heard they be burning in the north fields today and might need extra help." I remembered seeing smoke in the distance as I approached the mansion.

But I insisted, to her disapproval, that I wanted to see the earl in person and that he would know who I was. "Ye haven't heard, then? A few days after those thieves stole his famous horse, his lordship just fell over dead. The physician said it must've been 'is heart."

This was a surprise to me. Another tragedy tied to my own. "Well," I stammered, "then I'd like to see his son. He also knows who I am." I added, "We met last year." Hoping this piece of information would help, I gave her my name.

She seemed to take a moment to consider and then turned on her heels, indicating that I should stay where I was, just inside the doorway. After a few minutes, a well-dressed servant, probably the butler I had hoped to avoid, came to lead me into the house. He barely looked at me, and I just followed behind him, hoping he was taking me to William. I barely noticed the house outside of the hardwood floors and halls that we passed through. Finally, the servant opened a large door and indicated I should enter the paneled room. It was lined with bookshelves, and I guessed it must be a library. Under other circumstances, I would have loved to run my hands over the books and revel in the wealth of their numbers, but now I had to force myself to look up at the man who was sitting behind the large walnut desk. It was not William.

"Hello," Lord Anthony said in a mocking tone. "It's the little waif with the needle, I see," he added, obviously looking me over. "Kathryn Alexander, is it? I thought I recognized that name. You've certainly grown up since you, uh, had your hands on our...stallion." I perceived that he was intentionally trying to embarrass me; still, I couldn't help blushing. "What has brought *you* here today?" he finished.

My voice came out barely a rasp. "I was hoping to speak with the earl, but I just learned that he has recently passed. I was very sorry to hear that."

"Yes, yes. We are all sorry, etcetera," he blurted with no feeling at all. "Now, why are you here? I'm a busy man." He said this while leaning back in the chair and placing his feet up on the desk, mocking me again, it appeared.

I went on. "My father is also recently dead, my mother has consumption, and we are hard-pressed to earn our daily food. I was hoping your father would generously offer us some help."

Now he stood suddenly and came to my side of the desk. He spoke coldly, but with some strong emotion I couldn't name. "We *all* wish for some generosity, don't we? But we don't always get what we wish for. My brother, the great and all-knowing *new* Earl of Faringdon, has taken it upon himself to treat me and my brother with no generosity at all!" He was working himself into an icy fury and speaking in very precise syllables. "Now that my father is dead, I'm told I must find a 'worthy occupation' or my allowance will be 'cut off'!" he finished, looking daggers at me. "And so no, there will be no charity from this family to anyone. Now leave!"

I was grateful that he had gone back around to his chair and was sitting again behind the desk. On shaking legs, I retraced my steps back out of the library, where I found the servant/butler waiting just outside the door. He turned without a word and led me back through the halls and kitchen and saw that the outside door was shut firmly behind me.

I had come such a long way looking for help. I couldn't leave without at least trying to see William. I headed over to the barn and was surprised to find no grooms scurrying about. I went to peer into Cloud's old stall, but it was empty. I heard a scraping noise down the aisle and went to investigate. I found Smitty using a pitchfork, mucking a few doors away. When he saw me, he came out to the aisle with a smile.

"Miss Katie," he greeted warmly. "Good to see you." I was so overwhelmed to see a friendly face that I nearly cried.

"Good to see you too, Smitty. Where is everyone?"

"They're all out to the north fields. We were burning off brush, but the fire got a little bigger than we meant," he explained.

"Is Lord William out there too?" I asked hopefully. "I heard that the old earl is dead."

"Nah, Lord William has gone to London to receive his new commission," Smitty informed me, "and it's a sad state, it is, leaving us here to the whims of his brothers. I have no idea when, or if, he'll return."

I asked Smitty why he said that, and he went on to apprise me of the latest affairs of the estate. It seemed that Lady Middleton, William's fiancé, had come for an extended visit over the Christmas holiday. Things had seemed tense at times between William and her, especially after her disappointment in not receiving the family's heirloom emeralds as a gift. Three days after Christmas, in a blinding snowstorm, she had left Faringdon in a coach belonging to the Earl of Bath, formerly Viscount George Herbert. Apparently, Lord George's father had met some end also. The coach had overturned on one of the steep slopes heading out of the village, and Lady Grace and her maid and another servant had all been killed. Lord George was not in the carriage, but it was obvious that she was fleeing to be with him. Some thought it was because George had inherited his earl's title before William; some thought the two just suited each other better. All the servants agreed that William had escaped the lion's mouth.

William had seemed morose and unhappy after his betrayal and loss, and then, when his father had died, he appeared to be relieved to have a reason to flee to London. Smitty hated to see him go; there were still so many of Cloud's progeny to train, and Anthony and Clarence had no patience for or interest in overseeing the work. Smitty didn't mind doing the task himself, but William had possessed a talent for it that was rare.

When I asked about my cousin Alice, the groom's face turned sour. "Don't you know," he grumbled, "that she was in on Lady Grace's scheme? It was Alice who made her excuses the night she got away— it was Alice who had carried the note from Lord Herbert about their assignation. When Lord William found out, he fired her on the spot. I have no idea where she's gone." I wondered to myself why she had not come to us in Uffington, but I had no way of knowing.

At this point in our discussion, we both heard footsteps and turned to see William's youngest brother, the thin one with the shifty eyes, approaching. Lord Clarence gave no greeting but looked me up and down and then said to Smitty, "Go out to the north fields and help with the fire."

Smitty answered, "Your brother told me to stay here in the stables to see to the horses," the groom defended.

Impatiently, Lord Clarence amended, "Then go out to the well and begin gathering buckets of water against the barn. We'll need them in case the fire comes this way."

"Yes'r" came the answer, and Smitty left us, looking reluctantly back at me over his shoulder.

"Anthony told me we'd had a visitor, and why," he snickered, "but he didn't tell me it was a pretty one." I didn't know what to say, and I was feeling very uncomfortable with the way he was appraising me. "I know how you might be of service, if you're willing," he added, a glint in his eye.

I took a step back. He knew I knew what he was talking about. I shook my head.

"Now, now, nothing to be shy about," he said, advancing a step and taking ahold of my arm. "If you're a good girl, it'll pay well." With that, he grasped my other arm and closed his face toward mine.

I shoved him hard away from me and reached behind me for the pitchfork I had felt as I had fallen backward. I pulled it sharply forward and put the tines between him and me. Seeing the weapon and recognizing my determination, he backed up a step. "Now let's talk about this," he wheedled. Then he stopped talking and gazed over my shoulder. Turning to look, I saw Smitty standing in the light of the far door. None of us moved for an instant, and then Clarence turned and strode out of the barn.

When Smitty reached me, I stammered shakily, "Thank you. I hope Lord Clarence won't be hard on you for this."

"Never you mind—he's just a cub," he declared, and then added, "I wish I had a man to drive you home, Katie, but there's no one to spare."

It didn't matter. I needed the walk to calm myself and to try to think of what else I could do. It was a long hike, but even so, no answers came to me. I tried praying again to God, whose God, I wasn't sure. Mama's? Da's? The God of St. Mary's? But I didn't know if he could or would hear me.

Chapter 15

THE GOVERNESS

It was another lean week living on root vegetables and weak broth, the occasional stewed apples, but with no sugar. Then we had a second visit from Squire Baker. After asking about my mother's health, he went on, "Mrs. Baker has sent me to inquire if we might hire you to teach our daughter to play the piano—well, to actually fill in for our governess, who left last month?" he amended.

I was taken aback. I had no idea how to answer. "We were told your mother was the daughter of an earl? And she herself educated you?" He said this as more of a statement than a question. "We have a nanny for our two younger sons, but our daughter, Abigail, is of an age where it's crucial for her to be learning the skills of a gentle-woman. She's not entirely lacking, as we had previously engaged a governess for her and the boys, but now the woman has left." He didn't say why.

"How old are your children?" I asked, more to fill the time while I deliberated feverishly.

"Abigail is thirteen, John Jr. eight, and Robert seven," he answered, thinking for a moment before giving the ages of the boys. "My wife had thought that Abigail could pick up the music art on her own by simply practicing, but that has not been the case…unfor-tunately," he finished.

"I couldn't possibly leave my mother for any extended period of time," I explained. "I would need to see to her meals and be here every night." I knew that normally, governesses lived with the families where they were employed.

"We understand that," the squire continued. "We're willing to let you come five days a week and work with the children during the day but return home in the evenings. It's only a short walk from here to there. Why don't you and your mother consider this? And then you can come up to the manor tomorrow morning at eight and let us know your answer. If you decide positively, we can strike terms and you can meet our children then."

Was this an answer to the prayer I had prayed yesterday? I had no way of knowing. But there was really nothing to discuss with Mother—we had no other options. So the next morning, as St. Mary's bells chimed eight o'clock, I was at the squire's door. The manor house was large, but not as spacious by nearly a tenth as the estate at Faringdon. Still, it was impressive. Of course, I had been on the property many times, but never in the manor house proper.

The squire greeted me at the door himself, no butler being on staff. I would discover as the week went on that the Bakers employed a cook, a nanny, two housemaids, a number of grooms and farm workers, and of course, myself. The children were lovable, if not a little spoiled. I took to Abigail immediately. She was a thin, shy girl, not so different from how I had been at her age, with a sweet smile. She obviously adored her father, who mostly ignored her. The boys were clever but undisciplined, cute little rascals whom I immediately liked.

Mrs. Baker showed me around the house that first day, obviously impressed with her own status and possessions. But I was not offended. Indeed, I was most grateful to have the position. It didn't pay a fortune, but it still meant that Mother and I would have regular meals and maybe even some new clothes to replace our threadbare ones. As a matter of fact, Leona (which was how I thought of her in my head) insisted on giving me a uniform, which I changed into every morning when I arrived, her not wanting me to risk damaging it at home, but not wishing anyone to see one of her servants "looking like a ragamuffin."

The first floor of the spacious home contained the kitchen, hall, dining room, drawing room, sitting room, and the squire's office. The piano forte now held a place of distinction in the large paneled drawing room. The six bedchambers, five for guests, were located on the second floor. The third floor contained the children's bedrooms, nursery and schoolroom, and sleeping quarters for the house servants. I was enthused when I saw the schoolroom. It contained not only four desks with extra furniture in the corner but also several shelves full of books, which I couldn't wait to handle, writing and ciphering materials, and a world map on the wall. It was a wonderful room. There were large windows along one side, which made the space seem cheerful and airy.

Mrs. Baker described, in her thin, wheedling voice, what I would teach the children. She wanted Abigail to learn to play the piano forte, sing, learn needlepoint, French, and possibly drawing and other fine arts. I warned Mrs. Baker that while I played, sang, and sewed well enough, the other subjects were not my strengths. I also advised her that learning to play the piano, at least with proficiency, should be no problem, but whether Abigail could ever sing with much ability would depend on her own talents.

The squire's wife further required that I work with the boys at the general skills of mathematics and reading. I asked how far they had gotten with their last governess, but there seemed to be some uncertainty about this. Next, I met Nanny Hubbard and the upstairs maid, Missy. Nanny Hubbard appeared quite old and infirm. She did not stand from the rocker to greet me but rather gave me a friendly, but toothless, grin. I later would learn that Nanny had taken care of John Sr. when he had been a child, and he was determined to employ her to the end, much to his wife's chagrin. I was glad to learn that he could stand against Leona when it suited him. But I did wonder just how much influence a woman of Nanny's age could have on such active boys. No wonder they seemed rather undisciplined.

Missy turned out to be a blessing and a paragon of information and advice. She greeted me with genuine warmth. I realized later that since Nanny Hubbard was often indisposed, it had fallen on Missy to try to corral the boys along with accomplishing all her regular duties.

It was understandable that she was glad for my induction into the household, even if it was only five days a week.

It seemed that the children had been constantly relegated to the third story, where they took their meals and spent their days and nights. They were rarely invited to spend time with either their mother or their father, being only called down on special occasions and on Sundays for church and dinner, when they were expected to dress and behave accordingly. Because of this, the third floor had become rather a nightmare for the poor servants who had to put up with the boys' shenanigans and activity anytime they wanted to use their private rooms.

While Mrs. Baker had been fairly solicitous that first morning, our relationship soon cooled to one of mistress and servant. I often felt she was deliberately condescending toward me, often critical of my person and dress. I sometimes wondered if she felt threatened by my family background and wanted to be sure I understood my place in her household. No mind; I was determined not to let it bother me, so grateful was I to have work and an income. Mother was still doing well enough at home that I could leave her, and our future was looking a little brighter. I could sometimes forget the nightmare behind us or that Mama's improving health would likely deteriorate again when the harsher winter weather arrived.

Still, the first few weeks with the children were rocky. Abigail was eager to please and followed me like a shadow. She seemed so lonely and anxious for my attention; I hugged her often. The boys were not used to sitting and focusing on anything for very long. I soon learned that asking for their attention, requesting that they sit still for a lesson, was like trying to hold water between my fingers. I had no real means of discipline besides withholding their meals or using a switch, both of which I was loath to do. I needed to find a way to make them *want* to sit and study.

Their main goal, at present, seemed to be to ease their own boredom by tormenting me. That very first morning when I took my seat at the front desk, I suddenly found myself on the floor, the wind knocked out of me. I could hear the boys tittering in their places. I glanced over at Abigail, who only stared at her hands. Rising, I looked at the broken stool and said, "Hmmm, it appears this seat needs some work," and I exchanged it for one in the corner.

My second morning, when I opened the classroom door, expecting to see the children in their places, only Abigail was sitting at her desk, apparently reading. There was no sign of the boys, and Abby only shrugged her shoulders when I asked about them. I went to look in the bedrooms and the nursery. Nanny Hubbard was sitting in her regular chair in front of the fire grate, apparently nodding in sleep. The boys seemed to be nowhere on the third floor. Heading back down to the second, I found Missy and asked if she had seen the boys. "Oh, miss, this is their favorite game—they are such hooligans! Try looking in the large window seat in the schoolroom. That's probably where they've hidden."

Traipsing back up the stairs, I entered the classroom once again, and "Hah!" came the cry from behind me. I jumped with a start, my heart in my throat—both boys had been hiding behind the door as I came in.

Quickly reaching an arm around each of their shoulders, I grabbed them both and pinned them to me in a bear hug. Giving them a little shake, I chortled, "That was a good one," and with a smile, I sent them to their desks. I learned that the boys liked nothing better than to startle any adult who dared enter their domain, their parents included. No wonder they saw little of their mother and father.

Later that same week, I was bending over a desk, refilling the inkwell, when "Hah!" came the usual cry and poke. The ink sprayed and spattered up onto the bodice of my uniform. *Oh, no,* I thought, *it will be ruined.* Still, I tried not to provoke the boys. I had gotten to know them well enough by now to understand that their pranks did not come from meanness, only boredom and too much energy.

Presently, that same day, Mrs. Baker chose to come up to the classroom to see how we were progressing, something she had never yet done. At least the boys were in their seats, although they were having a paper wad contest. The squire's wife immediately noticed the ink on my bodice. Staring at it coolly, she said, "I see you've managed to ruin your new uniform. I didn't realize you were inept when I hired you." There was a disdainful look on her face as she finished,.

I couldn't help glancing over at my students, all of whom were suddenly intent on their folded hands. "Sorry, ma'am," I apologized. "It was clumsy of me. I'll take the garment home and do my best to erase the stain."

"You will never get ink out of it. Never mind trying, just give it to Missy and wear your own clothes until we can purchase a substitute, but I'll be taking it out of your wages at the end of the month."

"Yes, m…," I murmured, again peeking at the three children. When she was gone, I began again with the lesson I had been trying to teach, and my students remained somewhat subdued and attentive the rest of that day but were back in their usual, overexcited form the next.

I finally hit on two methods that eventually brought them around. The first was to establish a regular schedule, which they were not used to. We began each morning with a brisk walk "to get the blood moving" (and to expend some of that boundless energy), outside, if at all possible. Since the children had not been allowed to explore their own home grounds often, this was a great treat for them, as were the active games and races we engaged in. But if they misbehaved while we were on our hike, at our games, or in the classroom later, they would lose this privilege for the next day. All three children grew to love our time outside. I taught them the names of trees and plants, birds and insects. I believe I enjoyed this time as much as they did. I had quite a bit of trouble convincing Mrs. Baker of its importance, she believing we were wasting classroom time (and her money), but in the end we were allowed our exercise.

My second strategy was to have a quiet time after our noon meal. During this period, I encouraged the boys to put their heads down on their desks and just listen. Abigail and I were reading aloud *The Adventures of Robinson Crusoe*, a book I had found among others in the schoolroom and which I had read the year previously. I knew that the shipwreck, pirates, mutineers, and cannibals would appeal to the adventurous youngsters. As we got further and further into the story, the boys began to beg me to read longer each day. Instead, I encouraged them to increase their own reading skills so that they could begin to explore the fascinating world of books themselves. We had primers with basic (and fairly dull) stories that they learned to read quickly, but they were soon ready to work on (with my help) such books as *Jack and the Beanstalk*, *Guy of Warwick*, and *Tom Thumb*. Once they got started, it could actually become difficult to get their nose *out* of a book. Missy said the change was near miraculous, but I knew it was really the power of literature to lead the imagination. These children were starved for entertainment.

Getting John and Robert to work on their mathematics was another issue entirely. Working with numbers was really a matter of rote practice. I could set them to a page of additions or subtractions, which I especially liked to do when Abigail and I descended to the drawing room for our daily lessons at the piano. But I would often return to the schoolroom to find the boys at games and the math papers abandoned. I finally asked them what it would take to get them to apply themselves. What did they really want? I was expecting to be asked for sweets or playtime. After they deliberated together, their answer surprised me. They wanted to learn to ride horses.

I could certainly appreciate this sentiment. It was really *all* I had wanted as a child, too. And their father had so many beautiful animals right on the property. It amazed me that he hadn't seen to their riding education himself. I was a little disappointed when I approached him on the subject and he said he didn't have time for the boys. I honestly believe he just didn't have the patience to deal with their energy. But I asked if we might use one of the older, gentle horses and the help of a groom and if I could teach them myself.

"Ordinarily, I would never allow a woman to take on such a task," he answered, "but I've seen you ride that filly you owned, and I know you have your pa's skills with animals. If you think this will help get results in the classroom, then you can try it. But let's keep this between ourselves. I doubt Leona would approve." And so the boys began to learn to ride.

The squire had an old saddle horse that was past its useful days. The gelding had been retired to being a pasture mate for Diamond before he had been stolen, keeping the stallion company on the days when he wasn't in the breeding shed. Three days a week, in the evenings before I headed home, a groom would bring King out, saddled, and into the small paddock. There the boys would take turns learning to walk and rein at first, but later how to post the trot. The old horse was past his cantering days, but in just a month, the boys, who were both athletic and clever, had soon outgrown the aged gelding and had moved on to a younger horse who could teach them to take their leads and paces.

The day came when we asked the squire if we might mount the boys on Goliath, whom I knew to be gentle and dependable, even though a giant. The squire, who had not watched many of the boys' lessons, was doubtful, but I cajoled and encouraged, and the horse was finally brought out under the squire's vigilant eyes. He was amazed as, one by one, each boy took his first ride on the big horse and was able to walk, trot, and canter with some proficiency. The boys were in heaven riding a horse with such gaits and size. They were laughing with delight, and their father found he enjoyed the whole experience, viewing his sons in a new light. After that, I did not have to coerce the man into spending time with his boys. They were soon regularly riding out with their father on pleasant evenings. Oh, yes, and they did learn at least some mathematics.

Abigail was doing fairly well with her playing and sewing, although she had no talent whatsoever in voice. She completed her first cross-stitch sampler with the poem, "Patience is a virtue, virtue is a grace, both put together make a very pretty face." She presented the framed fabric to her mother. I wish I could say that Mrs. Baker had been as pleased with her work as the squire had been with his sons' riding, but it was not to be. Leona was critical of the girl's stitches, even though it was her first attempt, and Abigail spent that afternoon inconsolably in her room. I felt responsible but didn't know what I could do. She and I redoubled her efforts on the piano so that there would at least be no disappointment in that arena.

As well as things were going between the children and myself, they were not going well with Mrs. Baker. The better things went in the classroom, the more unhappy she seemed to become with me. I took to hurrying up the back stairs when I would arrive in the mornings, hoping to avoid any accidental meeting with the woman, but I believe she often watched for my arrival, because we met "by chance" so regularly.

She would look down her long nose at me and say, "You're going to be late if you don't get a move on," or, "Can't you do something more with your hair than just put it in that long braid? It's so unattractive!" or, "I can sometimes hear the stomping of the children as they clomp down the stairs of a morning. Can't you teach them to be more graceful?" or "My children are becoming vagabonds—all I see them doing is tramp around our grounds." At least she hadn't caught wind yet of our horse-riding ventures.

Sometimes I would see her standing just outside the doorway to the drawing room as Abby and I worked at the piano forte. I felt, surely, that she must be pleased with her daughter's progress at the instrument. Abigail was now able to play simple melodies using both hands, following the musical score with accuracy. She was also showing talent in playing with emotion, even passion, and I wondered if this was becoming an outlet for the shy girl's feelings. I hoped desperately that her mother would praise her for her accomplishment, but so far, that had not happened.

I grumbled to Missy one morning about all this, and she just shook her head. Missy's theory was that Leona was a "very unhappy" woman. She had birthed six babies during her marriage, three of whom had died in infancy, as so many did in our neighborhood. After Robert had been born, Mrs. Baker had decided she wanted *no more children*. She had set her foot down so hard that the squire had taken to sleeping in one of the guest bedrooms, and that had apparently been the case ever since. It was common knowledge among the servants that when Squire Baker hitched Goliath up to his gig, he was heading to the brothel in Red's Tavern at Faringdon, and probably, his wife knew it too. No wonder, I thought, that she took her frustrations out on everyone around her. I vowed to try to think more kindly toward her in the future.

Chapter 16

THE BIRTHDAY PARTY

I n the fall of that year, my mistress announced that November
12 would be the squire's fortieth birthday. Many residents of
our village failed to live to see forty years, especially the poorer
folks, and this achievement was considered to be worthy of note.
Therefore, the much-younger Mrs. Baker announced that we were
to have a party in celebration of this accomplishment. For a month,
the whole house was put into an uproar. The Bakers hoped to have at
least ten guests, the dining room service being able to accommodate
twelve at table. But a tent was also being considered as an alternative.
Weather might play a factor, both in who could travel and whether
the party could be held outdoors. With all the uncertainties, Mrs.
Baker was in constant agitation, and staff and children just tried to
stay out of her way.

All the landed gentry in Berkshire had been sent invitations;
Leona fretted every day as the replies and regrets came by mail, worrying that her table would not suffice. As it turned out, three squires
and their wives, one baronet and his two single daughters, and the
Earl of Faringdon, excepting his brothers, had replied in the affirma-
tive. Mrs. Baker was jubilant that her shire's lone representative of
the peerage had deigned her invitation worthy of acceptance. And
she noted, ten guests and the two hosts made a perfect twelve for her
table.

Mrs. Baker was so pleased and excited—she made sure that everyone in the village knew that Lord Stanley was coming to attend her husband's birthday party, although he would not be spending the night, living close enough to travel home that evening. But the squire would be hosting visitors in at least four of the extra bedchambers. When I first heard Leona talking about her special guest of honor, I had trouble catching my breath. My mind had been caught up all summer in taking care of Mama and keeping up with my charges, but William had never been far from my thoughts. Was it possible that I would see him when he was here for the celebration? Even though I no longer had dire need for his charity, my heart felt a yearning just to be in his presence again. Would he even remember or acknowledge who I was, especially now that he was an earl?

Once the guest list had been finalized, preparations for the party began in earnest. An extra cook and footman had been hired for the occasion, a menu settled on, and cleaning of every room in the manor (save the third floor) undertaken. One day, as Abby and I sat at the piano forte, Mrs. Baker came into the room. "I've been listening to you play, Abigail, and I must say, you are becoming quite respectable." This was high praise, indeed, from her mother, and her daughter beamed. "I will expect you to prepare something special to play for our guests after your father's dinner party," she went on. "You know," she said needlessly, "the Earl of Faringdon will be here." And with that, she swept back out of the room.

Abby looked at me in a panic. She had only been playing a few months. While she was progressing rapidly, still, this was going to put a lot of pressure on her, on both of us. She began to cry softly, but I put my arms about her and whispered, "You can do this. You have an exceptional talent at the instrument, and I know we can choose something that will make your father proud." And so we began to search through the musical pieces that Abby had already been practicing and settled on a simplified minuet by the composer Lully. I'm quite sure her brothers were not ungrateful for the additional free time they had as their sister and I spent many extra hours in the drawing room.

Two weeks before the squire's birthday, Leona had a seamstress, Mrs. Davis, come to fit each of the children with special attire for the party. All three were excited to know they would be allowed to attend for a short while after dinner. They would have their own meal in the schoolroom, of course, but when the adults retired to the drawing room, John and Robert would be introduced and permitted to stay at least until after their sister had performed her piano piece. Leona warned me that I would be expected to chaperone the boys, who needed to be on their very best behavior. And then it occurred to her that I would also need to be appropriately dressed. So she asked the seamstress to go through my mother's clothes, which were still packed in Grandmother's trunk, and see what could be done about modifying a simple gown for me.

As we looked through the chest together, Mrs. Davis kept tut-tutting. It was too bad, she said, that the beautiful silks had not been cared for, that the lace had been allowed to rot, the velvet moth-eaten. But ultimately, we pulled out an aqua-blue silk frock with an embroidered skirt that had not aged too badly, and I hesitantly tried it on. I was amazed when it fit rather well; I had begun to think of Mother as only the thin wraith that she had become, and it touched me to reflect that she had been much the same size as me at my age.

Mrs. Davis removed the old flounces and took the flare out of the skirt, belting it with a simple sash at my waist so that it hung demurely. She was sorry that the other ladies would all be wearing the new, umpire style of gown, fitted tightly at the bodice and then flowing smoothly down to the floor, but I didn't mind. I was thrilled to be wearing one of Mother's frocks, and silk, at that. I did tell the seamstress that she would have to do something with the low bodice, as a governess would not be expected to "show her bosom." And so Mrs. Davis created an undergarment from lace remnants that reached almost to my chin and effectively kept me very modestly covered. It was not anything that would be in style, but neither was the gown itself, so it didn't really matter. She told me that the blue of the watered silk did give my pale eyes a lovely color.

The day before the party, Mrs. Baker had the four of us don our party wear and parade for inspection. She spent a good amount of time going over Abigail's attire and brought out a pearl necklace and earbobs for her daughter to wear. Missy was to do Abby's hair, and Leona spent quite a while coaching her daughter on how to curtsy and address Lord Stanley, how to make small conversation, how to bat her eyes invitingly.

"Mother, I might think you were asking me to flirt with the earl," Abby worried, blushing slightly.

"Well, it wouldn't hurt anything. The man will have to marry sometime," her mother rejoined. "Just let him see your pretty smile."

"I'm only thirteen!" came the pleading reply.

"Well, I had married your father by the time I was fifteen!" At this, Abby, who was quite shy anyway, gave up the argument. She was already biting her nails over her piano debut, and more than that would be quite impossible to even think about.

When, finally, the squire's wife glanced my way, she took in a deep breath. It was difficult to know what she was thinking, but she said, "I really don't think silk is an appropriate material for a mere governess to wear, even if she is attending a party. Don't you have anything in black?"

"I apologize, but you had told Mrs. Davis to look through my mother's things, and this is all she came up with. Would you rather I just wear my uniform?" To be honest, I felt I might be more comfortable in something more understated than the silk. Even though I wanted to see William, I had no desire to call out undue attention to myself.

Mrs. Baker looked torn for a moment, but then relented, waved her hand, and shook her head, dismissing me and my garb. The next day was a flurry of activity in the manor. I arrived late. Mother had suffered during the night. As the colder weather came upon us, so did her malady again become acute. She had coughed so severely that neither of us had gotten much sleep. I was so worried about her that I considered not attending the party. But knowing that the boys might cause real trouble without an overseer, I relented my decision.

When I arrived and had changed into my new dress, I found that Abby and the boys were already clothed and fidgeting. I cautioned them for the hundredth time not to soil their new outfits.

Abby's hair had been pinned up on top of her head with little curls down the sides, and I found that it made her look quite a bit older. She was excited, giving her cheeks color, and she looked almost fetching in her pink silk frock. Missy had just finished with Abigail's hair and asked if she could do something with mine. I had worn my hair free of its usual braid, and it hung down my back in a long curly tress. Missy, who was an expert at dressing hair, went to get more pins, and she soon had part of my hair pinned up and part left in a long curl. I felt strange with my new look, but Abby, staring at me for a moment, told me I looked absolutely beautiful. Soon, our dinner had been brought up and I was too engrossed in keeping the children's clothing unspoiled to worry about anything else.

Then it came time to adjourn to the drawing room. Abby took my hand. She looked so nervous. I put my arm around her and told her she would do just fine. Then I grasped each boy's hand, and we descended the stairs. We were obviously the last guests to enter the room. The squire came to the door and conveyed the boys to its center. Abby joined her mother, and I discreetly stole into the far corner of the room, where three chairs and been specifically set up for us.

The squire introduced his sons to his guests and then named each visitor individually. Lord Stanley, Earl of Faringdon, was honored first, followed by nine other names I had not heard before, save Squire Baxter, whom I had met on the commons at Lambourne. He had been the owner of the Cleveland Bay that had raced there and now seemed to be a special friend of John's. I wondered if he had driven his coach and four to the party and if, even now, we had the team of Clevelands stabled in the barns. William had risen at his name, and I was pleased to see that he shook both John's and Robert's hands, nodding to them as if they were young gentlemen. He was still the most handsome man I had ever seen, tall with broad shoulders, his square jaw and blue eyes set in a perfect visage. And he had grown a goatee!

Mrs. Baker also introduced her daughter to her guests. Abigail did a nervous curtsy in front of William, and he graciously told her that she was going to be just as beautiful as her mother. I believe Leona might have just stood there rooted to the spot had not the servants come in at that moment with trays carrying brandy snifters and glasses of cold cider, which were passed around to everyone. The boys joined me in the corner, where I made sure they each chose a glass. I noticed that all the men held snifters save for William, who had chosen cider. Then Squire Baxter raised his brandy and made the toast. "Here's to Squire Baker and his forty years. May he have forty more!" And everyone raised their glasses and cried, "Hear, hear."

Our maids next passed trays of small plum tarts and jellies, while the hired footman offered port and sherry. Mrs. Baker was pouring coffee for those who wished it. And once everyone had plate and glass in hand or placed upon the myriad little side tables that abounded near the couches and settees, it was announced that Miss Abigail was going to play for her father and his guests. She had been sitting at her mother's side, but now she rose, and nervously glancing at me for support, she took her seat at the piano forte. I nodded and smiled, and then she began to play, a little haltingly at first. But soon the emotion of the music carried her, and she was able to do admirable justice to the piece.

I tried to keep my eyes on Abby, as I feared she might look up at me for support at any time, but I couldn't help glancing toward William now and again. He was seated between the two single young ladies who had accompanied their father to the party. They were both pretty and well-dressed. I noticed that each took turns whispering in William's ear, despite his obvious attempt to listen to the piano performance. It was hard, though, for him to ignore the lady who was now leaning practically into his lap, but he was doing his best. I had hoped that he might glance my way at some point, but up to now, I don't believe he had even seen me. And with everyone present seemingly desirous of his attention, I could understand why.

Before I knew it, Abby had concluded her performance and the guests were applauding politely. Mrs. Baker was nodding surreptitiously at me, and I knew it was time for the boys to make their adieus, which they did by waving, and we were back out into the hall. I couldn't help feeling disappointed as I led the two children up the back stairs. What had I hoped for? That William would see me across the room, rise, and come to take my hand? It was all a ridiculous dream anyway. But still, I had hoped for…something.

I handed the boys off to Nanny Hubbard and then wandered back down to the first floor. I was under no illusions that I was invited back into the party. However, so strong was my desire to observe William, even if covertly, that I went out the back and around to the small garden. This area was just outside of the double glass doors that gave entry to the drawing room. The rosebushes had all been pruned back for the winter, and the large stone bowl that held the reflecting water in the summer was now empty. But the two stone benches at right angles on either side beckoned me. And pulling my wrap tightly around my shoulders against the chill, I sat in the shadows, grateful now for the lace that sheltered my neck.

The light from the party spilled out into this area, but one of the benches sat partially in the darkness, and this was where I took my seat. From here, I could see my objective but felt confident that I was hidden from view. Someone else was playing the piano now, one of the wives, perhaps. William was standing, talking to Squire Baker, with the two younger women still flanking him.

The performer had switched to a sonata, but still, William stood, his attention now being summoned by Mrs. Baker, Abigail looking uncomfortable by her side. The subject of my attention continued to give gentlemanly courtesy to his hostess as another lady took to the piano. I'm not sure how long I sat watching, but suddenly, it seemed that William had asked to be excused for a moment, because he was bowing slightly and then heading toward the double doors to the garden. Leona watched him regretfully but did not follow.

The earl came out into the garden and stopped, standing by the empty stone bowl, just a few feet from where I was sitting. I didn't move; I couldn't breathe. It was obvious he hadn't seen me. He stood for what seemed like an eternity but was probably just a minute or two, looking out over the dead garden to the stables beyond. I heard him take a deep sigh, and then he turned slightly in my direction. Had I moved? Had the light caught my eyes?

I saw him twitch and take a step backward. "I'm sorry," he defended, "you gave me a start! I hadn't seen you sitting there." Now that I had gained my objective, I didn't seem to have a clue what to do. To fill the void, William tried again, "Are you one of the guests? I'm sorry, I can't see you very well there in the dark." Still, I seemed incapable of speaking or moving. *He must think I am unbalanced,* I supposed unhappily, still barely able to breathe.

Then William took a step closer and seemed to study my face. "Kathryn? Kathryn Alexander, isn't it? I wouldn't forget those extraordinary eyes." I stood then, and he continued to gaze at me. "You've grown up," he remarked. "I might not have known you except for your beautiful face." I was glad it was dark to hide my blush. I knew he was just being a gentleman, but still, the compliment thrilled me. I nodded and gave a little curtsy.

"I just came out for air. Please, please, sit back down and tell me what you're doing here. Are you a guest?"

I retook my seat and was glad to see him sit opposite me. It appeared he might stay for a little while, at least. "I'm the governess here," I finally managed to say and then explained. "I accompanied John and Robert to the party but left when they went back upstairs."

"The governess?" He looked confused. "Didn't you and your father treat equine illnesses…and even train horses, I thought I had heard? And how is Cloud's lovely filly doing, by the way?"

I took a deep breath and then explained briefly what had happened this spring. "I had no idea the same thieves who took our stallion had also taken your Snowflake," he replied after listening compassionately. "And your father…I'm so sorry, I just hadn't put it all together even though I knew there had been a murder involved. Again, my condolences for your loss. Patrick seemed a very good sort." We sat for a while in silence, and I thought about explaining about Mother, but he continued before I had decided on the words. "So you are a governess now?"

"Yes," I answered simply.

"And do you enjoy it?"

I thought for a moment and answered, "Yes, yes, I do, very much, although I miss riding." Going on, I said, "And I was sorry to hear about your father passing too. And so now you're an earl?" He nodded. "And do you enjoy it?" I rejoined.

William didn't answer right away. Finally, he said, "It is expected of me to say yes." Then he added cryptically, "Many things are *expected* of me. But for some reason, I feel I can speak plainly with you. Can I, Miss Alexander?"

"Please call me Kathryn, and yes, I'm at your service."

"The answer is no, then, I don't enjoy it, although I realize that it's disloyal and ungrateful of me to say that. I was happy being my father's son. But now I have so many responsibilities, not the least being my two younger brothers."

"Yes, I've met them," I said coolly.

"Then you know what I'm talking about, sad to say." He went on, "And then there are obligations to the House of Lords and obligations to my estate and tenants, and I am expected to…produce an heir, and on it goes. I find, like you, I miss riding and training horses very much!"

It was probably a breach of etiquette to mention his fiancé, but he had alluded to his possible marriage. "I was sorry to hear about Lady Middleton's death," I said tentatively.

He was silent for a moment. "Again, may I be candid?" he asked and went on when I nodded. "She was beautiful, and I had once imagined I was in love with her. But the more I got to know her, well…the more I expect that I escaped an unhappy marriage, although, of course, I wouldn't have wished her ill."

We sat again in silence for a while. "May I ask you something, Kathryn?" I nodded. "Are all women naturally disingenuous?" He didn't seem to realize that this would be an insult to my own self. "I expect you've heard enough gossip to know that my mother died an adulteress. And my own fiancé was eloping to be with that damnable George Herbert when she was killed. I now have married women flaunting themselves at me, and it seems every matron with an eligible daughter is at my door. All the women I meet seem to offer themselves without any thoughts to modesty or decency. Sometimes it overwhelms me. It was why I needed air this evening."

I had no idea what to say; it seemed he was lost in thought and had forgotten I was even there anyway.

"Every time I think of Grace, I can't help but remember a quote: 'Greedily she engorged without restraint and knew not eating death.'"

"Milton?" I interjected.

"Yes, *Paradise Lost*." He came back to the present. "Do you know it?"

"I've read it but don't pretend to understand it all. Your quote describes Eve?"

"Yes, again, the mother of *all* women." He spoke with distaste.

"*And* of all men, save Adam," I pointed out. "And men can be deceitful, too, although I feel most are honorable."

"I know I'm jaded right now," he admitted. "I'm told it will take time to get over Grace's betrayal, but I sometimes wonder, How long?" Then he seemed to be ready to change the subject. "I know your father was a tradesman. How is it that you know Milton and are educated enough to become a governess?" He was shaking his head slightly. "And you speak with the accent of aristocracy." He was looking at me curiously now, and the strong emotion had gone out of his face.

"My mother was raised a gentlewoman," I answered, having been schooled to avoid speaking of her family. "She educated me herself, at home."

Before I could say more, the glass doors opened and Leona was gesturing to William. By way of apology, he said, "I'm sorry. I met an old friend here in the garden and lost track of time."

Leona looked at me with surprise and what felt like disgust but then turned to William and said, "Well, I hope you'll come back in now, Lord Stanley? We were just getting ready to enjoy some singing, and I hear you have a wonderful voice."

William stood to go in but then turned to me. "Won't you come in and enjoy the party, too, Kathryn?" I was about to decline, but he reached out his hand to me, just as in my fantasy. And surprising myself and Leona, I took it.

Once inside, they called William to the side of the piano. I retook my place in the corner as he sang a solo with one of the young ladies accompanying him on the instrument. He did have a lovely tenor voice, I was not surprised to learn, and I sat very happy in my own world. For the most part, William gave his attention to those around him. But every now and again, I would catch him glancing my way, which always sent my heart fluttering.

After singing a second song, William begged to be released and called for another to take his place. But Mrs. Baker approached and made the request, "Just one more, Lord Stanley, please, a duet. We must hear 'I Saw My Lady Weepe'! It has such beautiful harmonies. And who should sing the soprano?" She only paused for a second. "What about my daughter, Abigail?" She was dragging Abby forward.

Oh, no, I thought. Poor Abby. The girl could not carry a tune and would be mortified. Abigail knew it, too, and she began begging her mother, begging for anyone else in the room to please take her place, saying she felt ill. Finally, she looked at me.

"Please, Miss Kathryn, please come and sing with the earl." I was nearly as mortified as Abigail, especially seeing the look on Leona's face. But then William joined Abby's case and called me up to sing with him. For Abby's sake, I thought, and I stood.

I didn't know the song and expected I would make just as much a fool of myself as the girl would have. But soon the pianist was playing the introduction, and William, guessing that I didn't know the melody, began to sing the soprano part with me while I watched the words on the page of music. By the second verse, I was comfortable enough that William began with his tenor harmony, and soon we were singing the chorus with smiles on our faces. Mother and I had routinely sung together when she was healthy, but never had I enjoyed a song so much, and I believed I could now die a happy woman.

This thought brought me immediately back to earth. What was I doing? Mother was deathly ill at home and needed me. As soon as the song was concluded, I made my apologies and nearly ran out the door. But quick as I had been, Leona was right on my heels.

Calling me back, she said through clenched teeth, "Who do you think you are? You had no right to spoil my party. How dare you steal Abigail's rightful place! You are a nobody, and I can't believe I subjected my children and household to your insolence!" She was nearly spitting now. "You have lost your position here, and if I ever see you on my property again, I'll call the constable. Do you understand?" She said these last words with such vehemence that it drove me backward. Nodding, I turned on my heels and ran.

Chapter 17

THE FALL

Mother had been so ill when I got home from the squire's party that she couldn't speak, only looked at me through glazed and mattered eyes when I could manage to rouse her at all. I stoked up the fire in the house and set to making soup, chopping a few vegetables and using the last of the bacon fat I had purchased last week. I was too worked up to sleep anyway. When the soup had simmered for an hour, I ladled some into a shallow bowl and took it into the bedroom. Piling pillows behind Mama's back, I held the steaming liquid under her nose, hoping the vapor might revive her a little. But I was never able to get her to swallow, even a spoonful. She wouldn't take water either. I still had a few coins left from last month and resolved to go and get the physician first thing in the morning. That night, my old dream returned. The white stallion with the thrashing hooves seemed to pursue me all night.

Mother was no better the next day when I set off for the village. Dr. Thomas agreed reluctantly to come back with me, but only on condition that I paid him in advance. After he took Mother's pulse, listened to her chest, and shook his head over her skeletal condition, he walked me back out to the front room. "I told yer pa last spring that there wasn't nothing else to do for yer ma. The only thing that I've heard of that can help consumption at this stage is to take her to one of them new hospices. The closest one is down at Lambourne. But I don't know how you'd get'er there without killing her. And worse, it'd take ten pounds just to get'er admitted! Who in our class has that kind of money?" he stated. "Best be planning for a funeral." He told me he was sorry and left, shaking his head.

Before I could recover from the physician's verdict, a knock sounded on my door. There was the squire, looking more severe than I had ever seen him. "We need your rents for this month, now that you are no longer under our employ," he demanded without looking me in the eye. I sent him away without answers.

I dropped down on a chair and put my head in my hands, too stunned to cry. I knew Mama was dying. What was I going to do? I had to get her to Lambourne to that hospice, but how? Who would help us? And then the answer came to me: William! William would have a coach to carry her in. William would give me the money necessary to pay for her treatment. I just knew he would! Kind William. (I put out of my head the niggling worry that I would become just another person who wanted something from him, another obligation.)

It had snowed overnight and turned very cold. I stoked up the fire, high as the chimney would allow. I knew I might be gone most of the day. I left a big bowl of soup on the table by Mama's bed on the chance she might wake hungry, kissed her cheek, and told her I loved her and where I was going. Then putting on my woolen dress and socks, pulling on my leather boots, which Da had made for me the winter before, and donning my father's heaviest long coat, I set out for the arduous walk.

I had a hope that I might catch a ride to Faringdon as I had on my last trip. The road appeared to have had some light traffic, which made walking in the wet snow a little easier. But I saw no vehicles until the last mile. By then, my trudging through the drifts had taken nearly all my strength. A farmer driving a large sleigh to a team of drafters was carrying a heavy load of firewood into the town. I could tell he was rather loath to add more weight to the overburdened sleigh, but he took pity on me. It was still snowing lightly, and I'm sure I looked like I was about done in.

He dropped me off in the middle of town, and then I made my way on north through the gates of Faringdon Manor. Since I knew William was to return home from the party the previous night, I made my way directly up to the front door of the manse, believing that he would see me if I gave my name. I was not surprised when a suited butler opened the door and admitted me into the wide marble foyer, but he allowed me to go no farther, taking a disparaging look at my soaked boots and rather-aromatic woolen clothes. When I asked to speak to the earl, he sniffed and said that the earl wasn't home at present. I wasn't sure what to do. I asked where the earl was, and he said he was out. When I became more distressed and begged him to tell me where the earl was or when he might return, the butler told me it was none of my business.

Evidently hearing our disagreement, Anthony opened a door to my left and stuck out his head. "What's going on, James?" he asked impatiently.

Then he noticed me. "You!" He spoke with a leer. "Is she begging for money again, James?" There was mockery in his voice.

Without waiting for an answer, he went on. "I told you last spring to leave, and I mean it now, too," he said, stepping toward me menacingly. I wanted nothing to do with either of William's brothers, and I knew there was to be no help for me here today. I backed out the door and had it slammed in my face.

Before I left the estate, I visited the stables, hoping to find Smitty. He wasn't in the barn, but another groom told me that Lord Stanley had indeed arrived home late last night and had gone out again this morning. He didn't know where he'd gone but told me to try at the Gentlemen's Card Club, where he often went in the afternoons, which it was at present.

I took a deep breath and reversed my trip back into town. By now, I could not feel either my hands or feet. The woolen coat, which had been so warm when I set out this morning, had sopped up the wet snow and was now both weighty and cold. But soon, I thought, I would find William and then everything could be made right. When I reached the club a quarter of an hour later, I knocked on the door and a rather-burly man answered. He was evidently the doorman. He looked at me and said, "Sorry, miss. No women are allowed in the Gentlemen's Club."

"I don't need to come in." My voice wavered. I was shivering violently. "I just need to talk to Lord Stanley…please," I added with as much fervor as I had in my waning strength.

"He's not here, miss." No, that couldn't be!

"Please, could you check? I was told by his groom to look for him at this club."

"I'll go and see," he said with sympathy. "Wait right here. I can't let you inside, though."

He was back in no time. "Sorry, miss, but I'm told he's gone to London for a fortnight. Is there anything I can do for you?"

I sank down into the snow and began to cry. "I need money, lots of money," I cried. "I'm fearful that my mother's going to die."

"Well, I'm afraid there's not much I can do about that," he said. I felt him take both of my elbows and begin to lift me to my feet. "Again, I'm sorry I can't help, but you aren't allowed to stay here on our doorstep. Why don't you go across the street to Red's Tavern? At least you can get warm there, and Red may suggest a way to solve your problems."

I looked across to where he was pointing and saw a low, sprawling building with a sign in the window. I was so cold. I really couldn't think about anything except getting warm. I directed my sluggish feet to head in that direction and somehow made it through the door of the tavern. I wasn't sure what I should do and was snow-blinded for a moment and couldn't even see where I was.

I heard a voice over to my right say, "Can I help you, ma'am?" I turned toward the voice and then collapsed onto the floor. It was several minutes before I became aware of my surroundings again. I was slumped in a chair, leaning over a table. A woman was holding something in front of my nose and telling me to drink. I opened my mouth and swallowed and then coughed. The liquid burned as it made its way down my throat—some sort of liquor, I judged.

"She's more alert now, Red," the woman called, and a man came and sat down at my table. They had obviously removed my wet coat, and a warm towel was wrapped around my head. Red (for I supposed that was his name) was looking at me.

"I don't think I've seen you here in Faringdon before, have I?" I shook my head, still incapable of speech.

"Are you lookin' for work?" he asked. He handed me the glass of amber liquid and said, "Drink some more of this," and I obeyed him, coughing. But I admit, it did give me a warm glow inside.

Now he asked again, "Are you lookin' for work?"

I tried to speak and found my voice. "I need money," I rasped.

The man Red looked over at the woman, and they eyed me carefully. The lady was shaking her head, but Red said, "She might do. Some men like them young, even though she's not very busty. And with Sally out, we could use another girl."

My brain had thawed sufficiently so that I guessed what they were talking about. I knew that Squire Baker visited "the brothel" here in Faringdon. The idea repelled me, but what was I to do? I had run out of options. If I returned home empty-handed, I would watch Mother die. The alcohol and cold might have been affecting me, but I was not unaware of the decision I had to make.

"Do you want to earn a few guineas?" Red asked, and I nodded resignedly. He sent me to a small front room with Gertie (I heard him call her), and she peeled me out of my wet clothing and tried to fit me in one of their costumes. Everything hung on me, but I was beyond caring. Somehow, she pinned and tied things up and then said it would work. I would have to wear my own boots, though.

"What am I supposed to do?" I asked weakly. I had stopped shivering with the cold, but now I was trembling in…exhaustion? Fear? Surrender? I couldn't name the emotion.

"Just sit at the tables here by me," she said. "If a man comes over, smile at 'im and be friendly."

"Then what?" I needed to know.

"Then go with 'im into one of the back rooms and do whatever he says." She reached over and took my hand. "It will be all right. You'll get used to it. And the money can be pretty good, if you're real nice!" Picking up the glass on the table again, she finished, "Here, drink the rest of this. It will help."

I don't know how long I sat there. Several men did come into the tavern, but they sat over at the tables on the far side of the room, drinking the ale Red brought them, and didn't even look our way. I was beginning to feel blurry eyed and worried I was going to weep.

Now another man entered. I could see he was tall and looked familiar. Oh, God in heaven, help me. It was William. I dropped my head and tried to make myself invisible. He had just sunk into a chair on the far side of the room, and I could hear him talking to Red, who had greeted him by name.

"Is Clarence still here?" William asked.

"Yep, but I expect he'll be out anytime now. Can I get you some tea while you wait?"

"Not today, but thank you." Now it got quiet again.

What was I doing here? I suddenly wondered. How could I be making this mistake? Mother would rather die than see me shame myself like this! She would *rather die*! I couldn't let William see me. I had changed my mind. I wanted to leave, but I would have to stand and go into the front room for my clothes. Perhaps William and his brother would just depart and never see me if I sat very still. I felt paralyzed with fear and embarrassment.

My next thoughts were, What if I went to William now and told him of my situation and asked for money? But I looked down at my bawdy red dress and realized there was no way out of this. Suddenly, the atmosphere in the room changed somehow. I peeked over to see that William was staring right at me. Even though I turned my back to him, I could feel his eyes boring into me.

Suddenly, he called, "Red, I believe I'll have a glass of gin."

"Gin, sir? Did I hear you right? But you never drink."

"Are you going to serve me or not, blast it?" the earl said angrily. Now I was quivering in earnest. Soon William called for another glass, and then a third. I couldn't turn to look at him but felt certain he was still staring at me. Then another man entered the tavern and walked directly over to our end of the room, greeting Red on his way. I couldn't look up, but he evidently stopped right in front of me.

"Who's this?" he asked, taking my chin and turning my face up toward his.

"She's mine," declared a loud but familiar voice behind him as Lord Stanley came around to grab my arm. The other man stepped back as the earl pulled me from the chair and dragged me toward the back.

I was so filled with shame and terror all I could say was, "No, no, please…"

William stumbled slightly as he towed me toward the rear and mumbled, "I thought you might be different. I thought…I thought…"

And then we were entering a room holding only a bed and a coat stand, and William was slamming the door. Again, he seemed to stumble, and I realized he was quite drunk. Still holding my arm, he flung me toward the bed, where I landed with a thump. He was having trouble unbuttoning his trousers with clumsy hands, and I was paralyzed, just lying partway across the bed, my boots dragging the floor. Once again I whimpered, "No, please."

Suddenly, I was hauled farther up on the mattress. William's strength surprised me. Then he was atop of me, pulling my skirts up about my waist. I knew what was about to happen and squeezed my eyes tight. The act didn't take long, the pain in my lower abdomen and grunts from Lord Stanley announcing its completion. And then he rolled over and began to snore.

I lay there for a long, long time, partially underneath his prone body, in shock, I think. Finally, coming more to my senses, I carefully extracted myself, pulled down my skirts, and looked about the room to consider my options. All I could think was, *I have to get back to Mama!* I didn't want to return to the front of the tavern but guessed there would be a back door. I would have to leave my own clothing behind. Thankfully, I still had on my boots.

I looked at William's warm, fur-lined overcoat and came to a decision. Donning it—no mean feat, for it was twice too big and long—I headed silently for the door. Then I became aware of a weight in one of the pockets. Dipping in my hand, I came out with a muslin bag—a bag full of heavy gold coins.

I don't know how many hours it took me to reach my little cottage, but it was well after dark when I got there. The fire had gone out, and the house was stone cold. The soup by Mother's bed was frozen. And Mama was dead.

PART II

Chapter 18

BRISTOL, 1735

W hy and how I came to be in Bristol in 1734, I can't really remember. It's possible that I was trying to find my mother's family, since my grandfather, the Earl of Avon, would have been from that district. But I can't be sure. As to how I got there, I have a foggy memory of riding in a coach for days, sleeping in inns along the way. I must have still possessed the pouch of coins that I had stolen from Lord William Stanley. But I know that when my "angels" found me wandering, destitute on the streets of Bristol five months later, I was penniless.

I call them angels because I'm sure, without their mercy and intervention, I would be dead. I *was* dead, dead for a long time even after they found me, dead in my soul, dead to the world. I was also five months pregnant.

They have told me that I couldn't speak, or wouldn't speak, for nearly six months after they brought me to their Home for Needy Children. It must have been three months after first coming to the Home that my baby was stillborn, but I have no distinct memory of that, only flashes of an intense physical and emotional pain, greater than any I had known. What horrors I endured wandering on the streets of Bristol prior to that, I may never, blessedly, remember.

But slowly, as the months progressed and I was cared for and loved by my dear angels, the fog began to lift. Mrs. Angel Cartwright (for that *was* really her name) and her husband, Samuel, ran the

Home for Needy Children. Samuel was also the pastor for their protestant sect, called the Way, a group of dissenters from the Methodist Church. There were about fifty members of the group, who met for worship in the same building that housed the orphanage. Angel and Samuel routinely perused the streets of Bristol and had gathered nearly twenty-five children who either had no parents or who had no one to care for them. These children ranged in ages from one to seventeen years old, me being the oldest. They also offered what medical services they could to both their charges and the poor and destitute residents of Bristol, free of charge. How and where they got the money to support this charity, I never knew. Perhaps they had a rich patron, or perhaps Samuel was wealthy in his own right? Either way, these were the most self-sacrificing people I had ever met, and I will be eternally grateful to them.

As I began to come back to reality, I started helping Angel to treat the sick among the residents of our Home and city. Mrs. Cartwright was still a youngish woman in her late twenties. She had a neat, trim figure, an open, welcoming countenance, and more energy and compassion than any woman I had ever known. When Angel realized that I had a knowledge of herbal remedies, she began to rely on me more and more. Beginning to feel that I had some purpose was probably what allowed me to start regaining more of my senses.

Angel and I would begin each day making rounds among "our children." Before breakfast was served, the Home residents would attend the morning devotions. It was at this time that we would treat any of the children who needed our help. Some had chronic illnesses, especially the children who had not been with us long. After devotions and breakfast were over, the residents would divide into various groups; the younger ones were taught basic reading and mathematics; the older ones were trained in a trade, mainly spinning and sewing for the girls and masonry for the boys. Members of the sect took turns overseeing these projects, and I, too, was soon ensconced as a teacher in the primary classroom when I wasn't attending to Angel on her rounds through the streets.

Once in a while, a messenger would come to our Home, requesting Angel's assistance. The poor people of the slums had no access to physicians, surgeons, or the hospital. Likewise, there were often accidents and burn victims at the myriad of factories that were springing up all over Bristol, and the need for medical attention was great. Angel, like me, had no formal training, only a basic folklore knowledge and a desire to help. When someone couldn't afford a physician, we were at least willing to try to assist. We had a storeroom stocked with herbs and potions for all sorts of common ailments. We kept ingredients such as dried cherries for gout, foxtail for heart conditions, cod-liver oil for rheumatism, laudanum for pain, and peppermint oil for headaches. If we had a need for something we didn't keep on hand, we would visit the apothecary. Angel was often impressed with my knowledge of herbs, for which I always silently thanked my da.

During my first year at the Home, I refused to attend either morning devotionals or the weekly worship service. I had no interest in hearing about a God who had seemingly abandoned both my mother and my unborn child, although I endeavored never to think about the babe, never even giving her a name. Angel and Samuel often tried to speak to me about the heavenly Father's love, but I didn't want to hear it. Besides, how could God, if there was one, possibly love me after what I had done and become? (I was under no illusions about the life I had lived on the streets of Bristol before the Cartwrights had found me.)

I might have continued in my fog, creeping through life without feelings, if it hadn't been for Esther. She was a three-year-old child we found shivering and sick on the streets of Bristol. People in her neighborhood told us her story—she had been born with a harelip, and her mother had rejected her at birth and put her out on the curb to die. But the child's grandmother had taken pity on the baby and fed and cared for her as best as she could. However, when the grandmother's life had ended, the little girl was again placed out in the streets, where she had somehow managed to live on scraps of garbage, an outcast. People would shun her because of her facial deformity, throw rocks at her to make her leave their doorstep. She was a sad little waif who continually held her hands in front of her mouth to hide her defect and cried piteously and continually for the first week she was at the Home.

I was instantly drawn to Esther, and I felt desperate empathy for her—it was the first emotion I had allowed myself to feel in a very long time. When she initially came to live with us, I spent as many hours as I could spare from my other duties just holding and rocking the small, weeping bundle. While I had not been able to shed my own tears in many months, Esther cried for both of us. Her tears only abated when she finally fell into sleep and began again upon awakening. She was desperately underweight, obvious signs of scurvy and rickets in her tiny frame.

We set about getting a good diet of milk and fresh vegetables into the child. Esther was lucky in that her cleft lip did not extend into her palate, as so many times such did, and she was thereby able to eat normally. However, she would cram her food into her mouth with one hand, still holding the other in front of her face. And all the while her tears would continue as she scanned from side to side, as if worried that someone was going to steal her food. I also supplemented her diet with lemon oil for her scurvy. Her physical disabilities began to improve long before her emotional ones. But slowly she spent less and less time crying, although we never saw the poor child smile that whole first month. She would not play or interact with the other children and would not return hugs but often just sat, rocking in a corner. It was a welcome day when she first uncurled and raised her arms to me when I went to pick her up. And as Esther learned to respond to affection, I felt my own heart thawing.

I continually worried about the little girl, though. While her scurvy was gone and her frame was beginning to straighten up, she continued to suffer other physical maladies, especially suffering from recurrent aches in one or both ears. Angel felt certain that Esther had other physical abnormalities, but we were not equipped to know how to help these. Still I continued to sit and talk with Esther as often as I could, and she eventually began to lower her hands and try to speak. As the months went on, she did learn to say a few simple words and expressions and, finally, even learned to smile and play. By the time she gave us her first tentative grin, I found that I had begun to smile again, too.

Chapter 19

EDWARD

Sometime after Esther came into my life—whether it was weeks or months, I didn't know, for time was still a hazy guess to me—we were summoned to a local alehouse. This was a nicer establishment than either the Fox and Hound or Red's Tavern. The place was fairly clean and not so dark and smoky, as many pubs were. However, the Crowing Rooster boasted a brothel in its upstairs compartments, and we had made calls there more than once. The pub serving girl who came to fetch us was named Nancy, and she reported that one of the "upstairs women" had been beaten by a client—rather severely this time—and the prostitute had no money for a physician. So Angel and I packed what supplies we thought we might need and followed Nancy to the establishment.

Every time I entered a pub, alehouse, or tavern, I felt uncomfortable. It reminded me too clearly of my own poor choices, my own fall from grace. However, I felt nothing but compassion for the women who worked in such places. I knew better than to judge; hard times could force a person into any situation, as I knew well. Still, as we entered the tap room, I kept my head down and tried to just concentrate on following Angel's willowy form. But she had stopped to talk to the owner of the Rooster, unhappy that he was not doing more to protect his working girls.

While I stood there in Angel's shadow, I became aware of a table not far from where we had stopped. There were four gentlemen seated there, evidently drinking ale, and I couldn't help recognizing a familiar voice, a voice that I had once longed to hear. It was Lord William Stanley speaking, I was sure. There were others in conversation, too, but I had no interest in them. What could I do? I wanted to run, wanted to pull my apron up over my head and flee back to the relative safety of the Home. But I felt rooted to the spot.

Angel's conversation seemed to go on forever, the gentlemen also conversing, until I noticed that the men's voices had ceased. Glancing as surreptitiously to the side as I could, I saw that they were all looking at me, or, in William's case, staring intensely at me. I took Angel's arm and propelled her forward toward the back stairs. "Come on," I whispered urgently, "let's go." She gave up on her conversation with the owner, looking at me with surprise. But she did not argue.

The whole time we were working on the injured woman, poulticing her bruises, applying honey to her abrasions, Angel kept glancing sideways at me. I was mechanically performing what needed doing, but my mind was elsewhere. Did the earl really recognize me? Would he call for the constable? What could he think of me? Did he assume I was just one more of the upstairs' denizens?

As we were making ready to leave, I held back, finally admitting to Angel that there was a gentleman below that I did *not* want to see. She seemed to understand my reluctance, although she looked at me quizzically and then called Nancy up to the second floor. The serving girl was glad to share confidences. Yes, the gentlemen were all gone now. They were not regular patrons but gentry in town because they were expecting a sailing vessel in port with a shipment of horses. But the ship had not yet arrived for some reason, and the men had come up from the docks and had stopped in to have a tankard.

"Ye should know, Miss Angel, that one of them men stayed behind and asked questions about you and Miss Kate."

"Was he tall and good-looking, with fair hair and blue eyes?" I asked anxiously.

"Nah, that gentleman left quickly," she replied. "But I saw him talkin' to the older gentleman who was the one askin'," she clarified. "He wanted to know who the two of yous were and what you were doin' here."

"Do you know who he was?" Angel asked, still obviously worried about me.

"Nah, I never seen him before. But he wanted to know if you'd be comin' back, and I told him I 'spected you'd be checkin' on Charlotte again tomorrow, her bein' so bad off and all. I hope that was all right?" she asked nervously.

"Of course, Nancy, and we thank you for telling us what you know," Angel added, patting the girl's arm.

The next day, I begged to stay behind while Angel went to check on Charlotte, which she respectfully allowed. When she got home, she reported that the injured woman was doing much better today and, unfortunately, planned to return to her trade right away. Angel had offered her a place in the Home for Needy Children, but Charlotte had declined the offer.

Then Angel told me that an older, well-dressed gentleman, presumably the one Nancy had mentioned, had approached her in the alehouse. He had introduced himself as Sir Edward Walker, a local baronet whose name Angel had heard mentioned before as being a charitable, respectable landowner.

"He asked about our Home, about our work with the sick, and about what we had been doing in the Crowing Rooster. And feeling he was a gentleman, I answered his questions. But when he asked about you," she said, laying her hand upon my arm, "I told him nothing save that you had been there that day as my assistant. Was that all right?" This she asked tentatively, and I assured her it was. But I was not feeling sure about it at all.

What had the man wanted? Was he a friend of William's? Why was he asking about us, about me? There were no ready answers.

The next several days, we were kept very busy treating two boys who had been burned badly down at the iron mill. The factory routinely used young lads to wheel hot lumps of puddling iron from the blast furnaces to the hammers. This was a difficult and dangerous job for boys only ten years old, and the barrow had dumped prematurely, pouring molten iron across their feet and ankles. The men at the factory had immediately emptied buckets of cold water, kept for exactly that purpose, over the children's burned extremities, but to no avail. And the families of the boys, who had sent them to work due to poverty in the first place, could not afford the attentions of a physician or hospital.

Angel and I trekked into the slums day after day, doing our best to save both boys, administering laudanum for their pain and applying extract of aloes to their burns, Angel praying fervently over them. But in the end, neither boy lived, having suffered excruciating deaths. Angel and I were both drained with exhaustion and sorrow. And while I grieved for the senseless loss of two young children, at least I had been too overwhelmed to have worried about William or his friend in days. That had not stopped the nightmares, though, which had returned in earnest.

It was not long after the boys died when we received a visit from that very same friend at the Home for Needy Children. Sir Edward Walker spent an hour conversing with Samuel, our pastor, in our worship hall before following him on a tour through our quarters, making introductions to the residents as they went. I was in the classroom with the younger children that day, and Samuel asked me to introduce each student to Sir Walker, stating that he was one of our new patrons. Feeling very self-conscious, I abided with Samuel's wishes and had each child come forward to meet the baronet. Sir Walker was polite and greeted each one with a handshake.

When we had finished with the students, the gentleman asked about the smaller children who were playing on a blanket in the corner, little Esther among them. Walking over to the group of five toddlers, I pointed to each and said their name. Esther immediately ran to me and hid herself among my skirts. Surprising me, Sir Walker bent his knees and squatted beside the little girl, or what he could see of her.

"Won't you come out and meet me, little one?" he asked in a gentle voice.

"Esther," I prompted.

"Won't you come out and meet me, Esther? I promise I won't hurt you." Esther only burrowed deeper. "I have a sweet in my pocket if you can come out to say hello." He looked up at me, as if asking my permission, and I nodded. At the mention of sweets, the other toddlers all walked or crawled over and began pulling at the man's trouser legs. Sir Walker had evidently come prepared for this, for he began handing out little pieces of candy. Esther, sensing the other children were receiving treats, also unwrapped herself but held her hand over her mouth as she accepted the sweet and then hurried off to the corner, still hiding her mouth even as the candy disappeared. I couldn't help being impressed with the kindness, gentility, and interest he showed toward my little ones.

While he was passing out treats to the rest of the class, I took the opportunity to steal a glance at the man. He was older than William, perhaps in his midthirties, and not as tall. As if making up for hair that was beginning to thin on top, Sir Walker had a thick beard, wider than a goatee, but still only covering his lower face. He had cheery brown eyes and a kind smile.

As the gentleman prepared to depart the class, he signaled for me to follow him to the door, which I did reluctantly. "I was wondering about the little girl, Esther," he began. "I didn't get a good look, but it appeared she has a cleft lip?" I nodded, not knowing where he was heading with his question. "Going through life with a harelip can be devastating to the child's future. I'm familiar with this because I have a niece who was born with the same malady. Can you tell me if the cleft is deeper than just her lip?" he asked gently.

"No, it appears to be strictly external but extends up to her nasal passage. It doesn't seem to cause difficulty in eating, but she's so self-conscious about it that she has trouble doing everyday tasks just using one hand. And she has difficulty pronouncing words," I added, more eager to talk to the man now that we were discussing a subject dear to my heart.

He nodded and appeared to be giving the subject deep thought. Then he made his adieus. "It was very nice to meet you, Miss Alexander." I gave a short curtsy, and he left our room.

That evening, I sought out Samuel and asked if we could speak. I told him I had some concerns about Sir Walker and his interest in our orphanage. The pastor asked me why, but I just murmured something vague about him being a friend of someone I knew from my past life. Samuel did not question me further. He probably assumed

I would tell him more when I was ready. He and Angel were like that, understanding and patient. How lucky I was to have them as my patrons!

Samuel went on to say that Sir Walker was a local landowner in the area, well-known in the community. But the baronet had not heard of our Home for Needy Children until the day he had met Angel at the alehouse. Sir Walker was a widower—his wife had died five years previous in childbirth—and he had no other children of his own. Why he had never remarried, Samuel didn't know. But Sir Walker seemed to have a great interest in helping children and had already made a substantial donation to our mission. Samuel asked me to be as gracious to our new patron as I felt I could under my own circumstances.

As it turned out, Sir Walker was back the very next day, and he brought a surgeon with him. Samuel, Sir Walker, and the surgeon all appeared just after our morning devotionals and asked me to fetch Esther so she could be examined. "Can you please tell me why?" I inquired, unwilling to go and get my little charge without knowing what was happening.

Sir Walker answered, "This is Mr. Thomas, the surgeon who corrected my niece's harelip so successfully. He's agreed to look at Esther and see what might be done."

"But surgery…" I couldn't finish. And then added, looking at Samuel, "That would be quite expensive."

"The expense will be nothing," the baronet reassured. "As for the surgery, yes, there will be pain, not during the operation itself, but afterward. Comparing that to a lifetime of social stigma seems a fair exchange, though. At least it was in my niece's case."

Samuel interjected, "Kate, why don't we let Mr. Thomas look at Esther and just see if he believes anything can be done? Then we can talk and pray about it." And so I relented.

After the surgeon's examination, his opinion was that the surgery to correct the condition would be relatively simple, and recovery most likely uncomplicated. But there was risk involved, and there would also be pain, but only for a week or two. Once our visitors had left, Samuel, Angel, and I talked the situation over. I was reluctant to put Esther through more trauma, but both Cartwrights, after praying together, felt the surgery would give the little girl her best shot in life. Knowing how attached I was to her, though, they left the decision in my hands. And in the end, I came to agree with them. Esther would have her lip repaired.

Chapter 20

SURGERY

It was decided that Mr. Thomas would come to the Home to perform the surgery, since it was to be relatively simple. And this way, Esther could remain in surroundings where she was most comfortable, to afford her the least distress. We made a bed of clean sheets on top of my desk in the classroom, where the windows let in lots of sunshine. The surgeon's intention was to induce a swoon using a dose of brandy and then to quickly perform the procedure. He would be using a knife to scarify the places on her lips that needed to be joined and then use waxed thread to stitch the two together. He said he had performed this surgery several times and felt it would go well.

There were four of us in the schoolroom besides Esther and the surgeon. Angel and Samuel were going to help restrain the child, who would be sitting on my lap, at least when we began. And Sir Walker had come to watch and help "in any way he could." I was surprised to see him, assuming his interest in the procedure had been satisfied once we had made our decision. But no, here he was. I wasn't as uncomfortable around him as I had been at first, but I still wasn't sure of his motives.

Mr. Thomas was getting out his equipment when I noticed the lancing fleam. "Are you intending to bleed her during the surgery?" I demanded.

"Of course," came his reply.

Since Esther was sitting in my lap, her head buried in my bodice, frightened of what was going on around her, I was hesitant to act too upset. I said quietly, "No, I don't believe that is in her best interest."

Angel put her hand on my arm. "But, Kate, this is what Mr. Thomas thinks is best. This is what is usually done, and he is the surgeon."

"I don't care," I said through clenched teeth. "I won't let you."

Suddenly, Sir Walker stepped into our discussion. "Miss Alexander has had years of practice in the medical field too," he said with quiet reserve. I wondered how he knew this fact. "And she knows Esther best. I think we should follow her advice and avoid the bleeding." And gratefully, his opinion carried the day.

Next, Angel and Samuel each took one of Esther's arms, and I put my arm around her waist and whispered reassurances into her ear. But still she began fighting, not knowing what was happening. We had added sugar to the brandy, but Mr. Thomas warned us she would still resist it. He was experienced in how much to administer but said we would try a lesser amount and then add more if needed, as he didn't want to risk giving her too much.

While he held her nose closed and the rest of us did our best to hold the struggling child still, he poured the sweetened brandy down her throat while she coughed and gagged. Then we waited, but it only took a few minutes before she had slumped in my lap and we laid her on the desk. The doctor quickly began to work. As I saw him cutting into the poor little child's split lips, I began to cry softly. Angel took one of my hands, and then Sir Walker took the other. I did not resist, and I noticed he was sniffling too.

There was a lot of blood, but that didn't bother me. I was relieved when the actual stitching began. I had not seen such a slender needle before and intended to ask Mr. Thomas where I might acquire one. The two sides were stitched together quickly, I had to admit, but Esther remained unconscious. While we waited, Mr. Thomas told us that when he had opened the child's mouth, he had seen that there was a cleft in the back of her throat as well, and he suggested that it might be the source of her earaches. But he said that he knew of no way to correct the problem.

Before she woke, we set to bandaging her face. We wrapped several layers of clean cotton cloth around her lower head, just below her nose. Mr. Thomas said this would prevent her from scratching at the stitches and keep them clean, but more importantly, it would keep her from being able to open her mouth wide enough to strain the surgical area. "If she cannot pull back her cheeks, her mouth cannot open much."

"But how will we feed her?" I asked.

"Several times a day, you must unwrap the bandage and give her as much soup or other liquids as she wants, but no solid food for seven days, and that is how long the bandage must stay on. Keep her dosed with laudanum so she'll stay quiet and comfortable. In another seven days, you can begin to wean her off the medicine," he concluded, but then added, "I'll be back each day to check on her progress." Once she was safely awake, the surgeon took his leave.

We did as Mr. Thomas instructed and kept Esther doped on laudanum. Sometimes it was difficult to get her to eat even soup. If I waited until some of the medicine had worn off to feed her, then the pain would return. Her tears and cries nearly broke my heart, and I spent as much time as I could holding and rocking her. But I had other responsibilities and could not be with her all the time.

To my surprise, Sir Walker came back each day, often bringing some little present or other with him. He sat beside her bed for hours, reading to her when she was awake. At the end of seven days, we were able to remove the bandage permanently and begin to wean her off the laudanum. The scar on her lip was healing nicely, and the doctor was especially pleased since it looked like she was going to be able to completely close her top and bottom lip when the healing was completed. He had warned us previously that sometimes a gap was left at the top of the mouth that could never fully close.

One day during that second week, I came into the dormitory to find that Esther had crawled into Sir Walker's lap as he was reading to her. The child's head was leaning on his shoulder, and both he and Esther looked completely at ease. I backed out of the room without either of them seeing me. I couldn't help wondering about this man—he brought up so many conflicting emotions in me.

After the second week, Esther was allowed to begin eating solid food. The scar was still quite red and obvious, but the pain had diminished, and we could pretend that she looked almost "normal." We had let her observe her reflection in a mirror, and she had fingered her upper lip and gazed at herself for a long time. After that, she slowly began to "forget" to cover her mouth with her hand. Her speech also dramatically improved. It was as if she had learned to speak already and had just been storing the knowledge in her head for the day that she was able to articulate it.

Sir Walker didn't come as often now but still visited several times a week. One day he caught me as I was entering my classroom. "It looks like Esther's healing is almost complete now."

"Yes," I admitted, and then added, "And if I haven't told you before, thank you so much for achieving this surgery. Her future is so much brighter now!"

"Well, no one could be happier about that than me," he answered and paused. "By the way, there is a carnival coming to Bristol this weekend. What would you think of taking Esther as a sort of celebration and attending together?"

This caught me off guard. I had heard something about a festival coming up, but I hadn't attended a fete since Billy had accosted me at the harvest celebration. "Do you mean we would take all the children?"

"No, I was thinking that just the three of us could attend one night. Of course, we might find a way to take all the children one of the afternoons, if we could talk the Cartwrights into it?" he offered.

"May I think about it?" I asked. It was Monday, and I had a little time before the weekend.

"Of course. I'll be back to see Esther in the morning, and we can talk more then."

The next day, I asked Angel if she could take over my classes for the morning, and I waited for Sir Walker, meeting him at the door of the Home. There was a teahouse just down our street, and when he arrived, I asked if we might step down the block.

After we were seated and he had brought us two cups of steaming liquid, I began. "Before I make any decisions concerning whether we go to the festival, I need to clear up some questions." I didn't want to sound too bold—he had been so compassionate toward Esther, and I was beginning to be very fond of him—but I simply had to know the answers. "We first saw you at the Crowing Rooster…and you were there with Lord Stanley," I faltered. "I have to ask, What is his part in all this, Sir Walker?"

He looked uncomfortable. "Please, don't we know each other well enough now for you to call me Edward? And yes, William and I are friends, good friends. He was staying with me at Rollinswood that week. We were both expecting the import of Arabian stallions aboard the *Star of Hope*, but she was late, and that was why we had entered the Rooster that particular day. And yes, William did recognize you."

I was waiting for him to go on, but he seemed to hesitate, so I asked, "Did Lord Stanley ask you to talk to me?"

"Well, he asked me to find out about you."

"What did he say about me?"

"Only that he had had dealings with you in the past that weren't pleasant and he wondered what you were doing here in Bristol."

"So…he asked you to follow me?"

"Well, not exactly. All I was supposed to do that first day was stay and ask questions. But then I met Mrs. Cartwright and found out about the Home, and then I became interested myself."

"And what did you tell Lord Stanley?"

"By the time our new horses had arrived and he left for Faringdon, I was able to reassure him that you were a teacher at the Home and, as far as I could tell, a respectable member of our community."

"Was he the one who told you that I'd been involved in herbal medicine for years?"

"No, that was Samuel. William said very little about you beyond what I've told you."

I sat and pondered this quietly for several minutes and then came to a decision. "Why do you want to take Esther and me to the festival? Is it just for Esther's sake?"

Now it was his turn to pause. "No, to be honest, it isn't. I may have set out to get to know you because William asked about you, but I've come to admire you very much, and my interest now is all my own," he finished.

I came to a conclusion. "I can't go on with this pretense," I stated. "I'm not who or what you believe I am, and it wouldn't be fair to continue with the charade."

"Please, Miss Alexander. I don't care what's in your past. I feel I know the person you are now, and that's the person I wish to be with."

I sighed again and came to a further decision. I told him my story, starting with my parents, not mentioning my mother's family, but including my Irish papist father. I talked about my childhood, my filly, and the nightmare of my father's death. Then I spoke of my mother's illness, my stint as a governess, and my firing. During my account, I mentioned my brief encounters with William and how much I had admired him and how, at the last, being totally without hope or help, I had gone to Faringdon to ask for his assistance. I did not spare words when I concluded with our last encounter and my theft of William's purse and escape. I spoke of being homeless on the streets of Bristol but did not tell him of my pregnancy.

He sat for a moment, not saying anything. I rose to leave, believing that our conversation was over, but he stayed me with a hand. "Please, Miss Alexander, please sit back down." I sat. "Nothing you have told me has changed the way I feel. Under the circumstances, you believed you had no other options. I cannot fault you for trying to save your mother's life, no matter what you felt you had to do."

This stunned me. "You'd still want to be with me, knowing I had sold myself…and stolen money?" I asked. "You can forgive me for that?"

"I believe you felt you had no other choice. And yes, that's easily forgiven," he concluded, looking me right in the eye. "Now, can we put the past in the past and talk about the future? Miss Alexander, can we please take Esther and go to the carnival this Saturday?"

With tears in my eyes, I replied, "Yes, and you might as well call me Kathryn."

Chapter 21

ROLLINSWOOD

The next Saturday, Edward and I did indeed take little Esther to the festival. She was so excited to go on an adventure with her two favorite people, but I could tell she was nervous about being among so many strangers. Many times, I caught her with her hand over her mouth, or flinching away if a bystander got too close to her, but for the most part, she greatly enjoyed herself, as did I. We both often smiled and even laughed, and I couldn't remember an occasion when I had felt so relaxed—not in a very long time. I believe Edward was having fun, too.

We stopped for treats several times—once for spiced bread, and another for potato custard, which Esther was able to eat with relish now. We walked among the myriad booths of vendors selling food and trinkets. Edward bought both Esther and me necklaces made of little colored shells, which we had both admired and wore proudly the rest of the afternoon. We avoided some of the entertainments— the cockfighting and bullbaiting, finding these both disgusting, not to mention inappropriate, for our small charge. But there were jugglers and tumblers, dancers, and mimes and too many things to see and do in just one afternoon. We did not stay for the evening music and dancing. Esther was so worn out in just a couple of hours that Edward had to carry her for the last bit, and we finally agreed that we needed to call it a day.

Once I had delivered Esther to her bed, I found Edward waiting for me in the hall. "I know you have duties during the week, and I don't want to impose, but you've told me several times of your interest in horses and about the filly you raised yourself. And I was wondering if, next Saturday, you'd like to come out and visit Rollinswood and inspect my stables and new stallion?" He paused, but when I didn't seem to know what to say, he hurried on. "We wouldn't have to stay all day. Just come for tea, and then we can have a look at the horses. My older sister who lives with me would very much like to meet you."

The mention of his sister gave me pause, as did the worry that Edward seemed to be getting too attached to me. But the thought of spending time with his horses was a temptation that was hard for me to resist; it had been so long, I told myself. And so I hesitantly made plans to ride out to his estate that next week.

Edward gathered me from the Home in his fancy calash pulled by a matched pair of bay hackneys. His liveried driver had dismounted and was standing in front of the geldings. Before mounting the carriage, I approached the near horse and held out my arm, allowing him to sniff my gloved hand. I could feel his soft muzzle and warm breath through the light cotton material, and it thrilled me. How I had missed this!

Edward handed me up into the carriage, murmuring, "You look lovely today, Kathryn," and I felt my cheeks blush. I knew I looked the same as always even though I had worn my best calico frock with my hair pulled back in a loose bun, but the compliment was still pleasant to hear. He had lowered the folding top on the convertible, as it was a fine day, and I reveled in the feel of the breeze on my face and the clip-clop of the horses' hooves as we trotted up the cobbled streets of Bristol and headed out into the country. With the driver up top, Edward was free to take the seat opposite to mine so that we could converse, which we did easily. He told me about his property, how many horses he owned, and his hopes for his new breeding program. It was the Earl of Faringdon's success at breeding and racing the crossbred Arabians, he said, that had gotten Edward interested in trying the same.

The baronet also told me about his two sisters. The older one, Lady Mary Walker, was unmarried and had lived with him all her life, even in the years before his wife had died. But Mary had her own apartments in the manor, and Edward was glad now to have her assistance in overseeing the house and staff. His younger sister, Lady Elizabeth Crawley, was also in residence on the estate at the moment, having come to stay in the Dower House for the summer. She had married the second son of an earl, and they lived in a town-house in London. But she and her three children regularly spent their summers at her childhood home in Bristol, claiming that the air in London precluded taking any outside exercise at all. Edward said he was always glad when his youngest sister came to visit; he was evidently very fond of her and her children.

As we pulled into the drive that wound up to the Rollinswood manor, I was impressed with the sloping lawns edged with stone walls, the green forest glens beyond. Edward had told me that he often rode out on the wooded trails of an evening, and I thought to myself how pleasant that would be. As Edward helped me down from the calash, I couldn't help noticing the two spaniels who were hopping up and down at the baronet's feet, vying for his attention. Reaching down at last, Edward stroked the ears of each dog in its turn. "This is Molly, and this one Rolly," he said, with obvious affection.

I had always wished for a dog, but with scarcely enough food to feed the three of us, Da had never even considered it. Now I reached down my hand, keeping my fingers protectively in a fist. Rolly approached first, sniffed, and then gave me a lick. Molly seemed a little shyer. I began stroking Rolly's long speckled hair, and he beamed up at me, lolling his tongue. "I can't believe how silky his ears are," I said incredulously, running my hand down his drooping appendage.

"Yes, these two are supposed to be hunting dogs, but they spend most of their time lazing in front of my fire grate in the house," Edward said, shaking his head good-naturedly. "They would both try and be lapdogs, if they were allowed, but my sister would draw the line at that!"

We next entered the manor house, the two dogs at our heels, being greeted formally by a butler, who showed us from the spacious hall into a brightly lit sitting room, its wall of windows facing down over a large colorful garden. An older woman clothed in an elegant green silk gown rose upon our entry, and Edward introduced me to his sister, Lady Mary Walker. Although she immediately asked me to call her Mary, still there was a stiffness about her, and her smile felt forced as I watched her assessing me.

Lady Mary said that tea would be served shortly and invited us to sit and chat. The two spaniels immediately plopped at Edward's feet. She asked about our drive and about the weather. I told her what a lovely room and view I thought was afforded there and asked if this might be a particular favorite of hers, as it seemed to me to be a perfect place to write correspondence or sit and read. She replied that, yes, it was a favorite and she hoped it would *always* be so and gave me a rather-piercing look.

At that moment, the door burst open and two young boys immediately sprinted toward Edward, who had stood and held out his arms. They were chanting, "Uncle, Uncle!" but their mother immediately called them back and warned them to behave like gentlemen, since they obviously had company. I was then introduced to Lady Elizabeth Crawley. Unlike her older sister, Lady Elizabeth greeted me with genuine warmth, her brown eyes, so much like Edward's, gleaming with pleasure. The two boys were presented as Harry and Michael, although I wasn't altogether sure which was which, as they didn't tend to stand in one place for long.

Behind Lady Elizabeth came her twelve-year-old daughter, Beth, whom I had already heard so much about. Beth's greeting was more tenuous. She politely said, "Nice to meet you, ma'am," but then immediately looked down at her feet. I recognized the gesture as one I had used so frequently in my own youth and felt an immediate bond with the girl. I also noticed that Molly had gone to rest her nose protectively against the girl's knee. Beth would never be considered beautiful—her upper lip was misshapen, her nose a little flatter than most, a faint scar below her nostrils. But knowing what she must have looked like before her surgery, one could almost forget that she might have once been considered disfigured. And later, as I sat and encouraged her to open up a little, I would think that she was almost pretty when she smiled.

When Elizabeth stood and said they needed to leave for an appointment, Edward complained, "Oh, Lizzie, do you have to go? And before tea?" The two boys, who had been perched on his lap, also expressed disappointment that they would miss the cook's biscuits, but they reluctantly followed their mother out the door. I was grateful when the maid brought in the tea set and cookies and Lady Mary proceeded to pour. Once we were seated again with cups and plate, she began to ask me pointedly about my family, where I had been raised, where I had been educated, where I was living now. For most of these questions, Edward would interrupt, "Sister, you know I have already told you that her father was a tradesman," or "Was from Uffington," or "That she had been taught by her mother, who was raised a gentlewoman."

I finally had to interject myself. "It's all right, Edward. I don't mind answering Lady Mary's questions. At present, I live with the Cartwrights at the Home for Needy Children in Bristol. I teach the younger children there and help Angel Cartwright in giving medicinal treatment to the poor of the city."

"I see" was her standard reply to each answer. I didn't blame her for being skeptical of me; her brother was a nobleman and obviously well-off. I'm sure she wondered how he could be interested in a commoner like me, even as a friend. I longed to tell her not to worry, that I had no plans for replacing her as lady of the manor, but of course, that would have been impossible to say out loud.

Finally, Edward stood and told his sister we had much to do before driving back into the city, and we left her with her own troubled thoughts in her beautiful sitting room. As we re-entered the hallway, he asked, "Would you like to have a tour of the house, Kate—may I call you that, Kate?"

"Yes, all my friends call me Kate. I was always Katie to my da, but…" I broke off for a moment as poignancy washed over me. "But, Edward, I would much rather see the stable and grounds." He smiled at me, and we left the house, the spaniels cavorting around us. The barns were a bit of a walk from the manor, but it was a beautiful day, and I was glad to be out in the sunshine. We walked through the main stable building, but the place was empty. His stalls and aisleway were not quite as grand as the ones at Faringdon but were still airy and clean, and I reveled in the smell of hay and the faint trace of manure. The horses, he told me, were all out to pasture, and we walked on out through the back door of the barn to where I could see at least ten horses grazing in the distance.

"These are my broodmares," Edward stated proudly. "My carriage and riding horses are stalled in the smaller stable," he said as he gestured to his right. "Most of my mares are of local stock, but I tried to pick the finest examples I could find. Several of them already have some Arab blood in them." One of the mares had ambled over toward us and had dropped her head over the fence. She was a golden chestnut color with a wide blaze down her face and a large, kind eye. "This is Kitty," Edward said and gently stroked the mare's nose. I held out my own hand for a sniff, and then the animal, realizing that we had no treats, dropped her head back to the grass and began grazing again. I inhaled deeply, scenting the rich, horsey odor that took me back to happy, earlier days.

Edward then took my hand. "Come on," he said excitedly, "I'll show you Chieftain. I asked my head groom to have him ready this afternoon. They should be back here in our training paddock." As we rounded the barn, I could see a servant standing outside a fenced pen that housed a beautiful, doeskin stallion. I had never seen a horse with this striking color before. His coat had the light tan hue of a deer, but his mane, tail, and all four legs were dark brown, almost black. His coat gleamed with shards of gold in the sunlight, and he took my breath away.

Upon seeing us approaching, the groom had entered the paddock and fastened a longe line on the stallion's head-collar. He now proceeded to ask the horse to trot in big circles around and around. "Watch Chief's smooth gait. Doesn't he cover the ground magnificently?" Edward asked proudly. Indeed, the horse looked like he was floating around the pen, his tail waving proudly above his back. Chieftain had the same dished face and proud arched neck that I had loved on Cloud and that had graced my own lovely filly. I could have stood and watched him show off for hours. When the groom asked him to move on into the canter, the horse tossed his head, snorted, and gave a little buck as he playfully charged into the graceful, faster gait. At last, the groom called for a walk, and the man and beast approached us.

"Oh, he is lovely, Edward," I gushed, reaching out my hand, but then reconsidering and pulling it back. "Does he bite?" Many stallions did have that nasty habit.

"No, not at all. Chieftain may look like a tiger, but he's wonderfully gentle. I'm hoping his progeny will get not only his speed but also his temperament." When we reluctantly left the paddock area, we walked back toward the house but then veered around to the back lawns, where I could see a landscaped reflecting pool and gazebo. Taking seats in the shade of the roof, Edward took off his hat and wiped his forehead. The afternoon had warmed considerably; the dogs lay panting at our feet.

And then he began to talk for the first time about his departed wife. He admitted to me that he had loved her deeply despite their arranged marriage. She was the daughter of a nobleman, and they had been intended for each other from a young age. Married for five years, she had experienced three miscarriages, her health failing more after each one. He divulged to me with remorse that the physicians had all warned them against trying to have more children—they said she didn't have the constitution for it—but his wife would not listen to them, would not listen to him, insisting that she would rather die than remain barren and not produce an heir. And he had given in to her. And it had cost them her life.

He went on to say that he had told himself he would never put another woman through that again. He had no interest in finding another wife anyway. One happy marriage was enough for any man, he had thought. "But then you came along, Kate. I didn't think I could ever find another woman I could love as I did Elsbeth, but I have."

I was shaking my head, looking at my hands rather than his face. "Oh, Edward." But I didn't know what to say or how to explain.

"Don't speak of it now, Kate. I wasn't expecting you to jump into anything. But I just wanted you to know my intentions. You are kind and beautiful, and I am hoping you will allow me to court you, even though I must seem old and unattractive to such a young woman as yourself."

I was still shaking my head, but at this last, I raised my eyes to look at him. "Your offer flatters me very much, Edward. Your own gentleness and kindness make you the very most attractive kind of man. It's just...it's just..." I was shaking my head again.

He reached over and took my chin, softly lifting my head to look at him again. "Please don't answer me now. Just think about it. Promise me you will." He kept holding my gaze, so I nodded, and we left it at that. But all the way home in the carriage, I could think of nothing but what he had said. His older sister had judged me correctly: I was not worthy of her brother. I was not "pure" enough for him. He deserved someone of more noble character.

My thoughts continued as we rode along in the fading light of the afternoon, he allowing me my silent contemplations. But hadn't Edward already told me that he could forgive my past transgressions? Hadn't he said they didn't matter to him? And hadn't I believed him? If he felt that my mistakes were not at issue, then what might be my answer? And still I found that there was an unseen barrier that I couldn't seem to decipher.

When we finally reached the Home, William handed me down from the carriage and stayed me for a moment with his hand on my arm. "One final proposal, Kathryn, please, please consider...we could bring Esther home to be our own little girl...bring as many orphans home as you wished. I would like nothing better than a whole houseful of children. That is, if I had someone like you to be their mother." And with that, he reached forward and kissed me lightly on the cheek and then remounted the carriage and drove away.

Chapter 22

FORGIVENESS

I slept little that night. This time, it was not nightmares that arrested my sleep. How wonderful would it be to have a husband like Edward, gentle and considerate, one who loved children as I did? How satisfying might it seem to have a field full of horses at my disposal, to ride into the woods of an evening with my husband, to never have to worry about my future? And best of all, how blessed to be able to give Esther a real home, and maybe others, too, maybe even my own babe? This last thought caught somewhere between my heart and my throat. No, I would never deserve another child of my own, as only I understood. But still, why not the rest?

Since Edward had absolved me of my past, then what was causing my reluctance? Deep in my heart, I knew the answer. I had asked my mother once upon a time how I would know when I was truly in love, when it was "right." And her answer had been, "When you know you can't live without that person, when you would give up anything to be with him." That was not the way I felt about Edward. There was only one person in the world who would answer to that description for me. And I couldn't marry Edward knowing that he wasn't the one.

I was not surprised to find the baronet at the door to my classroom the very next morning. His pretense was to inquire about Esther, but we both knew he'd come to judge my reaction to the previous day's questions. Leaving my students with a reading task, I walked out to the street with him. He started to say something, but I interrupted him. "Edward, I did a lot of thinking last night. You're a wonderful man, and you've offered me the most blessed future. I'm so grateful that you've honored me in this fashion, and it's truly caused a change in my heart—you *must* believe that. But I can't continue with a courting relationship in good faith. I can't marry you, and most likely, will never marry. This is something that only has to do with me, not you. Please forgive me, but we mustn't continue to see each other, not in that way."

He was silent for a long moment. I believe he had been expecting this answer and was doing his best to accept it. "Can we continue to be friends?" he asked quietly. "I'd hate to have to stop coming by to see the children."

"Yes, I would love that, as long as there are no misunderstandings. The students here all love to see you, especially Esther. Please don't stop coming on account of me." He took my hand and kissed the top of it and then departed without another word. He would continue to visit with us at least once a week, and both of us found it possible, as time went by, to ease into a more comfortable friendship.

My words had not been idle when I told Edward that he had helped to change my heart. I had started attending the Home's morning devotionals and weekly worship. It had occurred to me that if a human here on earth could forgive me of my past sins, then perhaps the Lord in heaven could also. Angel had been telling me about God's love for months, but her words had not been able to sink below my defenses. Somehow, hearing those same words of forgiveness from Edward had made God's love seem possible. Not everything that Pastor Samuel said from the pulpit rang true to me now, but at least I was beginning to listen.

Three weeks later, my world fell apart. Esther developed a severe illness in both ears. She would claw at the sides of her head and cry in frustration. Edward brought the physician by several times. I did not allow him to bleed her, but we used hot compresses against her head to ease her misery and he dosed her several times with evil-smelling medicines. We tried washing her ears out with spirits in case she had retained water, but nothing helped. I eventually started her on laudanum again, when the pain became so intense that she couldn't sleep at all. Angel and Samuel prayed over her ceaselessly.

Finally, her fever spiked and she went into convulsions and lost consciousness. We tried cooling her in a tub of water, but her skin continued to burn. I sat with her day and night throughout, but on the fourth of her illness, she gave up the fight. I wanted to die too. I was inconsolable. I pushed everyone, including Edward, away. Shutting myself up in my room, I sat and just rocked on my bed. I felt unable to attend the funeral that Samuel said for Esther, or her graveside ceremony. I wondered if this was just more of God's punishment for me. I could neither eat nor sleep.

Finally, Angel came and entered my room, disregarding my "Please leave me alone." Sitting on my bed, she said quietly, "I know how much you loved Esther. We all did, but you the most. And she loved you dearly, too." By this time, I'd cried so long and hard that there were no more tears in me. For the last day and a half, I had only been able to sit and stare. Angel's words were barely audible in my head. She continued, "You did the very best you could for her. You know, she got her life back here. Remember how forlorn the little waif was when we first discovered her? But she found love and acceptance, and her surgery gave her hope of a future."

"What future?" I murmured. "Why would God give her hope just to take it all away from her again? She never did a thing to hurt anyone else. Why didn't he take me instead?" I finally choked out the question that had been on my heart for days.

"We can't understand God's decisions and timing," Angel continued quietly. "I don't have that answer for you. But I *can* tell you this: Esther's hope has been realized. She is whole and beautiful and will never feel pain again. She is dancing with the angels in heaven. She was such a sweet child that I suspect she is sleeping in the very lap of our Lord."

I stared at Angel, hardly comprehending her words. What had she said? Something about Esther being in heaven? I asked her to repeat herself, which she did, and the words confounded me. "Both Mama and Da taught me church doctrine," I told her. "They said that children were born into sin and, until they performed their catechisms and sacraments, they could not go to heaven. A baby's death outside of the rites was hopeless."

At this, Angel went to retrieve her Holy Bible and showed me where it said that Jesus loved the little children, that he called the little children, and that we all needed to receive the kingdom of God as little children.[5] She explained that the members of the Way believed that children, although born with a sin nature, were innocent until they were old enough to really understand right from wrong and to make eternal decisions. At around the age of twelve, she said, or perhaps a little younger, God began calling them to repentance.

It was more than I could take in. But I asked her to clarify. "Then you are saying that Esther is in heaven right now?"

"Yes, I believe that with all my heart," she reassured. "Christ's blood covers all innocents, including us, when we have faith." I began to choke on my sobs. This was not merely about Esther. Ever since the stillborn birth of my own child, I had buried the fear that *my* choices, *my* failures had brought an innocent life into the world only to have that soul lost eternally through no fault of its own. The guilt over this had been slowly eating me alive.

I could not completely believe what Angel was telling me, but I felt a glimmer of hope stirring in my breast. Angel left me with her Bible and encouraged me to try reading the New Testament for myself, and that was exactly what I began to do. The change in me did not happen overnight, nor was I able to overcome my grief over Esther's death immediately, but it was not long before I was at least back in the classroom and going on missions of mercy with Angel. And eventually, I was baptized into the Way, finally coming to the belief that I could be and had been forgiven for everything through Jesus's blood and that, someday, I would see both Esther and Anne—I had finally named my baby girl after my mother—again one day in heaven.

---

5. Holy Bible (NIV), Luke 18:15–17; Matthew 18:2–4; Ezekiel 18:20.

PART III

Bristol, 1736

Chapter 23

THE HOWARDS

That next spring, my world changed again. Angel and I had been called to stitch up a man who had fallen through a rotten staircase while drunk and had no money for a physician. When we had returned to the Home, Edward was just finishing his weekly visit with the children and asked if I might enjoy taking tea with him. We hadn't gotten to spend any time together in the last month, and so I agreed, just asking for a few moments to go and put on a clean apron and jacket.

We walked down to the nicer part of town, where there was a "pleasure garden" that I had never visited. This was an outdoor shop that boasted paved pathways through ornamental flower beds interspersed with tables, where one could sit, order tea, and listen to roving minstrels. It was still a bit chilly for early April, but the sun was bright and Edward was in a cheery mood, telling me all about his new crop of foals and how pleased he was with them.

Several couples had wandered by, enjoying the early budding flowers, mainly tulips, lilies, and flowering shrubs, that had been planted along the paths. As a pair of older women came abreast of us, the younger of the two stopped abruptly and seemed to be staring at me. Edward stood and addressed the older one. "It's Lady Howard, isn't it? Sir Edward Walker at your service. We met two years ago at your cousin's estate in Bradford."

The lady in question looked at him rather severely but then seemed to recognize him. "Oh, yes, I do remember." She seemed a little vague. "And this is my sister, Lady Marguerite Smithson, whom I am visiting," she finished. Both women were dressed in the clothes of the aristocracy, the older one tall and thin with a narrow face and grey eyes, the younger one, shorter and rounder with blue eyes that were staring at me.

Edward then took the opportunity of introducing me. I stood to give a brief curtsy, acknowledging the two ladies. But at the mention of the name Howard, I had tensed. I had not heard my mother's maiden name since I was a little child. The younger woman was still staring at me. "Marguerite, whatever is wrong with your manners?" her sister asked stiffly.

"Bethany, I feel like I'm seeing a ghost. This young woman looks exactly like our sister Anne the last time we saw her. I can't get over the resemblance. And now I've noticed that she's wearing a pendant with our family crest. What can this mean?"

Edward was looking at me questioningly. I'm sure my face, which had gone pale, was giving away its secrets. So he suggested, "Why don't we all take a seat and perhaps sort this out?"

When we were settled, I spoke first. "My mother's name was Anne Marie Howard Alexander." At this, both women gave a little gasp. I reached back and unclasped the silver chain and placed the locket on the table, opening it so the picture of my grandmother was revealed.

"How can this be?" the older woman started. "Why have we never heard before that our sister was alive?"

"My mother died only three years ago," I answered. "I believe your father disowned her when she married."

Now the younger woman spoke. "We never knew what became of Anne—no one would tell us anything. I just assumed she was dead. I don't know why. Oh, won't Mother be surprised and pleased to hear that we have discovered Anne's daughter?"

At the news that my grandmother Howard was still alive and might want to meet me, my heart gave a squeeze. But could it really be so? We all went on to briefly exchange family narratives. My older aunt, Bethany Howard, had never married and still lived at Howard Manor at Bradford on the River Avon. After my grandfather Richard Howard had died, leaving no male heirs, his nephew, Lord Eugene Howard, had inherited the title and estate and was kind enough to allow Bethany to continue in residence in the Dower House with my grandmother, Lady Clarista, the dowager countess. Lord Eugene and his wife, Lady Estelle, had three children, a boy and two girls.

My aunt Marguerite lived right here in Bristol and was a widow. Her husband had been a third son of a baronet and had become a banker but had been dead some ten years now. Her two grown daughters were both married and lived in London. "I tried living there with my eldest daughter, but that city is just too busy and dirty for me," she explained. "So I came back home to live, and my daughters travel to see me once a year. I miss them terribly, but I'm happier here," she concluded.

Then it was my turn, and I gave them only the briefest account of my life, merely saying that I had come to work and live at the Home for Needy Children here in Bristol after both of my parents were gone. I did explain about Mother's consumption but did not mention how Da had died. Hearing my short history, Marguerite seemed to have an idea. "Kathryn, you *must* come and stay with me, at least for a while. It will give us a chance to really get acquainted. And I'll be traveling to Howard Manor for the Feast of St. George in less than a fortnight, and you should accompany me. Mother will want to meet you, I'm sure!"

As we parted ways that afternoon, I had many thoughts waging war in my head. Would my grandmother really want to see me? Did I want to get involved with the family that had disowned my mother and disdained my father? And how would they feel toward me if they learned my full history? Edward, for his part, encouraged me to go and stay with my aunt, at least for a little while. "What can it hurt, Kate?" Indeed, I thought, it might hurt a great deal.

Angel urged me to pray about the decision and seek God's will. She reminded me that I was welcome to come back to the Home at any time. There would always be a place for me there. But if I didn't go and see my grandmother now, I might never have the chance again. I struggled with the question, Where did God really want me to be? Prayer and listening for the answer were still so new to me. Eventually, as much as I hated to leave the children and the Cartwrights, I packed up my few belongings and began a new chapter in my life. If I had known of the danger awaiting me there, would I have gone? I was still such a coward.

Aunt Marguerite turned out to be a delightful host, albeit sometimes almost childish in her enthusiasm. She seemed truly glad to have me as her guest, and I believe I eased some of her loneliness. She lived in a large two-story house attended by a maid named Nancy, a cook, and a caretaker. My bedroom contained a charming, canopied bed and had a window that looked out over the small but well-tended garden. That first morning, we took our breakfast in the sunny morning room and chatted happily for several hours. I listened to the stories of the mischief her girls had gotten into as children. And she seemed quite interested in my life at the Home, the orphans, and the medical cases that Angel and I had attended to. But she especially wanted to hear about my mother.

After lunch, she brought up the subject of my wardrobe, which she felt needed to be refurbished. To be honest, she sought to discard all three of my frocks and begin anew. For my part, I did not want to accept her financial assistance, and we did have a bit of a disagreement over this. But in the end, she convinced me that I couldn't possibly travel to Howard Manor or meet my grandmother unless I was properly clothed. She was so very excited about the trip! So I reluctantly agreed to allow her seamstress to come and measure me, and we eventually settled on two muslin day dresses and two evening gowns, one of dark-blue silk trimmed in contrasting pale-blue taffeta, and the other a floral Chinese pattern. Both would have a full, hooped skirt gathered at a narrow waist, with short matching jackets. I found I also needed a chemise of thin linen and lace, both silk and cotton stockings, and new slippers. I drew the line at heeled evening shoes, jeweled pins, and hooded velvet cloaks. I simply couldn't accept that much charity, and besides, I knew I would probably never wear most of the things again.

Aunt Marguerite and I spent the next several days visiting the shops in Bristol that catered to the gentry, looking at fashions and picking out the materials that would become my new wardrobe. I must admit that this was a novel and instructive experience for me, and one that I enjoyed. But judging from her enthusiasm, I believe that Aunt Marguerite's enjoyment was even greater, as she almost skipped from store to store, chattering to the shopkeepers about our upcoming trip. The first time my aunt introduced me as Lady Alexander, I was caught completely off guard and politely requested that she just use *miss* instead, but she wouldn't hear of it. I was a Howard and a lady, and that was that! The week and a half of preparations for our trip seemed to fly by, and before I had caught my breath, we were in a hired coach on our way to Howard Manor.

Chapter 24

HOWARD MANOR

I t was only a few hours before we had clattered through Bradford, the coachman blowing his horn, and then we were pulling up the long drive that was the entrance to the Earl of Avon's estate. I was too nervous to note much about my surroundings. The entrance, lawns, terraces, even the manor house itself all reminded me of Faringdon Manor. But I had never before arrived at any manse in a coach and four. As the carriage pulled up in the circular drive before the great house, several liveried servants scurried out to head the horses, lower the steps, and assist my aunt and me out of the passenger compartment, her maid, Nancy, following behind us. The grand treatment had me feeling nervous and out of place.

We were greeted by a butler and shown through the large marble-floored foyer into what I presumed was the library, where a tall, thin man with a mustache stood from behind his desk and greeted my aunt. I had walked in behind her, keeping my eyes on her back, as was my usual comfort-custom. But she stepped aside and said, "Cousin Eugene, may I present Lady Kathryn Alexander, my late sister Anne's daughter. Kathryn, this is Lord Eugene Howard, Earl of Avon."

I dropped into a curtsy and then forced my eyes up to look into his face. He registered such shock that I could tell Aunt Marguerite had not given him any forewarning, which surprised me. Lord Howard soon regained his composure and greeted me coolly. Without any further conversation, we were ushered back out into the hall and led upstairs to our rooms to "freshen up from our trip" before meeting with Lady Estelle. Since they had not been expecting me as an extra guest, the housekeeper was fluttering around, trying to make new arrangements. The house was large, with many guestrooms, but I was made to understand, by tomorrow, they were all to be full and every bedchamber on the second floor already assigned.

The housekeeper was very flustered. "I'm so sorry, Lady Alexander, we just weren't expecting you." The poor woman was almost stumbling over her words. "We could either have you share a room with your aunt or we can put you in a small bedroom on the third floor." Aunt Marguerite and I both knew that the third floor would be relegated to the children, nanny, and governess, along with servants' quarters, which might also be located in the attic.

Aunt Marguerite said immediately, "You must come and share a bed with me, Kathryn. I won't have you sleeping abovestairs with the servants." But I was feeling rather overwhelmed and believed the privacy on the third floor might be more to my liking. I reassured my aunt that this would not be my first time sleeping with servants. I reminded her that I had been a governess myself at one point, and so she relented, and I found myself following the housekeeper through a closed door at the end of the hall and up a narrow flight of stairs, which I knew would be the one the maids used. I was shown into a small chamber, which seemed comfortable enough to me. And shortly, Nancy came up, carrying my small trunk of clothing, and told me she would be staying right next door so it would be convenient if I needed anything.

Once I had washed my face and hands in the basin provided in my room and had smoothed my hair back into its bun at my nape, I met Aunt Marguerite at the door to her room and we proceeded together back down the grand staircase to the main hall.

The butler then showed us to Lady Howard's sitting room, where we were expected for tea. Lady Estelle was the opposite of her husband physically, short and plump where he was tall and thin, but her cool expression seemed to mimic the one I had seen on him just a half-hour earlier. It was obvious that she had been "warned" of my presence. And while she was not unfriendly, neither was she welcoming. Aunt Marguerite seemed not to notice this, or else she was just choosing to ignore it, and so I took my cues from her.

"And how has my mother been since I was last here?"

"I'm sure you will see for yourself when you take your supper tonight with the dowager. But I believe you will find her tolerable enough. We do not see much of her here in the manor these days."

"And how are your children? Mark must be, what, thirteen now?"

This was a subject the countess seemed to warm to, and she told us proudly of his educational prowess, what an excellent equestrian he was becoming, what a handsome gentleman, etc. They were expecting to send him off to Eton to attend boarding school in the near future, a prospect that made his mother quite sad. "I will miss him dreadfully when he goes. He is just my dearest boy." Turning to me, she added, "I believe you will be introduced to him before you leave to sup with your grandmother."

Tea was served then, but I remember wondering why nothing had been said about her two daughters, and I resolved to bring up that subject when the opportunity presented itself. Lady Estelle poured and served, and then I asked if I was to be introduced to her daughters as well as her son tonight.

"Oh, I doubt it," she said, shaking her head. "Their governess rarely brings them downstairs. They are so young, you know." I had been led to believe they were nine and eleven, old enough, surely, to meet visitors, especially relatives. But then I remembered how the squire's children had been sequestered away in their schoolroom and wondered if this was common among the gentry. It wasn't long until Lady Howard stood, our interview obviously over, and Aunt Marguerite and I took our leave.

But as we neared the door, the countess called my aunt back for a moment, and it was clear I was to step on out of the room. The butler was nowhere to be seen, having carried out the tea tray not long before, and I wondered if I should wait for my aunt or leave, but go where? I didn't really mean to eavesdrop, but the door to the sitting room hadn't been closed, and though I'd moved a few paces on down the hall, I could still hear their voices.

"But how do you know she is who she claims to be?" Lady Howard was asking.

"Why, she's the very image of her mother, my sister. I should have known her anywhere!"

"But that's no proof. Anyone might look like a Howard. My husband is very concerned that she might be an impostor, seeking us out for monetary or social gain."

"Estelle, I can assure you that Kathryn did not seek us out. We found *her* sitting with Sir Edward Walker, taking tea, when we were passing by, and I was the one who recognized *her*. She also bears the family locket with my mother's picture in it. Please, rest assured. Lady Kathryn *is* my sister's daughter. There's no doubt!" And with that, my aunt came out of the room.

Before we left for the Dower House, we were indeed introduced to Lord Mark Howard. He was going to be tall like his father and already had the same disdainful look on his face upon our introductions that I had seen on both of his parents' visages. He stood straight and tall next to Lord Howard and might have been handsome if he had been smiling. It was obvious that he knew he was going to be an earl one day and was already practicing his airs. I was glad that we did not stay long in any conversation but excused ourselves and headed out through the gardens.

The house where my grandmother took her residence was much smaller than the manor, but still a good-size, two-story brick made in the same style as the mansion. It was situated behind the larger house, and one had only to traverse through a garden and down a few steps, an easy journey unless one was an invalid. The Dower House had its own small staff, and of course, Grandmother Clarista also had her daughter Bethany in residence to help care for her.

Aunt Marguerite and I were shown into a small sitting room, where we found both older ladies waiting for us. Grandmother did not rise, but Marguerite went immediately to her and kissed her cheek. Then, holding out her hand to me, she said, "Mother, this is Kathryn, Anne's daughter." It was obvious that the old lady—and she did look very old—had been expecting me. With her hand on her bosom, she gazed at me through rheumy eyes and then began to silently weep.

"Come here, my child," she invited through her tears. "I've waited a very long time to meet you." And then I began to cry, too. I bent down and put my arms around my grandmother, Marguerite put her arms around both of us, and we wept together for just a bit. I noticed that Aunt Bethany just stood off a ways, and it was hard to read her expression. After we all regained our composure, I sat on a little stool at my grandmother's knee, and we began to get acquainted. At some point, our dinner was brought in on trays and placed before us on small tables, and I realized that we were to eat here. I would learn later that it was very difficult for my grandmother to get around and she often took her meals this way.

We talked all through our dinner, and then, stating that we were wearing her mother out, Aunt Bethany told us it was time to take our leave. But I promised to come back again the next day, and then Marguerite and I retraced our steps through the darkening garden and up the stairs to our rooms. Nancy attended to her mistress first, and I was already in my bed and reading my evening scriptures when she knocked and asked if I needed anything. I assured her that I was fine, and then she asked what time I wanted to rise in the morning. She informed me that the men usually breakfasted at eight o'clock, the women somewhat later in the morning room. I replied that she wouldn't need to call me as I was used to being up before dawn, and then I gratefully blew out my candle and laid my head on my pillow, thanking God that I had made the decision to come to Howard Manor.

Chapter 25

LORD MARK

The next morning, I heard the pad of servants' feet moving down the hall before sunup. Rising, I availed myself of the chamber pot and washstand and then made my morning devotions, a habit from the Home that I was determined to keep. Since I knew it would be several hours before the women of the household were to breakfast, I donned my warmest shawl and decided to explore the grounds of the manor.

Leaving by the massive front door, I traveled back down the gravel drive and headed for the river, which I could see in the near distance. The drive crossed the stream via an old stone bridge over arched spans that reminded me very much of the bridge in Uffington. I spent a while looking down into the water and thinking about my mother and the probability that she had stood on this very bridge when she was young. Grandmother had asked me so many questions about Mama the evening before, and it had provoked memories that I had not recalled in years.

I spent the next hour exploring the gardens and terraces that I had seen so briefly on the drive yesterday and then went back to my room to prepare for breakfast, although Nancy warned me that Marguerite and most of the other women were not yet up. So I wandered down the hall to the door of the classroom, which was ajar. I could see two girls, who must have been Jane and Martha. I apologized for interrupting their class and introduced myself to

Miss Smith, their governess. Her thin frame was draped in a black uniform and she had pulled her hair into a severe bun at the nape of her neck. I felt instant empathy for her.

I was a little surprised that Mark wasn't in attendance, but exchanging glances among themselves, they quickly explained that he had a private tutor, as he was preparing for entrance into Eton. At my mention that I had once been a governess for three children, Miss Smith invited me to sit and chat, and the three of us were soon sharing information about our favorite books and subjects. I found the two girls, aged nine and eleven, to be very polite, if a little shy, but the more we talked, the more they opened up. All three of them seemed starved for company and attention.

As we got to know one another better, they began to speak more freely, and I soon discovered that, indeed, they had been mostly relegated to the third floor, although Miss Smith was allowed to take them for walks in the gardens. But they were not often invited to join any adult functions in the house, nor did they attend church services on Sundays. This must be a very lonely, isolated life, I thought. When I asked about Mark, again they shared glances. Their brother, it seemed, had been invited into the adult world from a much earlier age and had studied with a private tutor for the last three years. He no longer slept in his third-floor bedroom but now had lodgings down near his parents, a change that had greatly relieved his sisters and governess. When I asked about this, they confided that Mark had been a spoiled, mean brother who often tormented and abused the girls and his teacher with absolutely no repercussions. They all seemed glad that he was mostly out of their world now, although he still came up to the classroom on occasion and could still be cruel.

Once Aunt Marguerite was finally up and dressed, we breakfasted together in the morning room. This was a very casual affair, the crullers, sausages, and egg tarts being just left on the buffet for the ladies to serve themselves as they appeared in the room. There seemed to always be a maid on hand to pour tea and carry away plates, but we saw no one else, either hosts or guests. After we had finished eating, Aunt Marguerite gave me a tour of the house she had been raised in, at least those rooms where she felt we would not be intruding on the Howards. There were servants scurrying everywhere, performing last-minute cleaning and preparation for the guests who were scheduled to arrive later, and we did our best to stay out of everyone's way.

With its mirrored walls and multitudinous candle sconces, the ballroom was clearly the most impressive room in the manor. Its length ran down almost one full side of the first floor, although it was not nearly so wide, with arched, paneled beams running across the ceiling at regular intervals. The floor was gleaming, Dutch oak hardwood. Across the hall was the large drawing room, wainscoted and painted with a marble slab over the fireplace. It also contained a spinet piano at one end. Not being able to help myself, I found I was approaching the piano, opening the keyboard and running my fingers over the ivories.

"Do you play, Kathryn?" my aunt asked.

"I haven't touched a piano in three years, but Mama taught me from an early age."

"Yes, she always loved our piano forte. Won't you please sit down and play something? I used to love to sit and listen to your mother practice." I didn't need any more encouragement. Sitting before the instrument, I let my fingers decide what to do, and soon I was playing one of Bach's psalms that I must have played hundreds of times as a girl. It took me back to the days when Mother and I would worship together on a Sunday morning. But soon, maids were entering the room, bearing large vases of flowers, and my aunt and I decided it was time to visit the Dower House.

We spent several very pleasant hours with Grandmother. We lunched on soup and braised fish with jellies for dessert. The dowager countess stressed to me that she had never wanted to disown my mother but that her husband had insisted on it. She admitted that it had been her own decision that had sent the oxcart with the piano forte to us and that the earl had been furious when he had found out about it. During all our conversation, Aunt Bethany remained stoically uninvolved. And when Grandmother began to nod after lunch, she suggested it was time for us to go.

Aunt Marguerite and I took our time walking through the lovely gardens, which sported roses and lilies already in bloom. I asked her why Aunt Bethany seemed so distant. "Don't you know, dear, she was always so jealous of your mother. Anne was the youngest, the prettiest, the favorite of both our parents. When Father announced her betrothal to the marques, Bethany was furious, feeling that being the eldest daughter, she should have been chosen. It made no difference that we all knew the grandee was a horrid man, but very rich."

She paused and then went on. "And of course, then there was your father. He taught the three of us young ladies how to ride, and I think we were all just a little smitten with him, although neither Bethany nor I would have done what your mother did in choosing to run off with him. But I believe my older sister was even a little jealous of *that*. I'm afraid that when she looks at you, she can't help but feel some of her old resentments, especially now that life and marriage have seemingly passed her by." I was very sorry to hear that and determined to try to win my oldest aunt over with kindness.

When Marguerite made her apologies and headed off to her room for a nap, I decided to wander down to the barns to see what horses might be stabled there. Entering the largest barn, I observed a horse standing in crossties about halfway down the aisle and a stable hand busily grooming him. As I headed toward them, I passed by an open stall and a movement caught my eye. A young man—I saw it was Lord Mark—was looking at something in the corner of the cell. As my eyes adjusted to the dim light, I saw with delight that it was a mother cat with what looked to be several newborn kittens. They were mewling and paddling their little paws, their eyes not yet open.

I was drawn to the little family, perhaps just as Mark was. As I entered the stall, Mark was bending down to pick up one of the small animals. I saw the mother cat draw back her face in a hiss, showing her gleaming, needle teeth, but he ignored her. Right as his fingers closed over the fuzzy kitten, she struck out lightning-fast with her claws and connected with Lord Mark's arm. It was obvious he had been scratched, because he jerked back his arm, the newborn still clutched in his fist. He howled in fury, calling the mother cat a filthy name, and then, in a pique of anger, hurled the tiny animal he was holding against the wall of the stall.

I cried in outrage and grabbed his arm. "Stop it! Why did you do that? The mother was only trying to protect her kittens."

The boy shook my hand loose and turned his fury on me. "How dare you touch me! Don't you know who I am?" Now the groom had come to stand in the doorway. I had let go of the boy's arm and was bending over the prostrate kitten. It was dead, its neck probably broken.

"Yes, I know who you are. But no one has the right to treat an innocent animal so," I said, standing upright again.

"I can do anything I wish. These are my animals—all of them!" he said, making a grand gesture indicating the whole barn. "And if I want to kill them all, I will."

Now he was striding out of the stall, the groom stepping back quickly to get out of his way, and Lord Mark marched on down the aisle and out of sight. The stable hand just shook his head and gave me a pitying look. I wasn't sure if the commiseration was for me, for the dead kitten, or for himself having to work for such an unbearable master.

Chapter 26

THE GUESTS

That afternoon and evening, the Howards' guests began arriving amid much excitement and commotion as servants scurried about, carrying trunks and showing visitors to their rooms. Tonight would be an informal evening. Tomorrow was the St. George's Day celebration, and there would be a parade in town, followed by a formal dinner and dancing at Howard Manor. Aunt Marguerite also informed me that in two days following the holiday, there was to be racing at Baringfield, the estate of the Earl of Bath. Many of the visitors who would be staying with us for two nights would then travel to Lord George Herbert's estate, as he had invited all the gentry who owned racehorses to lodge with him at Baringfield Hall for two more nights.

Hearing Lord George Herbert's name again made my stomach jump. And then another thought crossed my mind. Would Lord William Stanley also be among the guests there for the racing? Would he be among the guests here? Suddenly, I had a profound interest (and dread) in who was arriving in the fancy coaches and carriages that were pulling up in front of Howard Manor. I made my excuses to Aunt Marguerite and went to sit in a quiet corner of the front parlor, facing a window, so that I could watch the guests' arrival without notice. With the door to the parlor open, I could also hear the announcements made by the butler.

The visitors' arrivals took all afternoon. I counted fourteen guests in all, besides my aunt and me. There were three baronets, two with their wives, one single (Edward was not among them); a second son of a baronet, also single; the Marques of Stratford, his wife, and his two daughters; a baron and baroness; and finally, the Earl of Bath and his countess, the Lady Melinda Herbert. Evidently, after the demise of William's fiancé, Grace, Lord George had married someone else, a very beautiful woman, indeed, the most beautiful woman that had arrived that afternoon. There was still no sign of William, for which I was grateful.

I finally gave up my vigilant post and went upstairs to change for dinner, choosing my Chinese-print gown. Nancy came to help me dress and to do my hair, but I encouraged her to leave it in a simple bun and attend to my aunt. At the presentations before dinner, as we sipped wine in the drawing room, I was introduced as Lady Kathryn Alexander, granddaughter to the late Earl of Avon, second cousin to the present earl. I had not previously met any of the guests, and there were no surprises. I watched closely for any recognition from Lord Herbert as we were introduced, but he gave me only a cursory glance as I curtsied in front of him, and then his attention moved back to his wife. I had not seen the earl in the years since Lambourne, but his imperious posture and contemptuous countenance left me feeling as uneasy as ever. Lord Howard's son, Viscount Mark, was also among the dinner guests, and he delivered a very cold greeting indeed, as did his father. I wondered if Mark had described our encounter in the barn to Lord Howard.

Just as we were about to go in to dinner, two late arrivals were announced: the Earl of Faringdon and his brother, Lord Clarence Stanley. Whatever appetite had survived the other introductions now left me. As we proceeded on into dinner, I found myself concentrating on my feet, on the chair, on the china and plated silver in front of me. I had been seated between Aunt Marguerite and the baron and his wife, Lord and Lady Rothschild, at the foot end of the table. Lord and Lady Herbert were down near the head of the table, next to Lord and Lady Howard and their son. The marques and marchioness had been given the seats of honor next to the hosts. Lord William and his brother were next to them.

Even though there was quite a distance between us, given the twenty-one diners, I still found myself glancing down the table, watching for a glimpse of William. And I fancied that he was sometimes doing the same thing, but I saw no smile, no hint of any emotion, positive or negative, between us. He must be surprised and conjecturing at what I was doing here among these gentry, I thought. I was also waiting to see if there would be trouble between William and the man who Lady Grace had purported to run off with. But the two earls seemed to ignore each other, which I hoped was for the best.

I could not say what was served at that evening meal, whether roast beef or fowl, vegetable or fruit. I merely picked at the food on my plate, serving out the time before I could escape to my room. The kind, older gentleman sitting to my right did his best to engage me in conversation, as did my aunt, but my mind was too preoccupied to do much more than just be polite. Aunt Marguerite, however, was having a grand time and possibly a little too much to drink. I could forgive her for this, knowing the lonely existence she usually led. And besides, her chattering made it easier for me to be contemplative.

After desserts had been served, we were all directed across the hall, many of the men heading for the cardroom, while the rest of us went into the drawing room. I was relieved to see William leave with the men, although his brother and two of the other single gentlemen attended the women. Footmen were serving brandy, sherry, and port from silver trays, but I took nothing and chose a seat in a corner where I hoped I could watch the proceedings without attention.

Aunt Marguerite came and sat near me, as did the baron and his wife, our companions from dinner. The Rothschilds were an older couple, very kind and friendly, and they helped keep my aunt occupied. The marques' daughters were called upon to play at the spinet, and our conversations were soon accompanied by competent, if not exceptional, music. I noticed that Lord Clarence was giving most of his attention to the more attractive of the two sisters, a fair-haired girl with a very low-cut bodice. He was also sharing remarks and even a wink or two with the beautiful Countess of Bath.

At some point not long after we had entered the drawing room, the single baronet (he reintroduced himself to me as Sir Thomas Stanton) approached our corner and began making conversation with our little group. He asked me if I was planning on attending the racing in three days, and I shook my head. But Aunt Marguerite interrupted with a chortle and said that, most certainly, we *would* be going, that everyone from the Howards' house party was expected to continue to Baringfield and she was looking very much forward to it. I worriedly noticed that she had another glass of sherry in her hand.

Sir Stanton, who had dark, curly hair and was not unpleasant in appearance, asked me if I had seen any races. I told him I had seen the one at Lambourne four years ago. He admitted that he was only recently involved in racing horses but that he was enjoying it immensely. He went on to tell me that he had a two-year-old colt entered in the Baringfield competition.

"They're racing two-year-olds?" I asked, rather shocked. "Aren't they a little young to be put under such pressure?"

"Well, the main race at two miles is for the older horses, but there is a special competition for the young stock. It will only be one mile on the flat," he explained. "There's begun to be so much interest in breeding for speed here in England in the last few years. It seems all the gentry now are importing stallions to cross with our mares. I, for one, am very excited about the sport."

The room had now gone silent, as it seemed that both sisters had finished their turns at the piano. To my horror, my aunt stood and announced loudly that her niece played remarkably well, and I realized that she was speaking of me. I shook my head and tried to decline, but she had me by my hand and was not taking no for an answer. I could not refuse without seeming to be very ungracious, so I rose and took my place at the instrument, Sir Stanton coming to stand nearby. I resolved to play the same piece I had practiced that afternoon and, giving my full attention to my performance, managed to finish the musical score without problem. Rising to leave when I had finished, I noticed with a start that William had entered the room and was watching me intently. Feeling overwhelmed, I turned to my aunt and, claiming a headache, which was not far from the truth, begged to be excused. The young baronet offered to see me to my bedchamber, but I declined and fled the room as quickly as possible.

Once I reached the darkened third floor, I was startled to run into a familiar figure. It was my cousin Alice. She was just leaving one of the maid's quarters down the hall, and the candle illuminated her face so that I recognized her instantly. "Alice!" I exclaimed. "What are you doing here?"

"Is that me cousin Kathryn Alexander?" she answered back with equal excitement. "Surely, I could ask ye the same thing." Retreating into the room she had just exited, we both sat on the bed and hugged. She explained that she was now lady's maid to the new Lady Herbert, and I explained my newfound family connection to the Howards. We just sat and stared at each other for a moment and then laughed and hugged again.

She didn't have time for a long conversation; she had to get back down to the countess's bedchamber and prepare to help her mistress with her evening duties—that is, whenever Lady Herbert decided to retire. Rather than lords and ladies sleeping together in one bedroom, I was surprised to learn that they all had separate bedchambers. Some things just didn't make total sense to me. We promised to try to find time to make a connection and have a long talk in the next day or two, and then she hurried off downstairs.

I made my way back to my own room and began preparing for bed. It had been a long day, and I had much on my mind. How was I going to continue to avoid William if he was staying here as a guest? What if he still hated me? Should I try to find a way to get back to the Home at Bristol? Right now, that seemed my most attractive option. Could, or would, the Lord help me in all this? I wished Angel were here to counsel me and guide me in approaching God on such matters and in understanding how much the Lord was active in my life.

After saying my prayers, I blew out my candle and pulled back the covers to my bed. But as I crawled in, I felt something cold, stiff, and foreign underneath me. As I quickly exited the mattress, it took a moment with shaking hands to relight the candle with flint and steel. Pulling back the covers, I suppressed a scream: the dead kitten lay discarded upon my mattress.

Chapter 27

ST. GEORGE'S DAY

I didn't sleep well that night, too many thoughts crowding my wakefulness and too many nightmares of thrashing hooves chasing my sleep. Even so, I was awake before dawn, old habits clinging to me, and again I dressed and headed outdoors. I had made the decision in the night to beg my aunt to find a conveyance to take me back to Bristol sometime today. I had no desire to stay any longer.

Walking around the mansion, I noticed that there was a lot of activity down by the stables and went to investigate. Indeed, there were a number of grooms feeding and brushing the assembly of horses that had not been there the day before. It seemed now that every stall was full. Even so, I was surprised at so much activity so early in the morning and asked a stable hand to explain.

"Well, at least six of the gentlemen who are guests here have horses entered in the race at Baringfield in two days, and they've brought their racehorses here with them, and grooms, too. Later this morning, after the gentlemen have breakfasted, we expect most of them'll be out to see their animals take exercise, some of them even doing the riding themselves." Oh, I thought to myself, that would be a sight I would like to watch.

As I wandered down the barn aisle, a beautiful chestnut with a white mane and tail and that characteristic dished face caught my eye. Baron, I realized! So William might be here to race, too. There were horses of all shapes and colors, and my mind could hardly take in their magnificence. God, when he made horses, created something truly majestic.

When I reached the stalls at the farthest end of the barn, a young groom not more than a boy stopped me. "Ye can't go beyond here, miss," he warned.

"Why not?" I inquired.

"These last two stallions belong to Lord Herbert, and he don't want anyone near them," he answered in a firm yet boyish voice.

This surprised me a great deal and also troubled me. I retreated, as the boy stood watching me go. Then I left the stable by the entry door and circled back around until I could see into the stall windows that had been opened to the warm April air. I made sure not to get too close, just near enough that I could get a look into those last two cells. I wasn't sure exactly what I was looking for, but something just didn't seem right.

I was not surprised to see that Ahkil stood in the nearest stall, the slender and tough-looking Turkomene that George Herbert had ridden in the race four years ago. But I had to strain to see the horse in the last stall. It looked like a young animal, another bay like Ahkil, but probably just a two-year-old colt. As I squinted through the window from a little distance, I could see a stable hand with the horse. It looked like he was grooming the animal. But no, he was applying something to the hip of the colt with a rag.

What was he doing? I had to know. Moving stealthily, I crept right up to the window but bent underneath it. What was that smell? Coal tar, I was sure. We used it sometimes for a poultice. But it would leave a dark stain, a gooey mess. Why would the groom be applying that to a hip? Was there an injury? And then in a flash, I knew!

I jumped as someone tapped me on the shoulder—it was the boy. "What're ye doing, miss? Lord Herbert would be angry if he knew ye was here."

I backed quickly away from the window. "I'm sorry," I apologized. "I just wanted to see the horses. I'll leave now." And without looking back, I walked quickly, nearly running, back toward the house.

I didn't really feel like encountering anyone at breakfast, so instead I made my way around to the entrance of the Dower House and was shown again into the same sitting room as before. My aunt stood when I entered, but without greeting, and said, "The dowager doesn't rise for another hour at least. You'll have to come back later." Bethany had obviously been taking tea, but she did not invite me to join her.

Disregarding her apparent intent to have me leave, I asked, "Would it be all right if I sat and visited with you for a few minutes?" She looked as if this made her uncomfortable, but she finally nodded and sat back down. She still didn't offer me tea. "How is Grandmother doing?" I asked, searching for a way to begin.

"She does pretty well for her age most days" was the noncommittal answer.

"I believe she's very lucky to have a devoted daughter taking care of her in her retirement," I said, wanting to say something positive.

"Well, it's not like I have a lot of other choices," Bethany said, frowning.

"I'm sure that's not true. You could live with your sister, for one, or in your own house. Surely, Grandfather left you an allowance. But instead you've chosen to take care of your mother, and I know Marguerite and I are both grateful."

"What would either of you know about the life I lead?" She sighed, shaking her head, and then she was silent.

Quietly I asked, "Why, then, did you never marry, Aunt Bethany?"

She sat for a long time, staring at her hands, and then began, still not looking at me. "I was never pretty like your mother, or vivacious and fun-loving like Marguerite. When Father overlooked me to betroth Anne to the marquis, I was hurt and furious. And then both Marguerite and Anne managed to marry for love. I decided I would not be satisfied unless I was able to marry either for wealth and title or for love, like my sisters. I turned down two proposals from decent men who offered me neither. And then...well, my opportunities passed me by."

"I'm sorry," I answered, not knowing what else to say.

"Why? It wasn't your fault. That was the problem. It was my own fault, and I knew it. And the angrier I became with myself, the more I withdrew." She paused. "I'm not sure why I'm telling you all this."

"I still think you've made an unselfish choice in serving my grandmother."

"Lady Clarista was a good mother. She saw what was happening to me and did her best to help, but since I couldn't have what my sisters had, I just chose to be unhappy."

"It's not too late now, you know. My mother suffered terribly with consumption during her last years. We had little money, and she worked night and day to take care of Da and me and help make ends meet. But she was always cheerful, always chose to look on the bright side. Aunt Marguerite, too, has lost her husband and rarely sees her daughters, but she chooses to stay positive."

"Well, at least both of my sisters had the joy of bearing children. That's the one thing I'll always regret."

"Do you enjoy children, then?" I asked.

"I've had the unpleasant duty of watching this viscount…Mark grow up here in the household, and a more spoiled and unkind child I've never seen. His sisters *are* very appealing, but they're rarely allowed out of their schoolroom."

"Have you ever thought of inviting them here to the Dower House? Perhaps for tea? I've met them, and they and their governess are quite lonely, just like you."

"I have no idea if my cousin would allow that. But even if it were possible, I have little to offer them."

"These are still choices that are within your grasp. All of life hasn't yet passed you by."

"Even if you're right, I just can't find the strength inside myself to make that choice. I gave up hope of happiness a long time ago."

"Aunt Bethany, there was a time two years past when I'd given up hope, too. You would be appalled if I described the state my life was in, living on the streets of Bristol. But then I met some Christian believers who took pity on me and showed me God's love. I had to learn to forgive myself and believe that my Lord loved and forgave me too."

"You sound like my mother. That's what she's always said, but I was too full of bitterness to listen. And I'm still not sure I want to forgive myself or believe that God could care about an old woman who has been so foolishly jealous."

Aunt Bethany did finally offer me some tea, and we talked for quite some time while I shared my story with her. My grandmother also joined our conversation once she had arisen. I left the two of them reading scripture from grandmother's own Bible, and I resolved to continue praying for my aunt.

When I re-entered the house, I realized I had missed watching the men exercising their race mounts, but I didn't regret my decision to spend the morning at the Dower House. Now everyone seemed to be preparing to go into town for the St. George's celebration. When I had risen this morning, I had decided to return to Bristol as soon as possible. But now I had determined to travel on with the house party to Baringfield. There was information that I needed to seek, and that was the only place I was going to find it. I hoped and prayed that I was doing the right thing.

Searching out Aunt Marguerite, I asked what the plans were for the day. There was to be a light lunch served for those who wanted to eat before going into town for the parade at one o'clock. Or we could choose to purchase treats from the stalls in town. And there was still the formal dinner and ball tonight here on the estate. So my aunt and I joined those gathering to walk into Bradford before lunch. The dark-headed baronet soon asked if he could accompany the two of us, and along with the baron and his wife, the five of us made our way over the stone bridge. My aunt was in a gay mood, the day was bright, and I found myself even looking forward to a little merriment, although I was still hoping to keep my distance from certain of the others.

We took our time walking along the main avenue of Bradford and admiring the wares for sale. Eating a delicious meat pasty while strolling along—I had never had breakfast—reminded me so much of other happy holidays with my family in our own village.

As the time for the parade drew near, we were ushered to a location on the central square, where a viewing area had been cordoned off specifically for Lord Howard and his guests. Since the Earl of Avon was the patron and landlord of this village, of course special honor and attention would be paid to him. I begged to just stand along the street with the villagers, but my aunt pointed out that benches had been set for us on the square and she preferred to sit. By the time we made our way to the seats, most of the Howard Manor guests were already gathered there, the ladies sitting, the gentlemen standing, and we were able to seat Aunt Marguerite and the baroness right at the edge of the group. Unfortunately, we were not far from the Howards, with William and Clarence just beyond them. I noted that, sadly, Miss Smith and the girls were not to be seen. At least Lord Herbert was at the far end from us. I still had no wish to cross paths with him, especially after my visit to the stables this morning.

The parade began with a group of children carrying a monstrous white flag bearing the red cross emblem of St. George. And of course, nearly every other element of the parade was draped in the same symbol. There were musicians with the flags sewn on their vests. There were riders dressed as warriors under the same banner. Several groups of dancers dressed in St. George's colors leaped and pranced by. One little girl was leading a sheep totally draped in white and red. The main course of the parade contained the group of mummers—those costumed players who would perform the mummer's play after the parade. Their regalia included masks that completely covered their faces. Judging from the costumes, it appeared that St. George, with his giant sword, was later going to slay a massive dragon who encompassed at least three hidden persons under the brilliant green of the dragon's costume.

While I had been watching the parade and finishing my pasty, a mangy dog had wandered up, sniffing along the roadside in front of us. His hair was falling out in clumps, and he was quite thin. Most of the others around me recoiled from the dog, who appeared friendly enough, but a little shy. Stepping forward, I fed him the last of my meat pie and was gratified to see his tail wag. Sir Stanton, who was escorting us, soon shooed the dog on down the street.

The parade was drawing to a close; the final entry, an enormous wagon draped in flags and flowers and pulled by two massive draft animals, was just drawing abreast of us. But my attention was drawn to a loud voice hurling curses just to my right. It was young Lord Mark, and as I watched in disbelief, he leveled a vicious kick at the mongrel, who was cowering in the street in front of him. When the dog still did not move away, he kicked it again. Then, in a blink, two things happened. I saw William grab the boy by the shoulder and pull him back. And the dog, when he saw his tormentor dragged away, took the opportunity to flee and ran right under the hooves of the near drafter pulling the wagon. The horse, being surprised, lunged forward, and the dray rolled right over the poor dog, both right wheels inflicting their horrific toll.

Instantly, William was in the street, kneeling by the dog. No one else moved. The dog was trying to lift its head, blood running from its mouth, no other movement from its body apparent. William knelt there for a moment, his hand resting under the dog's head. And then, he looked up directly at me, his eyes, I imagined, pleading for help. Immediately stepping into the street, I went to him, bent, and put my hand on the dog's chest. But it was too late. Even as I stood there, I felt the heart take its last beat; there was no more breath, the dog's head slumped. I looked into William's face, but he already knew. Then I turned and looked at the boy. He knew, too, and was smiling.

At that moment, a man, perhaps the local constable, strode up and began saying, "Here now, Yer Lordship. This is nothing for ye to worry about. This here's just a local stray, don't belong to no one. Been beggin' 'round here for weeks. Good riddance to the poor bugger." William had risen, and the constable began hauling the dead body out of the street, people going back to their business.

I returned to my aunt, tears in my eyes, and she gave me a hug. Sir Thomas, seeing I was upset, asked if I would like a glass of water or cider, and because I didn't want to talk about what had just happened, I nodded consent. He had only been gone a moment when I became aware that someone else had approached very close, just behind me, and I turned to come face-to-face with Lord Clarence. He was smiling.

"Just now when I saw you with that dog, I realized who you were." He smirked. "Look at you in the garb and company of a gentlewoman. I would never have guessed. You look very 'good' in those clothes, too." He said this last with a leer. "Perhaps tonight we can pick up where we last left off—do you remember, in our stables?" With that, he tried to give me a little pinch, but I slapped his hand away. I was grateful that no one else had been close enough to overhear our little conversation.

Turning my back on him, I approached my aunt again. The baronet had just come up with a glass full of cider. Thanking him, I took a small sip and nodded my appreciation. But then motioning to Marguerite, I whispered that I wanted to return to the manor without staying for the mummer's play. I was so grateful when she agreed, saying she was tired of the crowds anyway. Sir Thomas claimed the honor of escorting us home, but I insisted that he should stay and enjoy the play, explaining that we preferred to walk alone just now. And so we were allowed our leave-taking, the baronet reminding me that he would see us that evening at dinner and the ball.

Chapter 28

THE BALL

O n our way back to Howard Manor, I told Aunt Marguerite that I wasn't planning on attending the ball that night. She tried to talk me into going, but I held my ground. However, I did divulge the other project I had in mind. Telling my aunt of my visit to the Dower House that morning and describing my idea to her, she readily consented and we each went off in different directions to see what could be done.

First, I went to my room to compose myself. The incidents at the parade, both with William and then Clarence, had unnerved me. I also wanted to pray, asking for direction and assistance. Next, I went to visit at the schoolroom, where I found Miss Smith, Jane, and Martha busy reading. When I described what I had in mind, Miss Smith was skeptical, but the girls were so excited that she finally relented. And soon we were all on our way downstairs. The house was empty save for servants at their tasks, and no one stopped us from leaving and heading through the back garden.

Aunt Marguerite met us at the door to the Dower House, nodded assurance to me, and then showed us to the now-familiar sitting room. Aunt Bethany greeted the girls and Miss Smith, and then they were formally received by the dowager countess. All three of them gave polite curtsies, and subsequently, we all sat down for tea, which Bethany poured as our hostess. I was surprised that, on such short notice, the tea tray also contained picklets and assorted sweet breads, treats that the girls helped themselves to generously, much to Miss Smith's disapproving glances.

Grandmother assumed control of the conversation at first, asking the girls questions about their studies and what subjects they liked best, but once everyone relaxed a little, my two aunts began regaling the younger women with stories from their own childhood in that same schoolroom, and soon we were all laughing and enjoying ourselves. When teatime was over, Miss Smith and the girls took their leave, but I noticed Aunt Bethany made them promise to come again soon. I hoped they would. Before we left, Aunt Marguerite reminded her sister that she was invited to the ball that evening. Bethany declined the offer, but her younger sister begged her not to say no but to please think about it. And then she and I left to go and prepare for dinner.

I had agreed to sup with the other guests that evening, knowing that not to do so would be considered rude. But I was still determined to miss the ball later. Dinner went smoothly enough. I was again seated next to Marguerite and the kind Lord and Lady Rothschild, and conversation mostly centered around the parade and the mummer's play, which was described to me in detail. As soon as we had finished eating, most of the ladies excused themselves to go and make final preparations with their attire. Aunt Marguerite and I retreated to her bedchamber, where we found Aunt Bethany waiting, dressed for the ball, her tall frame draped in a dark blue, silk gown that made her look very elegant.

I was so glad that she had decided to rejoin life, at least in this one small step. But when she discovered that I had declined the evening's festivities, she put her foot down and said she would not go either. In the end, of course, I relented. With Nancy's help, they dressed my hair and chose the blue silk gown for me to wear. They were not happy when I insisted on tucking a lace modesty scarf into the top of my bodice, which had been cut fashionably low, but I knew I would not feel comfortable otherwise. Aunt Marguerite had chosen to wear her green gown with the embroidered flowers decorating the hem and sleeves, which she felt made her look "less portly."

Then the three of us descended the staircase together, for my part, and perhaps for Bethany's, with some trepidation.

Most of the other guests were now in the ballroom, and the five musicians were already playing, although no one was yet dancing. Footmen were passing the requisite trays of drinks, and people were talking in small groups. We had not been in the room long when it was announced that the branle was about to begin. One of my aunts explained to me that this would be the opening dance—the couples would form one long line of pairs who would then perform a series of sideways steps. They said it would be interesting to see who headed the line, as it was customary for the most important of the peers to lead.

While the three of us were discussing whether the branle would be led by Lord and Lady Howard or the marques and marchioness, the dark-haired baronet approached and asked me for the pleasure of the dance. Politely, I answered, "Lord Stanton, thank you for the compliment, but I should've warned you this afternoon. This is the first ball I've attended, and I'm afraid I don't know any of the steps. The only dancing I've done previously has been folk dances at the celebrations in my home village." Thomas looked disappointed. Then I added, "I don't believe you have met my elder aunt. Aunt Bethany, this is Sir Thomas Stanton. Sir Stanton, this is Lady Bethany May Howard, daughter of the late Earl of Avon."

Thomas, in utter gentlemanly fashion, bowed over her hand. "It's a pleasure to meet you, Lady Howard. Since Lady Alexander claims inexperience, would you do me the honor of this dance?" I thought my aunt might faint, but she accepted the young man's hand, and Marguerite and I had the satisfaction of watching Bethany perform her first dance in many, many years. When the branle was over, she returned to us flushed and smiling. "That was the most fun I've had in years!" she admitted. And then she went off to sit in one of the chairs lining the back wall and rest herself.

Aunt Marguerite was invited by Lord Rothschild to dance another one of the more sedate dances, as his wife, the baroness, sat and watched with Aunt Bethany. Sir Thomas came to stand by me, but I begged him to re-enter the dancing, pleading that I would observe and try to learn how to perform at least one dance. The other nonmarried gentleman in attendance, a second son of someone, also came and asked me to partner with him, but I declined. I really had little interest in dancing.

Mostly, I was watching William. He was standing with several of the other men. Clarence was dancing, first with one of the marquis's daughters, and then the other. But both girls seemed to have more interest in his brother and kept drifting over to try to talk with William. Often when this happened, I would catch a glower on the younger brother's face.

Midway through the ball, after the dancers had performed the very courtly minuet, the minstrels began an Irish jig, most definitely a country dance I was familiar with. And sure enough, here came Thomas. Grinning, he held out his hand, and I really had no other excuse. We began the dance near the end of the ballroom, where I had been standing. I was surprised that the baronet was familiar with the jig, and told him so, but he replied that there might be lots of things about him I didn't know. We laughed, and then I gave myself up to the joy of the music. Many of the older couples had stepped out, and those few of us dancing had nearly the whole floor to ourselves. When the music ended, we received a bit of applause and hooting, and we all took a bow. Now it was my turn to be flushed and breathing a bit as I retreated to the end of the room and the musicians began another round. As he had this afternoon, my gallant partner offered to go and bring me some refreshment, and again I nodded.

"Is it my turn now?" a churlish voice said beside me. I knew who it was, Lord Clarence. "I saw how my brother was looking at you," he stated, but I had no idea what he was talking about. "I think you owe *me* a dance now."

"You are mistaken, sir. I owe you nothing. And besides, I don't know how to perform this dance."

"You danced just fine with Stanton. You can dance with me." And with this, he took my hand forcefully.

"No, and let go of me now!" I said coldly, jerking my hand back.

Leaning close, he began to whisper in my ear. "You forget, *Lady* Alexander, I know exactly who you really are. And I've been asking questions about you. If you don't give me what I want, I'll expose you in front of everyone here." Again, he took my hand, and again I pulled it from his grasp.

At that moment, Sir Thomas returned, carrying two glasses of punch. "What's going on here?" he asked, looking from my flushed face to Lord Clarence's angry one.

The musical set had now ended, and in the momentary quiet, Lord Clarence cleared his voice and pronounced loudly, "Excuse me, attention! I have an announcement to make." The room became silent as all eyes turned our way. "This woman"—he indicated me with a sneering nod—"is a fraud. She's no lady and does not belong among gentry such as us. I knew her back when she and her father were mere servants on our estate. She used to help care for our horses. Not only that, but I heard a rumor that she had been dismissed from our local squire's household staff for unbecoming behavior! She may claim some connection to the Howard family, but she was disinherited long ago and has not a farthing to her name!" That seemed to be his final insult, and he turned back to stare at me, victory apparent on his face. I secretly thanked God that William had apparently *not* shared my more-grievous failings. But still, embarrassment overwhelmed me.

The room was deadly quiet for an instant, and then I became aware of a presence beside me. It was Aunt Bethany. She already stood half a head taller than I was, but at that moment, she seemed even larger. Placing her hand on my shoulder, she proclaimed, "This young woman is the daughter of my sister, Lady Anne Marie Howard Alexander. Lady Anne, myself, and my sister Lady Marguerite were all raised in this very house, daughters of the late Earl of Avon. She has as much right and more than any person here to be in this room. What's more, she has more culture, breeding, and manners than some others who have been invited tonight!" With that, she aimed a withering look at Lord Clarence, and for a moment, neither broke the other's gaze. Then Clarence turned on his heel and strode away.

The musicians struck up the next dance, and I turned and thanked my aunt, who replied, "I know you want to leave now, Kathryn, but to do so would give that young scamp his victory. You must stand and prove your breeding." And so, the three of us remained at the ball for a while longer. The baron and his wife came over to speak to us, but no one else in the room approached. Sir Thomas seemed to have disappeared with the punch.

I briefly glanced over among the crowd of dancers and spectators, wondering what William might have thought of this latest spectacle. But he must have departed, following his brother. However, as I was scanning the guests, my eye caught two men, both glowering at me. The first was Lord Howard. Was he thinking of the scandal that I had just brought on his family? Or was he worried that I would be one more of the late earl's relatives who would be asking for a living from him?

But the glance that caught my breath and sent a shiver down my spine was from Lord George Herbert, owner of Ahkil, the man who had caused Milty's death, the man involved with Lady Grace. His gaze was cold and menacing as he stared in my direction. And now, he obviously remembered who I was, too.

Lowering my gaze, I quickly left the room, not waiting to beg my leave from the hosts. Stopping at my aunt's room to be sure she was settled—Nancy assured me she was preparing for bed—I quickly ascended the back stairs to my own chamber. But in the upper hall I again met cousin Alice coming down the passageway toward me. I asked her if she had time to talk, but once more, she complained that she had duties to perform, and she left me to my own devices.

It was a while before my nerves had settled enough even to prepare for bed. I prayed again for wisdom and strength and spent some time in the scriptures. Once ready for bed, I turned down my covers, set to jump should there be something unexpected lurking there. But the bed was empty. Crawling in, I blew out the candle, although it was a long time before sleep overtook me.

And then, suddenly, the white stallion was rearing over me, threatening to end my life, thrashing with his front legs. I felt the jar and shudder as those hooves met the ground around me, and I opened my mouth to scream. Coming suddenly wide awake, I knew that something besides the nightmare had awakened me. I lay completely still; the room was in total darkness, but I sensed another presence. I was sure I could hear someone breathing. I lay like that for what seemed like an eternity, searching desperately in my head for anything I could use as a weapon. Did someone mean me harm? Why were they in my bedchamber?

I reached my hand tentatively over for the candlestick as quietly as I could, but it still made a scraping sound as I dragged it off the nightstand and into the bed beside me. Then I heard a rustling, and I could imagine my door being opened and then closed again quietly. Since there was no light coming from the hallway, I caught sight of no one, not even a shadow. There was nothing to tell me whether my intruder had been male or female, young or old. Was it Mark again? I could not tell. I only knew that I now could count several enemies in this house who might wish evil upon me. I wondered, *Lord, are you here with me? Can I trust you to protect me?*

Once I was sure that my room was empty once again, I rose in the dark, found my way to the chair that sat against the wall, and dragged it over in front of my door and propped it against the doorknob. This probably would not keep anyone out, but at least they could not enter without creating a noise. Even so, it was many minutes, or was it hours, later before sleep found me again.

Chapter 29

BARINGFIELD HALL

T he next morning, I slept later than I had in days, probably because slumber had eluded me the night before. I found on waking that the sun had already risen, and I was quickly out of bed, looking around the small room to see if I could find any trace of the intruder from the night before. Sure enough, a note lay on my bedside table—this would have been just a foot or two from my head last night. I realized that if the person had wanted to do me real harm, they had certainly had the opportunity. The note simply read, "Get out before it's too late!"

This gave me pause to reconsider my plans to stay with the party of guests and travel on to Baringfield Hall. What if the person who left the note really did intend me harm? But if I didn't make the trip to George Herbert's estate, I would never know if my suspicions were correct. This was my only chance, and I knew it. So folding my clothing and other items, I had my traveling case packed in minutes.

I breakfasted at the Dower House with Aunt Bethany, later taking my last visit with Grandmother and then my tearful leave from both of them. I also went to bid farewell to Miss Smith and the girls, encouraging them to continue spending time at the Dower House, where I knew they would be welcome. Aunt Marguerite had planned to hire a coach to take us to the Baringfield estate, but the baron and his wife insisted that the three of us, Aunt, Nancy, and I, travel with them in their coach. The journey took several hours, and Lord

Rothschild enjoyed telling us of his property in northern Germany and of the Holsteiners that he raised there. He had brought a four-year-old stallion over for the racing, although he was aware of the reputation of the English Arabian crossbreds that were sweeping the competitions.

When we finally arrived, traveling through iron gates and up yet another long, sweeping drive, the dread that I had been ignoring suddenly hit me like an invisible force. My fear from last night sought to overwhelm me. Only prayer allowed me to step foot from the carriage onto enemy soil. Our hosts, George and Melinda Herbert, Earl and Countess of Bath, were there to greet each guest. And although they were pleasant enough to the Rothschilds, they barely glanced at Aunt Marguerite and me. As usual, Marguerite chose to ignore the slight, and we were shown to adjoining bedchambers. At least we were not assigned rooms with the servants.

Baringfield Hall was even larger and grander than any mansion I had yet seen. The four-story main building had two flanking wings projecting to the north and south of the tall main structure. The lawns, gardens, and terraces were also more extensive, which I found hard to believe possible. The rooms we had been assigned to were in the north wing and were comfortable and airy. Nancy had a smaller adjoining room, which was convenient for her.

We had arrived in time for tea, which was being served casually out on one of the terraces, since not all the guests were yet here. They were still expecting several additional owners of horses to arrive. I looked around as Aunt Marguerite and I sipped our tea and ate our buttered scones. The earl had even provided sliced, sugared lemons, a real treat. I couldn't help remembering four years ago when I had observed a similar tea being served on a similar terrace. But then I had watched from a servant's window, and now I was one of the guests. It didn't seem possible.

When Aunt Marguerite finished eating, she begged to retire to her room to rest before the buffet supper later. I decided to make a trip out to the stables to see if I could get near any of Lord George's horses. There was a lot of activity going on in the barns as new horses and grooms were arriving. I walked down the aisle of the main barn, admiring the animals, but I did not see any I recognized. Finally, I asked one of the stable hands who was grooming a horse in crossties if he knew where the Earl of Bath's horses were stabled. He pointed me to another groom, who told me that the earl's horses were not in these barns, but in several that were located on the other side of the racing area.

Lord Herbert had built a two-mile racing "track" around his large main pasture area. Although there were gentle rolling hills all along the course, still the race was considered quite flat comparatively. The barns I was seeking were apparently on the far side of the estate. Getting directions, I set out following the gravel road that led around in that direction. In about ten minutes' walk, I came upon the first barn. However, when I approached the wide double doors, a groom intercepted me, asking my business. When I begged to look at the horses, he told me it wasn't possible and said I would have to get permission from Lord Herbert.

Returning back up the road and nearing the manse, I saw that I was being observed by Lord George himself from his vantage on the front lawn, where he was greeting guests. I was sure he had no doubt where I had been, although what he might make of it, I could only guess. I had been frustrated in my quest and was going to have to make a new plan. Back in my room, washing up for dinner, I realized what I'd have to do. Tomorrow during the races could be the only time when it might be possible to approach the private barns with no one watching. Surely, all the stable hands would be busy with the horses in the races and the Earl of Bath occupied with riding his own animals. One more night, I thought, just one more night.

The buffet dinner was casual and served in the ballroom, where small tables had been set up for the guests. It was an uncomfortable scene for my aunt and me. The Rothschilds, being an older couple, were fatigued from the trip and had decided to sup in their room and go to bed early. Both the Howards and the Herberts were treating us coldly, their backs to us, making it eminently clear that we were not really welcome there. I would have preferred staying in our rooms, too, but Aunt Marguerite was always one to enjoy what could be enjoyed. She had marveled at the expanse of choices on the buffet table, remarking that she had never seen such a spread. There were at least five different kinds of meat dishes to choose from, including roast beef haunch, boiled leg of mutton, stewed rabbits, smoked fish studded with capers, and oysters still in their shells. And besides the potato and vegetable dishes, there were apple tarts, plum cakes, and best of all, chocolate pastries. To top it all off, there was a center-piece made entirely of fruits and vegetables, including little rosebuds carved from radishes, something my aunt exclaimed over all evening.

She and I sat alone at a little table to the side, no one else seeking to join us. Sir Stanton and the other gentleman who had asked me to dance the night before were busy engaging the marquis's two daughters and had not spoken to us once. I kept watching for William or his brother, knowing both planned to race on the morrow, but neither seemed to have arrived yet.

I knew that when the buffet was concluded, everyone would be invited into the drawing room and cardrooms, and I proposed that we take our leave. But Aunt Marguerite didn't want to miss anything, including the after-dinner drinks, I was sure. So I made her promise that she would not offer my services at the piano, if they had one, and we compromised. I knew my aunt led a quiet life at home, and I could not deprive her of our last night of entertainment.

As we entered the drawing room a little later, I saw that they did indeed have an instrument, and I was glad I had garnered the promise from my aunt. She and I took seats in the corner and set out to watch whatever amusements were going to be offered. Footmen came around shortly with their trays, and I decided to join Aunt Marguerite in a glass of sherry, hoping it would calm the discomfort I was feeling. I couldn't help wondering what we were really doing here and if I was being totally foolish. *God,* I thought, *please help me get through just one more day safely.*

And then William walked into the room, and beside him, not Clarence, but *Edward!* I couldn't remember being so happy to see anyone. They were obviously looking around the room, and when our eyes met, they came immediately to stand in front of my aunt and me. Both men made their polite greetings, Aunt Marguerite gushing over so much attention after being so ignored all evening.

For a few nerve-racking minutes, we made small talk. Edward had brought a two-year-old to race, although his hopes were really pinned on progeny from his new stallion, who wouldn't be on the ground until next spring. William explained that he had left Howard Manor last evening, angry and making sure that his errant brother was sent speedily on his way back to Faringdon Manor. Clarence would not be making an appearance in public anytime soon, or racing either.

Edward finally reached forward and took my hand. "I'm going to take my leave now. I only arrived an hour ago and have been speaking with William ever since, so there's much I need to attend to. But I hope to see you tomorrow, dear friend, and have a long conversation." And with that, he left the room.

Now William was looking at me with such intensity that I had to look away. "Lady Smithson," he said, addressing my aunt, "there's some private communication that I need to make with your niece. Would you mind terribly if we stepped away for a few minutes?" My aunt nodded permission, looking at me very quizzically. Rising, I took William's proffered hand, and we stepped out into the hall.

"Lady Alexander," he began.

At that same moment, I also began, "Lord Stanley..." If I hadn't been so nervous, wondering what William had to say to me, it might have been amusing.

William started again. "Can we be less formal? Would you consent to calling me William, or would that seem impertinent?"

I gave him a small smile. "I think Kathryn would be fitting, given our history."

He began shaking his head. "I'm so ashamed, and I owe you such an apology. Can you ever forgive me? Edward has just informed me of all you've been through...all you were going through three years ago. And I'm convicted of being an unforgivable brute and worse."

"No," I cried. "It is I who owe you so many apologies, not the least of which was stealing your purse."

"I think not. If I hadn't been consumed with my anger, if I hadn't overruled my better sense and gotten drunk, I might have stopped to ask why a circumspect lady like yourself was in such a predicament." And here, he looked down and became very quiet. After a moment, he looked up at me again and continued. "Kathryn, even through my drunken haze, I heard your plea for me to stop, but I ignored it." Here, he broke off again, the shine of tears appearing in his eyes, and he took a moment to regain his composure. "I guess I just wanted you too badly at that moment, or maybe I just wanted to hurt you. This is something I will be eternally ashamed of. And then, when I awoke in that bed after you'd left, I saw the blood on my trousers and knew what I'd done. I developed a rousing hang-over—served me right—but the next afternoon, when I was able to ride again, I came looking for you to beg your forgiveness and try to make things right. The villagers said your mother had died and you had disappeared, and no one could tell me where you might have gone. Not even the squire was any help." At this speech, I had no idea how to respond; his words had touched me so. He had come looking for me "to make things right!"

"And then when I saw you in Bristol last fall, it all came back to me…my own guilt and shame and my own doubts about you and about what had really happened. Edward has described to me your work at the Home for Needy Children and what a kind, compassion-ate, and genteel lady you are. He willingly admitted he'd asked you to marry him, but without success." Now we were looking at each other, both of us quite serious. "The first thing I need to know," he finally went on, "is whether you can forgive me so that I can begin to forgive myself? There can be no hope of a future relationship without that."

A future relationship…what was he saying? But I realized I had not answered his question. "Of course I can forgive you, if you can forgive me? I've learned a lot about forgiveness in the last year," I added.

We stood there for a moment, just looking at each other, a smile beginning to creep over both of our faces. Then one of the sisters came out into the hall, the beautiful, fair-haired one. "There you are, Lord Stanley." She pouted. "We've been looking for you. Everyone says that you have such a lovely singing voice, and we're about to have some music. Won't you please come and do us the honor?"

It was an awkward moment. We could no longer stand and have a private conversation. The time was wrong now. But perhaps when the party broke up? William turned and looked at me. "I'll come and sing only if Lady Alexander will accompany me. Do you remember the last time we sang together?" he asked. I nodded, and William took my hand and led me back into the room, the marquis's daughter remaining where she was, looking quite unhappy.

I went to stand beside William at the piano forte, where one of the wives was ready to play. He requested "I Saw My Lady Weepe," the same song we had sung together at the squire's birthday party, and she soon had the music in front of her and was starting the introduction. Glancing around, I spotted Aunt Marguerite still sitting in the corner with another glass in her hand. She smiled at me and waved encouragement.

The song was magical, even more special than the last time. William's tenor voice was indeed beautiful, and he was beaming at me with what I could only hope might be a reflection of what I knew was in my own eyes. The night had gone from difficult and painful to wonderful. William and I never took our eyes off each other the whole time we were singing. The rest of the room disappeared for me, and I let myself get lost in his gaze and the music.

Unfortunately, when the song ended, so did the mood. One of the other ladies had approached and whispered to me that my aunt had taken ill and needed to go back to her room. I immediately went to her side, William following. Aunt Marguerite looked at me apologetically, saying she thought she might be sick and wasn't sure she could stand, which turned out to be true. William supported her on one side, I on the other, and we managed to get her, staggering, out to the north wing and into her room. I thanked God we didn't have to manage any stairs. Once in the room, she went immediately to the chamber pot and began to retch.

I was going to have to take my leave of William. There had been so much I had wanted to tell him, how I had loved him since I was young and how I had come to faith in God. I knew I was going to have to confess about losing my baby, *our* baby, and how it very likely was my own fault. I dreaded telling him that. I also very much needed to tell him of my suspicions about Lord Herbert and my plan, but that would all have to wait. Aunt Marguerite continued to retch, kneeling on the floor, and my help was needed. I wasn't sure where Nancy was.

William took my hand at the door, kissed it, and promised that we would talk again just as soon as there was time, and then he was gone. I couldn't help but shake my head at how my prospects had changed in one short hour. It made me realize that God must truly be working in my life after all.

I helped get my aunt cleaned up and into bed, where she promptly fell asleep, but I was relatively certain she was not going to feel well in the morning. I went to find Nancy and warned her to check on her mistress during the night. And then I went to my own room.

As I prepared for bed, I thought about tomorrow and what it might bring. Had William really intimated that we might be able to go forward, as friends? As more? The fact that he had censured his brother after the scene last night and sent him home encouraged me. And what about my project tomorrow? Should I ask William for help, or Edward? But no, they were both entered in the racing and would be occupied at the very time I might need them. I was excited about what I could discover in those private barns, but also very nervous about Lord Herbert and the fact that I knew he was suspicious of me. I prayed very earnestly that night for God's protection and then drifted off to sleep.

The massive stallion, silvery in the moonlight, was rending the air again with his screams. As I lay on the ground beneath him, it appeared as if he were trying to claw a hole in the sky, his front hooves thrashing above me. Over and over, the horse reared and returned to earth, barely missing me. I had the sensation of several men struggling and shuffling around me, hauling on ropes, shouting, and trying in vain to control the colossal energy of the maddened animal. I knew I needed to concentrate. I needed to see the faces of the men. Even realizing this was a dream, I forced myself to focus, to look at the faces. Only one voice was familiar; only one face came into clear view. Lord George Herbert!

I came awake with a start. Had I really seen him? Why had it taken so long for me to recognize his face in my dream? Was it only because of my location now and the nearness of the man himself? Unable to return to sleep, I relit my lamp and sat up in bed. Not knowing quite why, I looked around the room and spotted something on the floor in front of my door. Rising, I realized a note had been pushed under the jamb. It read, "This is your last warning!" But now I was beginning to believe that I was no longer alone without protection.

Chapter 30

THE STABLES

Awakening at dawn, I spent a lot of time in prayer. I was nervous about my quest today, anxious about what I might find. If the vision from my dream had been correct, then I could very well discover the stolen horses here in the private barns this morning. I still believed that I had seen Lord Herbert's groom covering white spots on his colt's rump with coal tar, a sign that Cloud might have been its sire. The race for two-year-olds was scheduled for ten o'clock this morning, the race for the older horses later this afternoon. So I still had a lot of time to kill.

I decided to check on my aunt. Knocking quietly on her door, I entered the silent room. Aunt Marguerite seemed to be sleeping peacefully enough in her bed, snoring lightly. Poor Nancy lay curled on a pallet on the floor. Her mistress must have had a rough night. Rather than wake the exhausted maid, I decided to find my way down to the kitchen and retrieve a pot of tea and perhaps some toasted bread or some other light fare to help settle my aunt's stomach this morning.

Using the narrow servants' staircase located at the end of the hall, I descended into the bowels of the house, where I found the domestic staff in full swing. The chambermaids were already at table in a side room, having their own breakfast in preparation for their duties abovestairs. Grooms and stable help were also finishing up a quick breakfast and heading out. The cooks were all busy preparing what would probably be the food to be served to the hosts and guests later this morning.

As I was getting ready to ask for a tea tray, I heard a voice calling to me from the side room. "Cousin Kathryn, were ye lookin' fer me?" It was Alice, and surprisingly, she looked a little nervous.

"No, I was just coming to get a bit of breakfast for my aunt. But I'm glad to see you, cousin." I entered the room and went to give her a hug. Most of the other maids were rising to leave, and suddenly we were alone at the table. "I've been hoping we'd have a chance to talk. When I discovered three years ago that you were no longer at Faringdon and I had no idea where you'd gone, I was so distressed. I'm glad we've reconnected."

Surprisingly, Alice began to cry. "Yes," she said through her tears but didn't seem able to say more.

I gave her a little time to compose herself, and then tried, "So how do you like working here for Lady Herbert?"

"Oh, she's not so bad, not nearly as bad as Her Highness Grace." And with that pronouncement, she began to weep again.

"What's wrong?" I asked. Something was surely troubling her.

"Oh, Miss Kate, I've done so many things wrong I don't know where to start!"

"I've made a lot of mistakes in the last years, too, Alice."

"You have?" She looked at me in wonder, giving a small sniff.

"Truth be told, everyone does things they shouldn't, but mine were pretty evil. The good news I've discovered is that God loves us enough to overlook our mistakes, if we'll only ask him."

"Yes, but ye don't know all I've done, for sure."

"I'll be glad to listen if you want to tell me." She got very quiet, looking down at her feet. Then she began.

"It all started with that witch Grace. I was 'er chambermaid, ye know, when she visited at Faringdon over that last Christmas. One night she caught me goin' through 'er jewelry. I weren't goin' to steal nothing, honest, I weren't. But she told me she was gonna have me dismissed!"

"Oh, Alice, I'm so sorry," I commiserated.

"But then she offers me a way out an' says if I'll just do some-thin' fer her, I can make it all right." She paused. "I shouldna done it, I shouldna. Sure, I knew it was wrong. She was sendin' notes to Lord Herbert. I knew what she was up to, I did. And she needed me to see her notes got delivered down into Faringdon. But what could I do, I ask ya?"

"Poor Alice."

"And I always liked Lord Stanley, the young earl, that is. I told meself I were doing 'im a favor if I could get the witch out of 'is life. But then…she goes and gits kilt. And then they find out it's me been carrying the notes, and it all goes to 'ell."

I went and put my arms around my cousin. "You were put in an impossible situation."

She looked at me and began crying again. "And then…and then…"

"You don't have to go on, Alice. I can see this is hard for you," I said, trying to help her regain her composure. "Can I share a secret with you?" I said to take her mind off her guilt and help her to calm down. "I think Lord Herbert has been up to no good with his horses, and this morning during the racing, I hope to find a way to search those barns out behind his racetrack. Do you know anything about the animals he's breeding there?" I asked hopefully, but she shook her head.

"Please be careful, cousin. Lord Herbert can be a dangerous man!"

Suddenly, another maid entered the room and gestured to Alice hurriedly. "Her Ladyship is asking for you, Alice." Looking pale, Alice jumped up and hastened out the door, but glancing back, she said, "There's more I need to tell ye when I get a moment. Meanwhile, please be careful." And then she was gone.

Cautiously carrying a tray of biscuits and tea, I made my way back up the stairs and knocked on my aunt's door. I was bidden to come in and found Nancy tending to the older woman, who claimed a horrific headache. I asked the maid to fetch a glass of water and made Aunt Marguerite drink the whole thing. She said she thought she might be sick again, but she held it down, and I directed her to lie back and relax. I wished I had brought my herbs with me so that I could have dropped a little peppermint oil in her water, but I had nothing to help her.

Marguerite refused the tea and biscuits, but Nancy seemed glad enough for them, and I forced myself to eat one, too. I wasn't feeling much better than my aunt, my nerves playing Scotch-hop in my stomach. Sitting and trying to do nothing for an hour was going to be impossible, so I went back to my room and got out my Bible. Even though I had trouble focusing my mind on the scriptures, still it was closing in on race time when I finally exited the front of the mansion.

It was a pleasant, sunny morning, and villagers were walking up the front drive carrying baskets, children skipping around their parents. The whole holiday atmosphere would have been exciting for me on any other day. I walked around to the terrace, and I could see the spectators were beginning to line the fence that separated the pasture and track from the surrounding lawns and gardens. Families were sitting on blankets spread on the ground. Pendants were flapping in the gentle breeze, and horses and riders were already exercising and warming up out in the middle of the field. It was time, I thought to myself.

Walking back around to the front, I was surprised and frustrated when I realized that Lord Herbert had stationed servants at the entrance to both lanes that led right and left to the two stable areas. Of course, they would not want villagers and strangers traipsing through the barns. Now, what was I going to do? I scanned the grounds, looking for another way. The private barns were a good distance down the right road and back behind a copse of trees. I decided to head over into town and then see if I could cut around into those trees.

My plan worked, except that I had to traverse a small brook, getting my shoes and skirts muddy, but that was barely a concern. Perhaps a quarter of an hour later, I had drawn near to the first of three barns in a row. I scanned the area for servants but saw none. Neither did I see any horses. The second of the three barns had large paddocks running off from Dutch doors along the sides, but again, they were empty, the doors all closed tight. I decided to try the first barn and headed for the large double doors, which were closed.

Just as I reached the stable entrance, a servant rounded the corner and spotted me. It was the same groom/boy I had encountered in the Howards' barn. "What're ye doing?" he asked pointedly. "Ye can't go in there!"

I had to think quickly. "I just want to see the horses," I said truthfully. "You can come with me, if that would make you feel better. I won't steal anything." I was at the door, my hand on the latch.

"No'm, I can't let you go in," he stated emphatically, drawing himself up as tall as he could. I was still at least a head taller than him, but I think he was sizing me up for a fight.

I had come this far, and there was no turning back now. "I'm going in, anyway, but I promise I won't stay long. You can watch me, or not." And with that, I opened the door and walked into the dark interior. The boy stood there for a second, weighing his options, and then began sprinting away. Now I knew I had but a few minutes before he came back with bigger, stronger help. I had to hurry.

The barn had ten large box stalls, each of them holding a mare. Some were large and round, showing they were close to birthing. Others had already foaled, babies by their sides or lying in the straw. How I longed to stay and watch the cute, fuzzy creatures, but I had no time. I did glance into each stall for a moment and was not surprised to see that three of the foals had a sprinkling of white spots across their hips, making them look like little fawns. Quickly I opened the single door at the rear of the barn and headed for the second.

This stable was darker than the first. All the doors and windows had been shut tight, but there was still enough light coming through the cracks around the shutters to allow me to see once my eyes had adjusted. I could hear at least two horses stomping around in their stalls and located the first. It was Cloud! He was very agitated, pacing back and forth through his filthy stall. He was matted with manure, and I could not see any trace of hay or water. He whinnied plaintively, and another horse answered from down the way. I wondered how long he had been left caged in this stall without care.

Looking around, I spotted a water tank about halfway down the aisle. I knew I had little time, but I couldn't leave Cloud this way. He already had a head-collar on. I found a lead rope and opened the door, ready to clip it on. But as soon as I had the gate slightly ajar, the stallion lunged, pushing past me, scraping through the partial opening, and charged down to the water barrel, where he plunged his muzzle full into the liquid and began guzzling. Poor creature, I thought.

I went to catch him and had just gotten to the trough when the big double doors opened and a man came in, closing the doors behind him. Even in the dark, I knew it was Lord George.

"Well, well, I thought I would find my intruder was you," he said in a sneering tone. Cloud had also seen the man and now trotted down to the far end of the barn. "When the boy came and told me that a woman had broken in to my barns, I knew you had ignored my warnings, foolish woman." He almost spat these last words.

Speaking more calmly than I felt, I said, "I thought you would be riding in the race."

"Yes, you've cost me that, too! You've caused me a lot of trouble, and now this is going to end." He pulled something from his coat and held it out in front of him. My heart leapt into my throat. It was a pistol. He was advancing on me, and I realized I needed to keep him talking while I searched around for a weapon...or a plan. I said a quick prayer, begging for protection.

"It was you, wasn't it, the night my filly was stolen? It was you that I saw in the front yard?" Looking around, I couldn't seem to spot a pitchfork or even a bucket.

He had stopped now just a few yards away. "Yes, I was there, and three of my men. I wondered if you had recognized me. I would never have left you there alive, but I thought you'd been killed by that damned Berber stallion—you looked dead lying there in the dirt." So it had been Diamond in my "dream"! I was still stalling for time, so I was glad when the earl went on. "If my father hadn't been so taken with your damn filly, *insisting* on our stopping to take her too, we could have gotten the stallions away with no one the wiser."

"But I wasn't dead," I said, trying to keep him talking.

"No, and when I found out you had survived, I paid a man to watch you for a while."

"My cat," I said quietly, recognition dawning.

"Yes, a warning," he snarled.

"And my father? Was he killed by Diamond?"

"No, that was my doing." He sounded proud to admit this. "Even though I offered him money to keep quiet, he seemed intent on saving your horse, so that was that."

I still hadn't come up with a plan. My knees were shaking so badly I thought I might faint. But I had to keep him talking. "Why were these horses left here with no food and water?"

"Oh, that was an oversight," he said in a mocking tone. "After all, these are my prize horses. I had to work very hard to obtain them. I told my grooms yesterday morning that they were to let *no one but me* enter this barn, and then I must have gotten busy with my guests and forgotten to come and take care of things myself. How fortunate you came along. Now I can see to my horses…that is, after I finally take care of *you*."

At once he was advancing again, but a shaft of light fell across the aisle as the far door was opened and someone else entered the barn. I saw Lord George momentarily look away from me, trying to determine who had come in, and I took my chance and started to bolt. But he was one step ahead of me, grabbing me from behind and wrapping his arm around my neck, pinning my shoulders and dragging me back to the trough. "Who goes there?" he shouted.

Whoever it was had stepped behind Cloud, who was standing rather nervously at the end of the aisle. "Who is it, I say?" and he fired the pistol, aiming in the same direction as the person who had come in. I did my best to free one of my arms, but he held me in an iron grip.

Now the man—I could see it was a man—started sprinting up the front of the stalls, running low, but coming toward us. The earl dropped the first gun and pulled another pistol from his coat. The man was still moving. Now he stopped in front of the other occupied stall, and upon opening the door, the second crazed beast lunged out and came running directly toward us and the water trough behind us.

Lord George fired the second pistol as the big, white stallion reared and began thrashing those dangerous legs, banging hard into the two of us. As we went down, I rolled to the side, looking up to see the monstrous beast above me, just as I had seen so many times in my nightmares. I kept rolling, and I heard the hooves pound back to the ground, and then the only sound was the sucking noise that Diamond's lips were making as he drank in the water he was desperately craving.

I looked back to see the earl lying with his head in a pool of blood, the white stallion he had prized so much standing calmly over him. As I said a prayer of thanksgiving, I also found the strength to pray for Lord George, but in my heart, I knew he was dead.

Now strong arms were lifting me. "Kathryn, dearest, are you all right? Are you hurt?" It was William. When I shook my head, he left me for a moment and went to check on the man on the ground but came back looking stoic.

"How did you know where to find me?" I asked, barely able to catch my breath. "How did you know I needed you?"

"It was the maid, Alice. She came to me just before the race and told me you planned to go and search the barns while Herbert was busy riding. He and I were both mounted, ready to take part in the first race. When I saw the boy approach and then the earl dismount and head off towards the barns, I knew I had to follow. It just took me a minute to figure out how I might get in here without being spotted. But then I realized I was running out of time."

"I think he would've killed me if you hadn't come." And now I began to shake in earnest, and he let me gently crumple to a sitting position on the ground as my knees collapsed. Cloud had come tentatively up to us, and he dropped his head, sniffing my hair and then raising his muzzle to whiff at William's hand.

"Cloud, old fellow, I'm happy to see you again, boy. You look like you've seen better times. Come on, let's get these horses out where they can eat grass, and we'll go get help. Can you walk?" When I was able to stand again, we caught Diamond and were sorry to realize that one of the bullets had grazed him along the top of his crest, but the blood against his white neck made the wound look much worse than it really was. No wonder he had gone mad.

We had put the two stallions out into paddocks with hay and water when we realized there was another stalled horse at the far end of the dark barn. She had whinnied when we'd led Cloud and Diamond out through the doors. Peering into her cell, I realized it was another mare with a foal by her side. As I caught my breath, recognition hit me—it was Snow. She was a full-grown, mature mare now, and beautiful, just like I always knew she would be. Quickly snapping on a rope, I led her over to the water. She was more polite than the stallions had been, moving quietly and waiting for her foal, who looked to be only a few days old, to shuffle along beside her. But like the stallions, she drank for a good, long time. Once she had slaked her thirst, I threw my arms about her neck and had a good cry. Once I released her, she turned to nuzzle her baby and then gave me a little shove with her muzzle as if to say, "Where have you been all this time?" We also turned her and her filly out into one of the paddocks near the stallions.

As William and I walked together back up the road toward the manor, we could hear loud cheering coming from the race area. We both looked in that direction and could see in the distance the field of young horses thundering down the last part of the course toward the crowd. William had taken my arm, and he looked down into my face.

"I wonder who won," I said curiously.

"I did," he answered and held my arm tighter against his side.

The second race was canceled for that afternoon, and the crowds were sent home. The constable, JP, and magistrate all took turns questioning us, the guests, and the staff, but no one really doubted what had happened. Alice thankfully admitted that Lord Herbert had ordered her to leave threatening notes in my bedchamber the two previous nights. Lady Herbert claimed innocence of any knowledge of the plot. The grooms had just been doing what they were told. No one had any idea who "the three men" who had been in on the original thefts might have been, and I doubted we would ever know. But I was grateful that my father's name could now be cleared of all wrongdoing.

Most of the other guests were still no friendlier, but they were all packing up to leave, and I didn't mind anyway. William was all I could really think about—that and how God had used him to save me. And William had called me *dearest*. While I went to check on Aunt Marguerite and tell her all that had happened, William went to arrange to get his three stallions home, along with sending Diamond to the squire. There was also some question about the young horses on the property to be sorted out, but Cloud could now take his rightful place back at Faringdon.

While I was in my aunt's room—she was still under the weather—Alice came by. She looked uncertain as to how I would receive her, but I quickly rose to give her a hug. "Thank you so much, cousin, for telling Lord William about my plans. I know you were risking everything to do that, but you saved my life!"

"Oh, Katie, I wanted to tell ye everything this morning, sure. I felt so guilty for scarin' ye like I know I musta. I'm happy I could help in the end. But it doesn't make up for all the bad I done. Can ye forgive me?"

And so I reminded her again of the "bad things" I had done and how I had found forgiveness, and I think, in the end, she believed me. The Rothschilds also came to Aunt Marguerite's room to inquire about how we were feeling and to offer us the use of their carriage to return us to Bristol, which we accepted with much appreciation. We were to leave later that afternoon.

Edward came next, solicitous for our welfare and worried especially about me. I was able to reassure him that I was fine. He had heard all the news—I expected every person on the estate and even in the village had heard some version of it—and he offered to ship Snowflake and her foal to his farm in Bristol, which I gratefully accepted. I wasn't sure exactly what my future held, but I knew for now that I wanted to return to the Home.

William was there to see us off as we boarded the baron's carriage for Bristol. Disregarding propriety, he took me in his arms and kissed me gently, but not hurriedly. He promised that when things were settled at Faringdon, he would make haste to Bristol, and he asked if I would wait for him there. And of course, I nodded my assent. I knew that William was the man I had waited for my entire life.

Chapter 31

WILLIAM

I was relieved to settle back into life at the Home, where I could feel more like my true self. I packed away my new clothing and resumed my duties in the classroom, where my students greeted me with shouts, hugs, and kisses, as if I had been away for months instead of just a fortnight. And while I loved teaching and also being back with Angel and Samuel, who had become my family, William was never far from my thoughts. And all that had transpired during my visit with the Howards, and especially on that last evening, had changed me, perhaps in a very profound way.

Before I left to go to Howard Manor, I had come to believe that God had a purpose and plan for my life despite, or maybe even because, of all that had happened to me. I found that I had developed a deep compassion for the poor and the misfits and those forced into lifestyles not of their own choosing, and I felt I had a calling among these people and the destitute children that such life produced.

But for so many of my earlier years, I had harbored a secret love for William Stanley and a hope, no matter how improbable, that we might someday share a life together. That dream had been shut off, walled away, untouchable, in my heart for a long time. But now... well, now I wasn't sure what to think or hope for. Did we have a future yet? What was God's plan for me now? And despite knowing that God had forgiven me for my mistakes, despite hearing William say that he had forgiven me too, I still somehow felt unworthy of the relationship. I found myself on my knees morning and evening, praying about these questions.

It was less than a week after my return to Bristol that William made an appearance in my classroom. I was in the middle of our morning recitations when his face appeared at my door. I knew that both Angel and Samuel were away on business. There were other adults in the building working with the older children or cooking and cleaning, but no one was available to step in to relieve me of my teaching duties, and I could not leave the children. Besides, deep in my heart, I knew I was not yet ready to face this man. My love for him was sure, but what future we might or might not have together was unclear, and so I admit I was relieved that I couldn't just offer to talk with him privately.

Greeting him at the door felt awkward. "Lord Stanley," I uttered quietly, producing a self-conscious curtsy.

William reached out his hand and took mine. "Kathryn," he said warmly, attempting to catch my downcast eye, "I've been counting the days until I could come and spend time with you." Now he looked around the room at the dozens of small eyes fastened on his personage. "These must be your students. May I come in?"

I thought he would feel uncomfortable around so many strange children, and I expected him to immediately leave when I explained that I could not get away presently, and perhaps not at all that day. But instead, he took off his coat and, it appeared, prepared to make himself at home. "I've waited so long, for years, really, to find you. I'm not prepared to wait any longer. Surely, there is some way I can help here with your students?"

Again, this surprised me. As far as I knew, William had no experience with children. But suddenly, putting him to work in the classroom seemed an easier alternative to having a private meeting with him, and so I relented. At first, after he was introduced, the students seemed rather in awe of him. It was probably not so much that he was an earl, but they were just not used to having a man, especially a somewhat-austere man in gentleman's clothing, in their presence.

However, the toddlers were the first to overcome their shyness. Whenever Edward visited, his pockets were always full of candy. My youngest children were soon clambering at William's knees, begging for treats much as a dog might beg for a bone. William looked at me nervously, and I had to chuckle—he seemed so out of his element. "They're used to receiving candy from Edward when he visits," I explained.

Understanding dawning, William nodded and then knelt down to the toddlers' level. "I'm sorry, little ones. I'm afraid I'm quite uneducated when it comes to children. But I promise to bring you candy the next time I come." With that, the children tottered or crawled back to their customary corner, but one child, little Mary, seemed loath to leave him and clung to his sleeve. Standing up, William reached back down and gently picked her up, where she nestled against his shoulder, hiding her eyes. Seeing him like that with one of my beloved children broke open something inside me, and I had to turn away to hide the shine of tears that I knew had come to my eyes.

I soon had the oldest of my young children sitting in a circle around "Lord William." He sat patiently in a small chair, his elbows resting on his knees, and listened to them read. He was uncomplaining and kind, helping them with pronunciations and smiling at their small accomplishments. I was very taken with the way he assimilated into my world and seemed to enjoy my children, whom I loved very dearly.

We had lunch with the students, relaxing while sitting at the long tables, eating a simple meal among the babble of voices and clanging of spoons. William talked with the older youths who had joined us for the meal, telling them stories of life in London and patiently answering questions about all his travels. None of our inmates had ever been anywhere outside of Bristol, and they were avid listeners.

After lunch, Angel and Samuel returned and William went off with the two of them into Samuel's study, to my somewhat relief. I had loved watching him get more and more comfortable with my small charges, but I still wasn't sure what the future held, or even could hold, for us. I waited nervously all afternoon, teaching distractedly, but William never reappeared at my door.

When classes were over, Angel came to tell me that Lord Stanley had made the request to visit with me the next day, when I was to be relieved of my teaching duties after lunch. She admitted that she and Samuel had spoken for at least an hour with the earl and had searched his motives and his heart, but didn't say more than that. I gathered, by their tacit approval of his return on the morrow, that he had somehow passed their test. I had never told Angel much about William, but she knew he was the man I had sought to avoid that day in the Crowing Rooster when we had first met Edward.

I struggled with my decision on how to dress the next morning; should I unpack one of the new day dresses that Aunt Marguerite had purchased and dress as Lady Alexander or instead as the commoner I felt I really was? In the end, I decided to wear my old calico shift. I was most comfortable just being Miss Kathryn. But familiar clothing could not stem the nerves that threatened to overwhelm me all morning.

True to his word, William was waiting for the students and me as we returned from lunch, and he was bearing gifts of candy, which caused quite a stir among the children, as they had never tasted chocolate before. I admit I enjoyed several pieces myself. Angel soon shooed the two of us out the door, and William suggested we walk down to the same teahouse nearby that Edward and I had often visited. I still felt somewhat awkward around William, and we didn't say much as we strolled down the street, the warm spring sunshine splashing across our faces. I knew I should be floating in utter joy to be walking by his side on this beautiful spring day, but I could not get over my dread. It didn't matter that I had spent hours praying about this. I still had no clear answers to my distress.

We were soon seated at a table, with two cups of tea placed before us, and now there was nothing left to do, it seemed, but talk of more-serious subjects. We had already exhausted our small talk—the weather, the children. William had told me that I was even more beautiful than he remembered, but this caused more consternation than joy in me. I knew there were things I needed to say, but it was so difficult to find the words.

"William," I began. At least I felt comfortable enough to call him by the name that had been on my heart for years. "William, before we can pursue our friendship further, I feel there are things you need to know about me, things that may make you decide to go back to Faringdon."

Reaching out and taking my hand from where it was lying next to my cup, William looked so deeply into my eyes that I had to look away. "Kathryn...dear, I thought we had agreed to each forgive the other and let the past go? Both of us have admitted our deep regret, I most of all! I don't need to know anything beyond what I know now. You are graceful and kind, wonderful with both animals and children, and full of faith in the Lord. And I find you to be the most beautiful woman I have ever met, both inside and out."

"Please," I pleaded, interrupting his speech. "As I said, I believe you have the right to know more about me." Again, I broke off my gaze and stared down at my hands. And then, without looking at his face, I began to tell him, haltingly at first, how Angel and Samuel had come to find me on the streets of Bristol two years before. I admitted that my memories were untrustworthy, but I had been malnourished and homeless, to say the least. Most likely, I had been selling myself or worse to stay alive. Blessedly, my memories of that period were mainly darkness, but there was little doubt of what had most probably occurred. And perhaps worst of all, I had been five months pregnant, with his baby.

My voice caught in my throat as I told him this last piece. "Oh, William, it was my own failings that caused my beautiful Anne to be stillborn!" Large tears were running down my cheeks now. William had still said nothing, but he was continuing to hold my hand. "I know that God has forgiven me for all that I have done. Jesus has paid the price for that. And I also believe that I will see our precious child again one day in heaven. But how can you ever forgive me or think of me in the same way again?"

Finally, I found the strength to look up into his eyes. There were also tears running down his face, but he didn't seem to be conscious of them. "I already knew all of this," he said quietly. "Yesterday, the Cartwrights confided all that you had been through. They thought it was important that I know, and they wanted to be sure of my reaction before they would encourage our friendship."

"You already knew?" I was still trying to process this information.

"Yes, and it doesn't matter. If anything, it makes me all the more aware of my own guilt. Kathryn, I am so very sorry, for all you went through, for all I put you through. How can you ever forgive *me*?" We sat there for a long time, quietly weeping. Finally, he brought out a kerchief and handed it to me, and we each blew our noses.

"You already know that I don't hold you responsible," I tried to reassure him.

"You forgive me, then?" he asked, looking at me directly.

"Yes."

"Then let's put *all* this behind us. I can only thank God that he brought you through it all safely, and that we've been given the chance to start over." Then after a pause, he added, "Perhaps this has been enough for one day. But I believe Angel said you have tomorrow off, since it's Saturday. I'm staying at Edward's estate, and you have been invited to tea tomorrow. Would you allow me to pick you up after lunch and escort you to Rollinswood?"

"Yes." I nodded. I felt like a large weight had just been lifted off my shoulders, a weight I had been carrying for a very long time, and I gave God praise in my heart.

The next afternoon, William arrived in Edward's open carriage with the same pair of matched bays, the very calash I had ridden in the year before. I wondered if the driver was the same servant and what he must think of me. But I soon put it out of my mind. It was another beautiful day, my handsome William was sitting across from me, smiling a broad grin, and it was impossible not to be impossibly happy.

William took the opportunity to tell me the news from Faringdon. He had given Alice her old job in the manor, and she was working on inviting more of her family to immigrate since he had promised them jobs there, too. His brother Anthony had married a year and a half ago, and William had now turned the running of the estate over to him. According to William, his brother had finally matured and was showing promise. As for Clarence, William had purchased a commission for him in the Navy, and his youngest brother was now learning hard work and discipline aboard a sailing vessel somewhere south of England.

We arrived at Rollinswood just before teatime and were greeted by the spaniels Rolly and Molly, who seemed overjoyed to see William and who sniffed me politely. I was surprised to learn that Edward was to be "away" for the day, but his sister Lady Mary greeted us graciously at the door to the sitting room. I was amazed at how warm and friendly she was to both of us, showing great deference to Lord William, her houseguest, and seemingly genuine courtesy to me. How different this visit was from our last one!

Following tea, William led me out toward the barns. I guessed that he was excited to show me Snowflake, and to be honest, I couldn't wait to see her. She and her filly were grazing in a small field next to the barn. When I called her name, she lifted her head, gave a whinny, and came galloping over to the fence, her young foal kicking her heels in glee at the joy of running beside her dam. I soon had a head-collar on my beautiful girl. William had thought of everything and also had brushes and lead rope waiting. We set to work grooming the mare, although her coat was already gleaming and it was obvious she was enjoying very thorough care on Edward's estate. I knew I was probably soiling my frock, but I didn't care—it felt so good to have my hands on my horse once more.

William also helped me corral Snow's foal, and we spent a little time running the brush gently over her sides, talking quietly to her all the while as her mama picked grass quietly beside us. William said that he and Edward had already practiced placing a small head-collar on the young filly, and she was taking to being handled like a pro, just like her mother before her. "What do you want to name the foal?" he asked me.

I was surprised by his question and had to stop and think, honored by the idea that I would be choosing the name. "How about Snow's Beauty?" I suggested.

"I think Beauty is a perfect name," he answered, but he wasn't looking at the filly.

Once we had left Snow's paddock, William turned and said, "I have a surprise for you. How would you like to take a horseback ride out onto the estate?"

I caught my breath. This was something I remembered dreaming about the first afternoon I had visited Rollinswood. Riding was also something I had missed terribly for such a long time now. But I had nothing appropriate to wear. It turned out, though, that Lady Elizabeth, Edward's younger sister, also rode astride and her habit had been borrowed for me to wear. William had thought of everything, I realized, and there was no way I could turn this offer down.

Once I was dressed in Elizabeth's riding habit, a groom came to the front of the manor, leading Baron and the gentle mare I remembered meeting the year before, the golden chestnut named Kitty. William boosted me up on her back before gracefully mounting Baron, and we set off at a gentle walk, the groom riding a respectful distance behind us on a third horse. The sensation was exhilarating. I don't know which I was enjoying more, being on a horse again or being in the company of the handsome man I loved.

We soon turned off the drive and chose a path that meandered through the parklands surrounding the estate. I was surprised when we came out of a thick woods into a glen containing a small pond and another gazebo much like the one behind Edward's manor house. The groom came to hold our horses, and William helped me down off Kitty, holding me around the waist with his strong arms and gazing into my eyes for just a moment before placing me on the ground. I could see that refreshments were waiting on the small table at the center of the little building. As before, William had evidently thought of everything.

We sat on bare benches and nibbled at cookies and cider while our horses picked at grass. Once I had finished eating and had brushed the crumbs off my lap, William took my hand and looked seriously into my face. "Kathryn, I have already asked Samuel's permission to make this proposal, and his answer was that it is up to you." Here he paused and then asked just as gravely, "Would you do me the honor of becoming my wife, after an appropriate engagement period, of course?"

I could hardly catch my breath. I was already so happy. Even though this was something I had dreamed about for years, I could barely believe it was really happening. William was the man I loved and wished to marry. But how could I become an earl's wife, a countess, something I had no desire for at all? Still, I would have to let the Lord take care of that for me. "Yes," I said, breaking into a smile, and we sealed the bargain with a long, tender kiss.

On the ride back to the manor house, we couldn't seem to keep from catching each other's eye and smiling. I honestly couldn't get the grin off my face. The whole world seemed to be smiling. Coming out of the woods and onto the broad avenue leading up to the barns, I looked at William and asked, "Is there a reason we have gone at such a sedate pace this whole ride?"

"I was worried that it might be difficult for you to be back in the saddle after such a long time," he explained, slightly shrugging. With that, I kicked my heels into Kitty's sides, and off we went, perhaps not in a full gallop, as that seemed to be beyond what the mare had in mind. But still, the wind whipped my hair as we cantered up the hill, and I smiled gleefully over at William. He appeared to be having trouble holding Baron back from a full-out race, but he was obviously enjoying every minute of it, too. I couldn't remember ever being happier.

Epilogue

ATLANTIC OCEAN, 1737

Six months later, William and I were married in the small chapel at the Home by Pastor Cartwright. Edward witnessed for William, Angel for me. The children of the home were our special guests, and William provided a huge wedding feast in our honor. So many changes had happened in the last few months that I felt my head was spinning. I had gifted Snowflake to Edward, and she was already rebred to Chieftain. He was excited to see what her new foal might be like, even as her current filly was growing into a fine-looking crossbred. I was welcome to come and ride anytime I wished, and I had managed to get out to the estate on several occasions in those last few months.

William had contracted with Squire Baker to have both of my parents' remains exhumed and moved to the private cemetery at Faringdon, where we erected stones in their honor, and where I was finally able to pay my last respects with dignity. Aunt Marguerite and Aunt Bethany both made the trip to the estate for the special service we held, and we all stayed at the manor for several days, enjoying our reunion. Sadly, Grandmother had passed away, but I was grateful that I had taken the chance to get to know her. Bethany told us that she planned to spend the summer months in Bristol from now on, visiting with Marguerite, who planned to also return to the Dower House at Howard Hall as often as possible.

And best news of all, William had been studying the scriptures with me. He had always been a believer in the Lord but had never really considered what it meant to truly live for God. He was baptized by our pastor and became an active member of the Way, staying at Rolinswood with Edward for the last three months before our wedding. We spent our bridal tour in a rented cottage along the coast, taking long walks on the beach, riding horses up into the hills, or sitting on benches beside the shore, watching the waves break among the rocks. William was a gentle lover; regretful of the past, he made sure now to please me in every way he could. I couldn't get enough of him. Sometimes, when he was gazing at the ocean, I would just sit and stare at my handsome husband, hardly able to believe he was mine, and thanking God for every moment.

I still didn't have all the answers to my questions. Why hadn't God protected my da? Why had he let my mother and Esther and even my baby daughter die? But I was learning to trust his divine will, and I could see how God had used most of the things I had considered evil in my life to bring about good for my future, and also how the Lord had been with me, protecting me from the start.

Shortly after we returned from our marriage trip, Pastor Cartwright had announced that he and Angel and several other members of the Way were immigrating to America to start a new church in Williamsburg. Angel had a sister residing there who was discouraged to report that the Anglican Church was the only Christian establishment in the area. She had written begging her brother-in-law to come and preach his message of grace and forgiveness to the inhabitants there. The Home for Needy Children was doing well, and Samuel believed it could be safely left in the hands of other active members of the Way. Chief among these was now Sir Edward Walker. There was also further news in the baronet's life. He had begun courting a young widow who taught spinning and sewing to the girls at the Home. Marissa, a pretty mother of two young girls, was well loved by the children of the Home, and I was very happy for Edward. He had told me that our relationship was what had opened him up to the possibility of loving and marrying again.

Once the Cartwrights had announced their plans to sail to America, William and I both had felt led to travel with them, and we immediately packed the few belongings we would take with us. William had no desire to return to Faringdon, where his brother had taken charge. Besides my aunts and Snowflake, I had nothing to bind me to England. Both of my mother's sisters encouraged us to go and start a new and exciting life, and Snow was really Edward's mare now. Besides, William has promised me that, Lord willing, we will have new stallions and mares when we reach Virginia, which is purported to be a wonderful place to raise horses. So we gladly set sail together with few regrets left behind and many hopes that God would use us in this new homeland.

And today, as I finish this journal, I find that the nausea of the last six weeks has left me, and I'm beginning to enjoy sailing, even as I look forward to disembarking soon. I am reasonably sure of my pregnancy now, and William is like a boy with a new toy. He pampers me endlessly, although I tell him I'm healthy as a horse. We can't wait to start our new life in Virginia. We will no longer call ourselves lord and lady, but just Mr. and Mrs. Stanley, or better yet, Brother and Sister Stanley. William's purse is well stocked for the moment, praise God, and we hope to help the Cartwrights start another Home for Needy Children and provide free medical care wherever needed as we spread the Lord's "good news" of grace and forgiveness.

My dreams now are only happy ones. And when a horse comes galloping through them, it is usually my lovely mare Snowflake, a colt or filly cavorting by her side. There are no more nightmares of the white stallion.

About the Author

J ulia Oliver, like her heroine, has also loved horses from an early age. With her veterinarian husband, they have raised and trained jumpers, eventers, and carriage animals ever since their marriage in 1970. In her younger years, Julia was a high school teacher but, in the last decade, has dedicated her life to Meadowstone Therapeutic Riding Center, where she provides riding lessons to children with disabilities and also directs equine psychotherapy for adult clients from a residential addictions program. Julia has previously written two nonfiction books that have gained wide acceptance in her field of therapeutic riding and carriage driving. She and her husband (pictured with a horse they raised themselves) have lived on their Meadowstone farm for forty-three years and are active members and teachers in their nondenominational church.

CPSIA information can be obtained
at www.ICGtesting.com
Printed in the USA
LVHW021707181021
700767LV00003B/310

9 781645 445265